Books by C

Crossing Forces

Collision Force
Chance Collision
Calculated Collision
Collision Control

Collision Force

ISBN # 978-1-78651-899-6

Cover Art by Posh Gosh ©Copyright 2016

Interior text design by Claire Siemaszkiewicz

Totally Bound Publishing

Published in 2016 by Totally Bound Publishing, Newland House, The Point, Weaver Road, Lincoln, LN6 3QN, United Kingdom.

Printed and bound in Great Britain by Clays Ltd, St Ives plc

1

Crossing Forces

COLLISION FORCE

C.A. SZAREK

Dedication

For my husband, Shane. Looks like I finally came up with a story you're interested in.

Thanks to my cop buddy Jason for answering all my police questions, and former FBI agent Holly for helping me any time I needed it.

Thanks Amee for your enthusiasm for this story and for loving Cole as much as I do.

Thanks to Nicole for naming my town when I couldn't think of one.

Thanks Susie for telling me I was born to write this genre when I couldn't have disagreed more. Also for dropping your own writing to critique for me when I needed it.

Thanks to my critique partners Clover, Michelle, Jen and Gina for your suggestions, brainstorming and help when I was writing this book.

Thanks Michelle, Jo-Anna, Alanna and Kerry for always being there for me.

RIP Detective Tom Barnett. I miss you tremendously.

Chapter One

Cole cursed. He stared into the rear-view mirror in the busy parking lot, but saw nothing. He'd been so close this time.

The damn local police were breathing down his neck, and *that* was the last thing he wanted…or needed.

Cooperation, my ass. They needed to get the hell out of his case. He'd been too involved for too long, and he wasn't about to let some Podunk police chief tell him what to do.

Not to mention that dumbass detective getting himself shot. Cole didn't need the locals piecing it all together. He had to wrap up a few things before letting them in on his case. Full disclosure wasn't on his list at all.

That bastard Maldonado had got away from him. Even two months later, that still chapped. But he'd tracked him here and been in town a few weeks with no clues. Until the shooting. Two goons dead and a police detective shot twice. And Maldonado had slipped back into the shadows. Cole's gut told him the coward was still in town… He hadn't—or couldn't—move on. But where the hell was he?

Cole's cell phone rang, yanking him from his thoughts.

"Lucas," he said.

"Where the hell are you?" Olivia Barnes, his supervisor, barked at him. "Chief Martin called screaming at me. He said you told him to kiss your ass? What the hell, Cole? I told you to cooperate with them."

Cole snorted. Chief Martin had misquoted him, but not by much.

"I don't need them, Olivia."

"Oh, don't *Olivia* me. This was an order from higher

5

up. Get that through your thick skull, dammit. Get to that station and make nice. Now."

Cole sighed. His boss didn't respond. Though her tone had brooked no argument, he'd been tempted to tell *her* to kiss his ass. It wasn't like his record wasn't tainted, and it wouldn't have been the first time he'd told her off. But he held his tongue. He was damn good at his job, and Olivia knew it. Cole would play along, for now.

"All right," he answered. Olivia was silent on the other end of the phone. *Too silent.*

"All right?"

"You've ordered me, correct?" Cole said dryly. He could almost *hear* her eyes narrow.

"Just like that?"

"Just like that. C'mon, Liv, I can be a good boy."

She harrumphed. "Okay. Go kiss Chief Martin's ass."

"Can't promise that, but I will go to the station."

"Good. I can't afford any more damage control, Agent Lucas."

Uh oh, Agent Lucas? "Sounds like a warning."

"It is." Olivia lowered her voice. "I don't want to have to yank you off the case, Cole."

Like that would happen. "I'll call you later."

She started to say something, but he ended the call imagining her outraged expression—one he was quite familiar with. He smirked. Yes, he would play along...for now.

The drive to the station was short, but didn't alleviate his irritation with the whole damn situation. He slammed the car door and winced, berating himself. He loved this car. Cole patted the hood in apology, admiring the brand new, deep metallic blue Dodge Challenger. It looked mean as hell. Like it was made for him. He'd even contemplated keeping it when this was all over.

He groaned when he took in the smallish Antioch, Texas police station, but headed inside. The asshole desk sergeant practically growled when he introduced himself, as did

6

Chief Martin over the intercom. He ran into the female, literally, right after Sergeant Asshole-of-the-year had finally acknowledged his existence and buzzed him into the back. And although his head smarted, seeing a beautiful woman was the highlight of his morning.

"Whoa, sorry," she said, smiling. Her chestnut hair was pulled back into a ponytail and she had the bluest eyes he'd ever seen. She was tall and slender, and he liked what he saw. She was wearing a white button-down dress shirt and snug khaki pants, and the outfit was somehow incredibly sexy.

Cole almost missed the paddle holster at her waist, but when he saw it, he couldn't help but admire her subtly rounded hips. Her badge was on a chain around her neck, swaying gently with her movements. A detective.

"No, *I'm* sorry. You all right?" he answered, trying to tear his eyes away.

"Sure. You?"

He nodded. Cole bent and helped her retrieve the scattered case file contents. He latched onto a crime scene photo. Not only was she a detective, she was working *his* case—the pictures were all-too-familiar evidence. No doubt the local case was tied to his. He bit back a cringe.

"Ah, I don't think we've met."

They both straightened and she thanked him for his help. He tried not to stare at the items in her arms.

"Oh, I guess not. Detective Andi MacLaren. Nice to meet you." She held out her right hand, but he couldn't help but glance at her left before accepting her shake. No wedding ring. *Good.*

"Andi, huh?" He met her eyes.

"Well, it's Andrea, but not even my mother calls me that." She smiled.

Instinct told him she was a no muss, no fuss, hard-working kind of girl. Not overly feminine, but extremely appealing. A smattering of freckles spread across her high cheekbones and trailed over her nose. She wore little or no makeup — that drew him as well. Not his normal type at all, but gorgeous.

"And you are?" she prompted.

Cole jolted to attention. He'd been staring. And she looked as if she was oblivious. Should that bother him? *Yes.* Women *always* noticed him.

"Special Agent Cole Lucas, FBI."

Her eyes widened, then she flashed a grin that could have only been called impish. It rivalled one he was known to give from time to time. "*You're* Agent Lucas? You've had Chief in a tizzy all morning." Was that admiration in her tone?

He smiled back. "Guilty," he admitted, winking at her.

"Agent Lucas," Chief Martin shouted from the doorway to his office.

Cole caught Detective MacLaren's eye and shrugged. "Guess I'm being summoned."

She chuckled.

"Hope to catch you later…Andi." He flashed a grin, then trotted towards the angry police chief before she could answer.

Andi watched the FBI agent head towards certain doom and shook her head. He exuded cockiness. It took a great deal to rile Chief, but when Paul Martin lost it, look out. The whole force would avoid him for days.

She tried not to stare at Special Agent Cole Lucas' fine form as he jogged down the hall, but found it hard to avert her eyes. *God, he's hot.*

Tight jeans and a black T-shirt that clung to every muscle — and he wasn't lacking any. He was tall, probably three or four inches over six feet, and he had eyes the colour of steel. His hair was coal black and neatly trimmed. She grinned, remembering his name was Cole. And damn if he didn't have dimples when he smiled. He'd destroyed her image of proper suit-wearing FBI agents.

Unfortunately, he reeked of bad boy and he *definitely*

knew how good-looking he was.

A man to avoid.

She didn't consider herself *available* anyway. Noticing him meant she wasn't dead, right?

Glancing down at the fat case file, she sighed. She'd have to make sure it was all back in order. Andi headed to her desk. She had a few calls to make, and she was planning on stopping by the hospital to see Pete. Her partner had been shot twice a few weeks ago, but was recovering well and itching to go home.

They had no clue as to who had shot him...yet. But Andi was determined to catch the bastards. Working the case alone had been a challenge, though she was up to it. Pete would never blame her for the lack of progress, but *she* did. She couldn't wait until he was back at her side. She missed him.

She scanned his too-empty desk, then her own. A picture of Iain and a tiny newborn Ethan caught her eye and she smiled, her heart thumping hard. She still ached for her husband, who'd been killed in the line of duty just over three years before. She'd loved him and always would. Their son Ethan had only been six weeks old. Now three, he got her through each day. Andi was looking forward to getting home to him that evening.

The case file caught her attention and she scowled. *Duty called.* She opened it, biting back another sigh.

After signing into her computer, she opened her confidential informant database and scrolled down, scrunching her nose even though she found the phone number she needed. Calling CIs was her least favourite thing—Pete usually handled it.

About five minutes later, Andi hung up the phone, frustrated because she'd got nowhere with a lousy CI. She jumped when it rang again, then groaned when the caller ID flashed Chief's direct extension. She, like everyone else, was on avoidance mode with him.

"What's up, Chief?" she asked, keeping her tone light.

"My office, MacLaren," Chief Martin barked. Andi winced. What the hell? She'd done nothing to incur his wrath.

"Coming," she said, cringing as she heard the click.

Andi slipped into Chief Martin's office, smiling at his administrative assistant, Nikki. Her desk was right inside the door of the smaller room of the chief's large, two-room executive space.

"You can go right in. Beware..." the redhead said in a conspiratorial tone.

"I know it," Andi said, winking.

Nikki grinned, her brown eyes sparkling. Andi had liked her since she'd been hired about a year earlier. She was young and open, but she was skilled at keeping Chief Martin in line and everyone admired her ability to do so. But, evidently, the buck stopped at far-too-handsome-for-their-own-good FBI agents.

Swallowing hard, she headed into her boss's office. A scowl marred Agent Lucas' handsome face. What the heck? Their initial meeting had been light and friendly. What had she done to warrant that particular expression?

She looked away from him, meeting Chief's hazel eyes. His moustache twitched. He ran a hand through his thick, greying brown hair, and motioned for her to sit with the other. Andi slid onto the chair next to the FBI agent.

"MacLaren, this is Special Agent Cole Lucas."

"We've already met," Agent Lucas cut in, earning a glare from Chief Martin.

She glanced between him and her boss, nodding.

"It just so happens that your case may coincide with his," the chief continued.

The FBI agent made a low growling sound, and Andi ignored him as she met Chief Martin's eyes for the second time. "The guy who shot Pete?"

"Tip of the iceberg," Agent Lucas muttered.

Chief Martin scowled. "I want you to work with Agent Lucas."

Agent Lucas leant forward, his fists clenched. "I work alone."

"Not in my city, you don't. And not according to Special Agent Barnes." The two men stared at each other.

Andi had the urge to roll her eyes but forced herself to sit still. If it wouldn't have pressed her luck with Chief Martin's mood, she'd tell them both they could call her when their pissing contest was over. Although concerning her boss's order, she was with Agent Lucas. She was better off without him.

"I have a partner," Andi said.

"Detective Crane is unavailable, MacLaren. You're sitting next to your new partner. So get acquainted." Chief Martin intertwined his fingers and rested his hands on his desktop. "I have been *assured* that Special Agent Lucas will *fully* cooperate with your already on-going investigation."

"We'll see about that," the FBI agent said under his breath, earning yet another glare from her boss.

Great, not only did he *not* want to work with her, he was planning on being tight-lipped. Andi *really* didn't want to be stuck with him. "Chief, I don't think—"

"MacLaren, shut up. I didn't *ask* what you thought. You'll work with Lucas, no matter what either of you say. He will *not* roam around my city unchecked."

Agent Lucas rushed to his feet while Andi gaped. Chief Martin had never spoken to her in such a manner.

"Unchecked?" Agent Lucas growled, his fists tight to his sides.

Was he restraining himself from physically harming her boss? At another time, she might have been amused.

"I don't need a babysitter."

"I'm not a babysitter, dammit." Andi's words were out of her mouth before she could censor the statement. She glared. Both men looked at her.

"Lucas, sit down. MacLaren, I meant no insult," Chief Martin said. That was as close to an apology as she would ever get. "Lucas, MacLaren is my best detective. Second to her is her partner, Peter Crane, who is in the hospital recovering from his wounds. I am putting you with her because of her skills, not merely to keep you busy."

Praise? *Wow.* It didn't come often from her very *un-*touchy-feely boss. Andi flushed, taking a breath. But Cole Lucas didn't sit, and he damn sure didn't seem impressed by Chief Martin's little speech. He didn't even flinch. However, after several tense moments on his feet, he sighed heavily—insulting her a bit—and took his seat.

"There's no other way, is there?" he whispered.

He was musing to himself more than speaking to her or Chief, but it didn't stop the brilliant, triumphant grin that could have split her boss's face in two. He might have even looked handsome if he hadn't been gloating so hard.

Andi gave a sigh of her own. She looked at Agent Lucas then at her boss, who was staring at them both expectantly.

No one said anything.

"Well?" Chief Martin prompted.

"Well, what?" Andi grumbled.

"The case won't solve itself."

Was she back in high school in the principal's office? Though, at the moment, detention held some appeal. With a shake of her head, she rose.

Cole looked the female detective up and down again. Despite his irritation, he was drawn to her. Just gorgeous. He had liked her show of temper moments earlier, and had no doubt they would clash again. Andi MacLaren seemed like she needed to be in control. Well, he had news for her. He was *always* in control, and he'd have no issues making it clear, first thing.

He winked at the buxom redhead sitting at her desk in the chief's front room on the way out, and she gave him a knowing smirk. Cole hadn't caught her name, but she was stunning. Although, she was young—couldn't even be twenty-five. He glanced back at Detective MacLaren. Why was he so intrigued by her? The chief's secretary was much more his normal type, but he would prefer Andi MacLaren if he was forced to pick between the two. *That would be fun.* He bit back a grin.

"So, what do you have?" Detective MacLaren asked as he followed her down the hall.

"Meaning?" He quirked an eyebrow.

"Hmmm, I see you won't be making this easy for me."

She was already irritated with him. Should he answer her straight or push some more buttons? "What do you mean?" he asked, going for innocence.

Sighing, she shook her head. "Look, Agent Lucas, this will be a lot easier if we just cooperate with each other."

"Cole," he said.

"What?" Andi asked, eyebrows drawn tight.

"Call me Cole. And I will call you Andi," he said it slowly on purpose, dragging each word out. Her cheeks reddened. He'd ticked her off even more. She didn't speak, just turned away and headed down the wide hallway. Cole grinned and followed.

They passed through a door with a placard announcing 'CID', the Criminal Investigations Division, near the doorframe. He groaned when he observed the room. Though it was spacious, there were only seven cubicles, and one work area was empty save for the standard issue phone on the desk.

The only other person in the room was a man, probably in his forties, with dark hair and glasses. He sat at one of the desks, the phone to his ear, speaking in low tones. His workspace was neat and organised, and he wrote on a legal pad as he spoke.

Andi stopped at a cubicle on the far right against the wall. She leaned on her desk, crossing her arms over her chest and giving him a long look. "Well?" she prompted.

Cole looked around again, wanting to come off as nonchalant. "Where is everyone?"

One eyebrow shot up. "Pete's in the hospital. That's Detective Kurt Jamison over there. His partner is Detective

13

Sergeant Noah Sullivan—we call him Sully, naturally. No clue where he's gotten off to. Last but not least is Detective Jared Manning. He's on vacation, but he'll be back next week. Right now he doesn't have a partner. The department has an opening for a detective."

"Oh?" Cole grinned.

"Yeah. You interested?" That eyebrow went even higher, her tone sarcastic. Good. Cole was getting her all hot and bothered.

"Hell, no. This is Podunkville. I don't do small towns."

Detective MacLaren snorted. "Nice." Her lips pursed as if she was going to say something else, but she didn't.

He had a feeling it wouldn't take much more to make her really mad, and he didn't want to push her too far.

"So, a one-woman show, huh?" he asked a moment later.

"Actually, we have a female lieutenant, a female sergeant and several female officers. Do you want to see my case file?"

Cole shrugged. Her expression tightened, her full lips a flat line. She shoved the fat maroon file folder at him. He suppressed a chuckle and nonchalantly peered over the crime scene photos.

"Maybe you could tell me how big the iceberg is..." Andi said. Her chest heaved as she took a deep breath.

"Nice wish," Cole said. He skimmed her report. It was well written and informative, but didn't answer all his questions. How the hell had Maldonado got away? She'd returned fire. Ah, she'd hit the bastard. The CSIers had recorded four blood types at the scene, including her partner's outside the entrance of the warehouse where the two bodies were found. That might explain why Maldonado had gone into hiding. But Cole would find him.

"Look, I don't want to work with you any more than you want me around. Why don't we make the best of it and get something accomplished? Find out who shot my partner, and I'm guessing you have the key to your case."

Andi's voice pulled him from the plan he was formulating

in his head. Her blue eyes were wide and sincere. The case file still in his arms, Cole couldn't help but stare, trailing her body before returning to her face.

Arms at her sides, shoulders tight, she scowled. "Jesus."

Focusing on her irritation, he cocked a half-smile. His smartass comment died on his tongue as the detective who'd been on the phone appeared next to them.

"Morning, Andi. Who's your friend?" the guy asked.

"I would use the term *friend* very loosely," Andi muttered, shooting Cole a glare.

He let it slide and glanced at the other man.

"What was that?" the detective asked. He must have heard, though, because his eyes danced and a ghost of a smile played at his lips.

"Detective Kurt Jamison, this is Special Agent Cole Lucas, FBI. He's going to be...working...with me for a while."

"Nice to meet you, Agent Lucas," Detective Jamison said, putting his hand out.

Cole grasped it.

"Nice to meet you, too, Detective Jamison," Cole said, flashing a smile.

Andi harrumphed. Cole narrowed his eyes. She smiled sweetly at him. Any other time he'd have been pleased, but she was mocking him. Jamison glanced at her then back to him before giving a hearty chuckle. What the hell was so funny? Cole frowned.

"Well, I need to chase down Sully. We've got a promising lead in that big stolen property case." Jamison cleared his throat, but his tone sounded genuinely regretful. "Take care of Andi since Pete's not around right now, Agent Lucas. She's our girl."

"I'll take care of her, all right," Cole grumbled.

Andi glared.

Jamison laughed again then disappeared from the room. Andi crossed her arms over her chest. Cole made sure she noticed his eyes rest there before he flashed his best dimpled grin. Her breasts were too hidden. *What a shame.*

She rolled her eyes and let her arms fall to her sides. "Are we going to talk about the case at all?" Andi prompted.

Cole went back to reading the report but showed no reaction to it. He made mental notes of a few things and revised his plan. He put the case file down and gave it a pat. "Catch you later, MacLaren." He tossed his business card on her desk.

"What?"

"I have some leads to follow up on."

"Wait. *What?* Where are you going?" Andi's voice rose with each word. He flashed another grin and disappeared from the CID room.

Chapter Two

"Son of a bitch." Andi was torn between going after him and sitting at her desk, working on her own. What a pompous ass! She refused to go to the chief and complain. He'd told her to work with Cole Lucas, and work with him she would.

Andi hurried out of the room, muttering a few more choice words about Special Agent Cole Lucas. The hallway was empty, but he couldn't have gone far. She would head him off at the pass.

She scanned the parking lot. The only vehicle that seemed out of place was a Dodge Challenger, the most conspicuous shade of blue in the world. She rolled her eyes. Didn't it figure the FBI ass would drive something flashy? He wasn't in the car, but she wasn't about to let him ditch her.

The blue monstrosity wasn't locked. She slipped into the passenger seat, pulling the seatbelt on and fastening it with a click. Andi had no problem waiting him out. She would show him who was boss.

A clean, masculine scent tickled her nose. Pleasant, and all him, but she tried to ignore it. Andi didn't want to have even one positive thought about Special Agent Cole Lucas. No doubt he was convinced he was sexy. Not even a million dollars would get her to admit any reaction to him—even if she did have one, which she most certainly *did not*.

The conceited ape came sauntering out of the PD several minutes later, a steaming cup in hand.

He saw her in his car and gave a hoot of laughter. He said nothing for a moment, just slipped into the driver's seat, humming. Cole smiled and set his coffee gently in the cup holder. Andi remained silent, but she was seething.

"I've got to hand it to you, Andi. You've got balls."

"*Excuse* me?" she demanded. "Obviously, this is some kind of game to you, *Agent Lucas*. But this is not a game to me. My partner got shot. There have been two people gunned down. We have nothing. I realise that we're not New York City, or wherever the *hell* you come from, but this city means something to me, and I have a job to do, with or without you."

A low whistle filled the car and Andi almost lost it again. She was about to open her mouth to tell him off, but he spoke.

"This is not a game to me," Cole said.

She raised an eyebrow. "Then prove to me you can take something seriously."

"You have absolutely no idea what I can take seriously." His tone mirrored hers for the first time.

Good. She didn't care if he was angry with her. "Then *tell* me, for God's sake! We're supposed to be working *together*."

"Eighteen months. Eighteen months and three states. That's how long I've been working this case. *That* is what I can, and *do,* take seriously."

Andi pondered his outburst and the passion that flared in his steel gaze. He *did* give a damn about this case. "Then perhaps a new set of eyes may help your outlook on things," she said softly.

"Perhaps," Cole allowed, cocking his head to the side. He stared.

Her heart skipped a beat, which she promptly ignored. "Where to first?" Andi asked to take the focus off her.

"I'd like to see the place your partner got shot."

"Why? Crime Scene has already been through everything. Details were all in my report."

"*I* haven't been through it." His eyes narrowed.

"So my guys don't know what they're doing?" Andi snapped. Cole's silence was answer enough as to his opinion. "Dammit," she muttered. She hadn't got anywhere with him after all.

"What was that?"

She didn't answer him. The SOB really did think he was better than her whole department. "Fine. It's not far, I'll show you. Let's go."

Cole nodded as he started the car.

* * * *

The rest of the day proved more frustrating than fruitful. Andi and Cole had shouted at each other several more times. Chief Martin had given her orders, but working with Cole had to be a mission from God. The man had to be the most stubborn, pig-headed jerk she'd ever met. He wouldn't listen to her at all. She was an adult, a professional detective, and she'd covered all bases in her report. Why did Cole have so many *other* questions?

After several phone calls and following an empty lead that took them away from, instead of towards, the warehouse district, Andi was done. No warehouse at all. Running in circles with him was getting them nowhere. *What a waste of a day.*

She couldn't get past Cole's *interrogation* regarding what had happened that night. Guilt already chewed at her gut. She didn't need it from the FBI ass, too. Andi was just as angry the bastard had got away. But, like her partner, she hadn't got a good look at him.

"Just take me back to the station, please," she demanded as darkness approached, adding 'please' as an afterthought. "I have to get home, it's getting late."

"Police work doesn't stop because the sun goes down," Cole said, his tone amused.

Andi harrumphed. Why the *hell* did he think riling her was funny? Fists clenched, she forced a breath. "It does, today. Not that we actually did any *work.*"

No way she was telling Cole she needed to get going so she could send Bella home while the hour was still decent and get Ethan into bed.

Her stomach growled and she cursed. Had the agent heard it? Would he make the unlikely offer of sharing a meal with her? Andi wouldn't have gone anyway. The temptation to stab him with a steak knife would have been too great. Had she been with Pete, he would have probably offered to take her and Ethan to dinner, and she would have accepted.

That was often their routine when a case kept them working long hours. Her heart gave a sad pang. Andi missed Pete. She'd meant to go see him today, but it hadn't happened, either. Because of Agent Lucas.

"Something wrong?"

"No. Please just take me back."

"Fine." His word was tense and Andi took a bit of satisfaction that she'd irritated him.

When he pulled up next to her silver SUV, she slipped out of his car as quickly as she could.

"See you in the morning?" Cole asked after he'd lowered the driver's side window.

Andi quirked an eyebrow. "Oh?" *Was this his idea of an olive branch?*

"Do you want me to pick you up somewhere or meet you here?" he asked as if she hadn't spoken.

Andi sighed, resigned. She shouldn't be rude to him when he was asking almost nicely. "Meeting here is fine. I usually get in between seven thirty and eight."

Cole nodded. He drove off a moment later.

Andi stared after him. Was she upset that he hadn't flashed his dimpled grin? She ignored the voice that whispered *yes*.

* * * *

Limbs heavy, Andi set her keys on the end table in the foyer, glaring at the droopy plant. Damn, she'd forgotten to water it—again. She opened the closet in the hallway and put her gun in the safe with surprisingly deft fingertips on the combination pad, considering how tired she was. Her weapon would be quick to grab if she needed it, regardless.

"Mama!"

She smiled as she heard the little exclamation, and turned to sweep him into her arms, hipping the door shut. Ethan kissed her cheek, causing another smile. She tugged his pyjama top down over his belly and tickled him until he giggled.

"Hi, buddy." He beamed. Andi pushed his dishevelled copper curls—so like Iain's—out of his blue eyes. He was overdue for a haircut. It was a mess these days.

Bella stood close by, leaning on the doorframe leading into the living room, looking amused.

"Thanks for staying, Bells."

"Oh, no problem, Andi," she said, smiling. The girl had lived next door to Andi most of her young life. She was like a younger sister.

Andi reached into her pocket with a free hand, propping her son on her hip. She handed Bella a twenty dollar bill. The teen's eyes widened.

"But you've already paid me for the week."

"It's for staying late. Probably tomorrow night, too," Andi said with a grimace. "Besides, it is a school night."

Bella made a face. "It's not even seven-thirty, Andi. It's not like I have a bedtime... I *am* seventeen. Don't sound like my mom, please. I hang out over here because you're so cool."

Andi chuckled. "Right. Sorry."

Bella grinned pure mischief. "Well, gotta run."

"Okay. Thanks again."

"No prob. I made some cheesy mac Hamburger Helper, left you a plate in the fridge. He's bathed, too." Bella ruffled Ethan's hair. "See you tomorrow, squirt."

Ethan giggled. "Bye bye, Bell Bell," the three-year-old told her, using the name he'd called her since he could speak.

Bella made a face then grinned again, tossing her pretty dark hair over a shoulder. Andi watched her head out of the front door, slightly envious of the young and their energy.

She wasn't so old at thirty-one, but she sure felt it tonight. She glanced at Ethan, who just grinned.

Andi set her son to his feet. He dashed into the living room to his pile of toys. She watched him a moment before heading into the kitchen to warm up the food Bella had left for her. Thank God for the teen, or she would never eat.

She flipped on the TV and sank into the couch, her plate on her lap desk, smiling at Ethan playing as he whispered to his toys. He'd greeted her happily as she'd entered the room, but seemed loath to leave his play, so Andi didn't push. She'd put him to bed in half an hour and jump in the shower.

Normality was a welcome distraction. She'd almost forgotten about Special Agent Cole Lucas and his... *everything*. She shook her head, groaning to herself. How was she supposed to work with someone who had no desire to maintain professionalism and get the job done?

A city of about fifty thousand, it wasn't every day — thank God — that Antioch, Texas, had one murder, let alone two and she was determined to find the guy who'd shot Pete and killed the two men.

What she'd discovered wasn't encouraging. The men were from New York, and both had criminal histories longer than she was tall, with ties to drugs and suspected human trafficking. They'd never been in for murder, but Rodney Gains, one of the dead men, had done ten years for drugs. What did Cole know that he was refusing to share?

Andi had news for him. In the morning, it was disclosure time. How she would convince him was a mystery, especially given how today had gone, but she'd take him to the warehouse since he'd insisted on it and force him to open up. The case — his *and* hers — depended on it. He'd proved he cared about his case, so she'd have to get to him that way. There was no other choice.

She must have fallen asleep, because she awoke to Ethan calling her, and patting her knees with his small hands.

"Oh, I'm sorry, buddy." Andi glanced at the clock on the

cable box. After nine. *Damn*. Ethan was supposed to have been in bed an hour ago and his wide yawn indicated her little one was indeed tired. She stifled a yawn of her own.

In the short time it took to make it down the hall to his room, her son was already asleep in her arms, his head nestled on her shoulder, his little face buried in her neck. Andi smiled and rubbed his back for a moment before gently lowering him to his toddler bed and tucking him in.

"Sleep well, baby," she whispered, dropping a kiss on his cheek. Ethan didn't even stir. She watched him for a moment. *God, he looks like Iain*. Every day, he was looking more and more like his father.

Cole Lucas' dimpled grin popped into her mind. Andi frowned and pushed the image away. She didn't want to think about, see him—anything. Her heart fluttered and she berated herself. What the hell was that about?

She hit the shower. It wasn't very late, but she needed some sleep. Six in the morning was going to suck.

Right as she was rubbing her hair dry, her cell phone rang. *No, no, no*…she was off the clock, and she wasn't on call this week. She needed sleep.

She shuddered as Cole danced across her mind. *Oh, hell no*. But Andi relaxed when she glanced at the caller ID. It was Pete.

"Howdy, partner," he said by way of greeting. He sounded much too cheerful.

"Are you getting discharged or something?" Andi asked, a smile playing at her lips. She plopped on her bed, tossing the towel in a nearby laundry basket.

"Don't tease me, please. No." Pete sounded disappointed and she laughed.

"Then when?"

"Maybe a few days. Damn docs anyways. My arm is fine. I want to get back to work and get these bastards." He growled and Andi nodded to herself. He was minimising, as always, but that was just Pete.

"I would appreciate that as well, but you had a collapsed

lung, never mind your arm, buddy. Heal."

"You doin' all right?"

No, she wasn't. And Pete didn't know about Cole... "Listen...a Fed came by today."

"Oh yeah?"

"Yeah—" she paused, taking a breath. She'd rather not talk about him.

"Andi? You there?"

She ploughed on. "Chief's making me work with him. Evidently my—our—case has something to do with what he's working on. Something bigger."

She heard shifting, as if he'd sat up in bed.

"Like what?"

Andi groaned. "I don't know."

"You don't know?" Pete's tone was a mixture of amusement and curiosity.

"He... Well, he's an asshole."

Pete laughed and Andi was torn between a smile and a whine.

"Well, you're a real charmer, partner. I know you'll get him to open up. You know those Fed types, they can be territorial."

"If I didn't know you better, I would think you're okay with this," she said.

"Well, what can it hurt? Maybe he's got something we don't."

Andi frowned even though her partner couldn't see her. She wanted him to commiserate, not be logical. *Men.* "If I don't kill him, maybe we can investigate properly."

Pete laughed again. "Perhaps you've met your match, Andi MacLaren."

What the hell was that supposed to mean? "I'll solve the case," Andi said.

"How's the lil' guy?" Pete asked. The subject change was welcome. Her partner had always loved Ethan, and the adoration was mutual.

"Just put him to bed, as I will myself shortly."

24

"Ah. I didn't wake you?"

"Nah. Just caught me out of the shower, though."

"Woo-hoo. Nekked Andi." Pete chuckled when Andi made a noise in her throat.

"I'll forget you're injured and shoot you again." She bit back a laugh.

"I know what a mean shot you are, so I will remember that." Pete's tone was light, but Andi sighed as she was hit with another pang of guilt.

She was an excellent marksman, they both knew it. *Except that night.*

Her partner had not only heard it, but had interpreted it correctly. "Andi, don't even start. It's *not* your fault. And stop that feeling guilty crap, too. *You* didn't shoot me, and it's *not* your fault the bastard got away. You...I...*we*...will catch them. Don't beat yourself up."

"I know," she whispered. How was he always so spot on?

"Well, hit the hay, Detective MacLaren. Call me if you get anything tomorrow... *When* you get something tomorrow."

"All right, Detective Crane."

"Sleep tight."

"You, too."

"Hey, Andi."

She paused. She'd almost hung up on him. "Yeah?"

"Play nice with Mr Fed."

Andi rolled her eyes. "I wish a longer hospital stay on you." She ended the call shaking her head at her partner's parting laughter. The man laughed entirely too much.

She collapsed on her bed, sighing for what seemed the hundredth time that night. Her mind wandered. Iain danced into her thoughts, as always. His laugh had been almost palpable and she smiled. Andi missed him so much, but it was a hell of a lot easier than it had been. Her love hadn't faded, but time had helped.

Not wholly healed, but living. Working in a job she still loved, but a job that had been the reason for Iain's stolen life. A job he'd loved, too. She had their son to live for, and

Ethan was the only reason Andi had been able to hold it together. Then and now. If only Iain could have seen him grow up.

When Chief and Pete had showed up on her doorstep to take her to the hospital, denial, fear and desperation had settled over her. She'd had no idea how she was going to raise a child alone.

Then she'd closed her eyes—she remembered as if it was yesterday—and had seen Iain's smiling face. He'd had tears in his eyes and had told her he loved her, he loved Ethan and everything would be okay. Andi still couldn't explain it to this day, but it was almost as if he had really been there, and he had been trying to tell her it was all right to let him go. But she hadn't really let him go, not totally, even now.

Cole popped into her mind and she frowned. Handsome face, dimples that would make a nun's heart race. A man like him would never be able to fathom how she felt about Iain and Ethan. *No way.* He was rocking that 'I am an island' crap to the extreme. Did he have any family? Someone who cared about him?

"He was probably spawned, not born," Andi whispered to her empty bedroom, then shook her head.

How the hell was she supposed to make this work?

Chapter Three

His hand shook as he tried to pour whisky into the shot glass. He almost dropped the bottle – twice.

"Fuck it," Carlo muttered under his breath and chugged the Jack. It burned a path down his throat. The warmth that spread neither comforted nor covered the pain that radiated from his leg and scorched through his side. "I'm in bad shape. *Worse.* I'm talking to myself."

Blood pooled at his feet and he cursed again. His leg started bleeding every time he hauled his ass up. A tremble slid down his spine. *It's just the alcohol.*

He swiped the back of his hand across his mouth and tried to set the bottle on the counter of the house he'd broken into. It was more of a slam and the amber liquid swished inside the bottle.

Carlo clutched his side, wincing as he made his way to the bathroom of the sprawling ranch home. When he pulled his hand away, the red slickness on his palm told him he'd reopened the wound there as well.

"Fuck. God damn it. *Fuck.*"

Sitting on the closed toilet proved a feat that almost had him on the floor on his ass. He scrambled for the sink, his bloody fingers slipping before gaining purchase. He righted himself but his head swam.

Fever gripped him, which meant that infection was probably settling over him. Carlo didn't need a doctor to tell him how screwed he was.

If he'd had a cell phone, he actually might have called Mike Amato – Cole Lucas, or whatever his real name was. FBI or not, the bastard would get him the medical attention he didn't dare try to get for himself. His former boss wasn't a dumbass. Like the police, they checked hospitals first. Gunshot wounds would attract cops like flies.

He was lucky he'd been able to take care of Reese and Gains, the first two guys Caselli had sent after him. Reese had shot him in the leg first, but Carlo would always remember the look on the big man's face as he went down—Carlo had shot him, too. Only *his* bullet had counted. He didn't regret it for even a second—he'd never liked that asshole.

Then the police had shown up. He'd got a few rounds off at them and escaped, but not without a second wound. One of the cops had shot him in the side. It was more of a graze, but had torn his skin as it passed through. It hurt like a bitch and bled like one, too.

Carlo was stuck. He'd used most of the gauze and medical tape he he'd found in the house. He'd tried sewing himself up, but the hole in his side was wide and he couldn't twist enough to reach it. His leg still had a slug in it and it hurt too badly to try to dig out himself.

Reese had missed his femoral, but not by much. Carlo was a lucky bastard. He wouldn't bleed out, but if he didn't get some help, the infection could go from bad to worse. The idea of gangrene scared the shit out of him.

He couldn't stay in the house forever. Piled up mail and newspapers suggested the owners were on vacation. *Yeah, how long could that last?*

The longer he stayed, the more evidence of his presence he left behind, and the more risk he had of being caught. He was too weak to clean up after himself.

Carlo struggled with the last of the gauze on his leg. He didn't have enough to redress his side. The starburst stain there spread as he moved, but he gritted his teeth and finished with his leg.

The damn homeowners must be saints, there wasn't so much as over the counter pain killers anywhere to be found. He really needed some Vicodin or high powered Ibuprofen, but he would take Tylenol at this point. Breaking into a pharmacy was out. It was a sure way behind bars — he wouldn't be able to flee any scene.

He gripped the sink with both hands and shoved himself up, cursing as his side burned. He shifted his weight back and forth, his leg throbbing.

Carlo collapsed on the couch as his vision started to close in on him. He was about to pass the fuck out. Good damn thing he was lying down. He fought to maintain consciousness but lost the battle.

* * * *

Andi stared at the coffee cup Agent Lucas held out to her.

"Truce?" he asked, flashing his dimpled grin.

Heat crept up her neck, but she ignored it. "You think such a small offering will do the trick after yesterday's disaster?" She raised an eyebrow.

"It's a French vanilla cappuccino..." he teased, dragging out the last word.

How did he know her favourite flavour? It was all she could do to not snatch the treat from his hand, but she did take it. She wanted it, but damned if she'd admit that to him.

"I'm sorry about yesterday."

"Which part?" she asked, heading down the hall towards CID. Cole was on her heels.

"Look, I'm...frustrated with how this case is going. It's not often someone gets one over on me."

Andi glanced over her shoulder in time to see him cringe. She sipped the cappuccino he'd bought for her, savouring the sweet flavour as it danced on her tongue. *Delicious.* She hadn't had one in ages.

"You gonna let me in on what's going on?" She kept her tone light as they reached her work area. She settled in her chair.

Cole propped himself on the edge of her desk, crossing his arms over his impossibly broad chest. Andi averted

29

her eyes as his black T-shirt stretched across his abs. Her stomach fluttered.

"I'm fairly certain the bastard that shot your partner is my guy. His name is Carlo Maldonado, and he got away from me a few months ago."

Andi sat taller in her chair. "Got away?" He didn't have to explain how unusual that was for him. She was just certain of it.

"He turned state's evidence when a deal for his boss went south. He's got more worries than me on his ass."

"Deal? Drugs?"

Cole's steel gaze was level and about as serious as she'd seen him. "Girls. Young ones. He's a trafficker. But he's low on the totem pole."

Andi gripped her coffee tighter. "Bastard..." she breathed.

"No doubt." Cole shook his head.

Andi saw him in a new light. Was it because he cared about the case and the girls? Or because he'd failed...lost his prize?

"I was undercover for over a year. It took me six months to get in with his boss, Tony Caselli. Just when I thought I had them all trusting me, Maldonado pulled a stupid."

"What happened?" she asked.

"Saw a girl he wanted to keep."

"Keep?" From the look on Cole's face, she didn't need him to clarify. "How old?"

"Fourteen."

Andi's stomach lurched. "No."

"I got her out. And got us exposed. Maldonado didn't know I was FBI before then, but he's a coward at heart. I was escorting him in when they came after us, and I convinced him to turn to save his ass. We were almost home free when they found us. Shootout. He got away from me."

"Are they after you, too?"

Cole shrugged. "Probably. I'm not worried about it. I know how to disappear."

She cocked her head to the side, studying him. "And

now?"

"I tracked him. I don't know what brought him down here. He's got no ties to Texas I could figure out. Hate to admit it, but I had no clue where he was until he shot Gains, Reese and your partner. I know he's still around somewhere."

"I got him. I just don't know how badly," Andi said.

"Bad enough to make him bleed. Four types at the scene."

Andi nodded. "Thanks…for the info."

Cole stared as if surprised by her comment. She flushed. Damn, what was wrong with her? Andi cleared her throat.

"You taking me to the warehouse?" he asked, his tone nonchalant.

She frowned. "I thought we went through this." If he insulted her department again, she would—

"I suspect that Maldonado tried to make a quick buck."

"Meaning?"

"Vacant warehouse. He could have contacts in the south. Get a few girls through, and bam. Some money to move on. But Gains and Reese found him. Or it was a setup—Maldonado is a greedy bastard so, dangerous or not, he would've tried it."

In her city? Human trafficking? *Damn*. She didn't know what to say.

"It can happen anywhere, Andi," Cole said softly, as if he'd read her mind. Had his tone not been so low and *un*-mocking, she would have snapped at him.

"I still think the warehouse is a waste of time. There've got to be other leads to follow. What else do you know? Crime Scene already—"

"I want to see it for myself." His tone brooked no argument.

Andi's frown deepened. "Our Crime Scene guys know what they're doing." She set her cappuccino down and crossed her arms, her posture mirroring his.

"There's no need to get defensive. Relax, babe."

"Babe?" Andi rushed to her feet. "Do *not* call me that." What gave him the right to be so casual with her? She was a

31

cop. His *equal*. He was treating her like a chick he'd picked up in a bar.

Cole grinned. She stared, heat rushing her face. He'd *grinned* at her? He could go to hell. What a mistake she had made thinking he was anything but an asshole.

"We going or what?"

"You know what? You can go to—" Andi stopped as she took in his expectant gaze. This was what he wanted. Cole *wanted* to piss her off so she would let him ditch her. No. Fricking. Way. *Not* going to happen. "Yeah, let's go."

His mouth was a hard line, his handsome face tight, but he straightened to his full height.

The drive to the warehouse made her twitchy. She didn't want the reminder, the guilt of that night.

Andi and Pete had happened upon the scene anyway. Neither of them had been on call that night, but Pete had had a nervous informant who'd insisted on meeting him not far from where the shooting had happened. The guy was notoriously unreliable, so she hadn't wanted Pete going it alone.

They'd heard the shots, called it in and headed into what had ended up being two warm bodies and a fleeing shooter. Neither of them had even seen Maldonado—if he was indeed the shooter—but he'd seen *them* and fired. Shot Pete.

She'd got off a few rounds, but hadn't wanted to leave Pete to give chase in the dark when, at the time, she hadn't known how badly her partner had been hit.

The uniforms had arrived quickly enough, but the scum had escaped. She regretted not going after him. Andi would have caught him.

"Hello? Andi?" Cole's tone held irritation. He must have called her name a few times.

"Sorry."

"You okay?" His gaze was actually concerned.

Andi bit back a scowl. What the hell did he care? "I'm fine."

He frowned and cleared his throat. "Where to?"

Oh, we're here already. "Pull in to the right, and it's the first warehouse on the left. It was owned by an office supply distribution company, but they went under a few years ago. It's been empty since, though we've had to clear out squatters a few times. Usually of the drug dealing variety."

He didn't comment, but followed her directions, pulling the Challenger to a stop in front of the vacant building.

The entrance was still covered with yellow police tape, but Cole wouldn't care about that any more than he gave a damn about anything Andi had told him. She leaned on the car.

"You coming?" He arched a brow at her, a frown marring his handsome face.

"Why bother?"

Cole shrugged and turned away, heading into the warehouse without another word.

Damn him, he'd called her bluff. Andi cursed him to hell and back and pushed off the car, resisting the urge to key the damn thing. She followed his path into the building, forcing her feet into an even pace, not rushing after him like she was inclined to.

Cole squatted down next to where the bodies of James Reese and Rodney Gains had been found. He didn't even look up.

"I would bet this is Maldonado's blood right here. So, looks like you're not the only one who shot him after all."

Andi didn't get a chance to snap *No shit* at him because his cell phone rang.

"Lucas," he said into it as he got to his feet.

She busied herself with looking around, drowning out the sound of Cole's voice as he carried on his conversation.

What had she missed in here? *Had* she missed anything at all?

The scene played in her mind. Pete had been right outside. She'd been tight to him, guarding his back. Routine for them. He always led. She could still see his wide eyes and

33

pale face as he'd gone down. Andi had returned fire. The bastard shooter had cursed as he'd shuffled around the dark corner of the building. She'd hit him, but he'd been gone before she could make out the slightest detail other than male and thin, average height. She'd failed.

Andi sighed, studying the vast room. Why the hell would anyone pick the place to trade anything, let alone young girls? Wouldn't it be obvious kids didn't belong in the area? Even in this part of the city, there was always that one nosy neighbour who was a bit nine-one-one happy.

"Thanks." Cole's voice grabbed her attention as he ended his call. His expression was unreadable.

"Anything I need to know?"

"No." He arched an eyebrow and smirked.

"Okay, let me rephrase that. Was that about the case?"

"Nothing helpful."

"Dammit, I thought we were over this."

"This?" Cole's tone was a pretty good representation of *innocence.*

"You know what? I'm done. I'll be in the car." Andi forced a deep breath and an even tone. She wouldn't give him even one inkling that she was fuming, though her face was hot and stomach tight.

She turned on a heel, not waiting for his answer. Andi didn't give him the satisfaction of rushing out. *Breathe. Just breathe. He doesn't need to know he got to you.*

Restraining the urge to slam the car door was almost the straw that broke the camel's back. Andi made a fist but stopped herself from punching the console. What good would it do? Sore knuckles wouldn't improve what was obviously going to be the longest day of her career. Would she still be gainfully employed at the end of it, or in jail for murder?

Cole watched Andi go. She slammed the door and he shook his head. He really shouldn't have messed with her. The phone call had nothing to do with the case at all. His older sister Cassidy—Cass—had called. He'd not talked to her in a month or so. It'd been too long, and had been good to hear her voice. Husband great. Two daughters perfect. End of call. His only family shouldn't be abbreviated, but Cole had work to do. Cass understood. She always had.

His sister never excluded him. Despite the miles that constantly separated them and how Cole always played it off, Cass kept him grounded, connected to the real world— outside whatever case he was working.

Staring at the door, he almost hoped Andi would come back. So far this morning, he wasn't scoring any brownie points, not even with the cappuccino bribe. He *did* want to solve the case. He gave the mostly empty room a scan. Office in the far corner, glass windows so black he couldn't see inside. The door's grey paint was scraped and stripped, the 'O' and one 'f' missing from the metal letters affixed to it. A lone maroon rail container on the far side of the room, one door open. Four bays to his left, roll-up doors down and padlocked.

"Why this place, Carlo?" he whispered.

It was out of character for a coward like Carlo Maldonado to jump ship into the unknown. Cole had hung out with the guy for over a year. Carlo liked predictable, routine, his own semblance of *safe*, considering his career choice. Texas had never been mentioned.

Like Andi had stated, the bank owned the warehouse now. Cole had done his homework—he'd already looked into that. And none of the names on the former company roster looked familiar. The office supply distributor hadn't been a cover for anything illegal that he could figure out. Nor did anyone involved with it come with a criminal background.

He looked back down at the remainder of the bloody stains where Gains and Reese had fallen. The shootout had been at close range. It wasn't like Carlo to go in guns blazing. Perhaps he had known it was a setup, if it was. Greed aside, the man was a save-your-own-ass type through and through.

"Surprised you had it in you, Carlo. Killing Big Rod and Jim…"

Where was he now?

After a few more mental notes, Cole sighed. There was nothing more to see. He squared his shoulders. There was the rest of the day to get through with Andi. Getting somewhere on the case would be good, too.

Chapter Four

"You have *got* to be kidding me!" Cole took a deep breath. It didn't help.

The kid behind the counter took one look at him and blanched. His brass-plated name tag had 'Assistant Manager' etched under 'Michael'. "I'm *very* sorry, sir. We've been calling all the guests that weren't here all day. Both of the numbers we had for you were bad."

Cole groaned. He was about to demand a valid reason why they hadn't called the police department, but the hotel chain had no idea who he was, or why he was in town—exactly the reasons they didn't know his real name or have a real phone number for him. It was his fault, but couldn't have been any other way.

"Look, Mr Parker, I'm very sorry, as I've already said. The sprinkler system went haywire for hours. This situation is bad for all involved. Imagine our loss of business, and loss of money with all the refunds. And the damage. All of our beds, furniture—everything—it's all ruined."

"I don't give a damn about *your* inconvenience, *Michael*," Cole bit out, restraining the urge to poke the punk in the chest. Assistant Manager? He couldn't be more than twelve. Was he even out of high school?

"Bruce…may I call you Bruce?"

"No." Cole didn't even grin at his alias. He'd booked his room under the name Bruce Parker, a combination of two of his favourite superheroes' real world alter egos.

"Mr Parker, then. Once again, I'm s—"

"Like I said, *once again* I don't give a damn."

"I would be happy to help you get other accommodations."

Michael put his palms up, brown eyes wide.

"Where?"

"I can transfer you to another of our hotels, free of charge. It's about thirty miles from here…"

"Thirty miles? Hell, no."

"The annual rodeo is in town, so I'm afraid there's nothing closer."

Cole cursed and snatched his black duffle that some hotel employee had so *graciously* cleared from the room he'd been staying in since he'd arrived in Antioch. Good thing he'd never unpacked. He didn't stop to inspect his things to see if the sprinkler disaster had ruined them. He'd just deal with it.

He shoved the automatic doors open instead of waiting as he exited, but it didn't give any satisfaction or relieve any annoyance.

"Dammit," he muttered, tossing his bag in the back seat before climbing into his Challenger.

He dug his cell phone from his jeans pocket. Cole selected a number from his contact list, pushing harder than necessary on the touch screen.

"Cole?" The voice on the other end sounded surprised, but friendly.

"Hey, Dex. I need a favour." He heard a giggle in the background that was decidedly female. "Are you busy?" Cole hesitated, suddenly guilty. It was well after business hours.

"Not for you, Cole. Hold on." There was a muffling sound as if Dex had covered the receiver with his hand. "Be right back, babe," he heard his friend say, also garbled. "What's up?"

"Dex, baby, hurry back," the giggler called out.

His long-time buddy and fellow FBI agent, but on the technical side, as a computer expert and analyst, had always been a ladies' man. Cole was no slouch, but Dex put his antics to shame. His friend certainly didn't fit the stereotype of computer nerd.

"I need an address."

"Okay…" Cole could hear the patter of typing and Dex would be ready for him in a moment. They had done this hundreds of times. "Name?"

"Andi — Andrea MacLaren. But it's 'Mac' not 'Mc'."

"Umm…a woman?" Dex asked. His buddy was far too curious.

"My…partner…from the local Podunk PD," Cole answered.

"Same city you're in?" Dex asked without missing a beat.

"Yeah."

"She hot?"

Cole sighed. "Just give me the damn address."

"She's hot all right."

He growled and Dex laughed. He was hit with a sudden wave of jealousy. What the hell? Dex was fifteen hundred miles away, and his friend would never come between him and a woman. Not that it mattered. Andi was off limits for so many reasons. Besides, he wasn't even into her. At. All.

"Well, I've got it."

"Thanks," Cole said, jotting down Andi's address as quickly as Dex had recited it.

"Need help getting there?"

"Hell, no. This place isn't that big."

"You're dying, aren't you? What did you do to her?"

"What the hell does that mean?" Cole snapped.

"God, Cole, you haven't been this tightly wound in a while. Dude, you need to get laid."

"Jesus, Dex. Shut the hell up. Thanks for the address. Later." He hung up, shaking his head at Dex's parting laugh. Damn Dex anyway.

He hadn't had sex for a while, but so what? He wasn't *tightly wound* as Dex had said. He was fine. Just fine, considering the circumstances.

* * * *

Andi looked up when the doorbell rang and she glanced at the clock. It was just past nine. Who could possibly be at the door? Maybe Bella had forgotten something, but then again, she barely ever knocked, let alone rang the doorbell.

Checking the peephole, she let out a string of curses. She was crazy to even consider opening the damn door.

"Howdy, partner," Special Agent Cole Lucas said brightly from her doorstep, a black duffle bag in hand.

Andi blinked, but the jerk didn't disappear.

Not a good sign. His statement was reminiscent of Pete, but Cole was *not* Pete, and he hadn't wanted to be her partner for either of the last two days, so why now? She eyed him warily.

"Have a couch?" he asked, flashing an almost charming smile.

No way would she let those dimples affect her.

"You have *got* to be kidding me!" Andi exclaimed.

Cole laughed. "I was saying that, not twenty minutes ago, really."

She scowled. "Cut to the chase. What do you want?" After the day he had put her through, she didn't even want to see him, let alone have him at her home.

"I need a place to stay."

"That's my problem, how?" She smirked. He was an ass, but when *he* needed something, now they were partners? *Hell no.*

"Look, I'm not happy about this. I hate to admit it, but I'm desperate. I don't have a place to stay."

"Why the hell not?"

"The hotel kicked me out."

"What did you do?" Andi bit back a smile at the wave of satisfaction from Cole's situation. There was such a thing as karma, after all.

"Well, it wasn't just me. It was everyone that was staying there. They had to close down because of some sprinkler system disaster. There's nowhere else vacant because of some rodeo."

"Oh?" Andi said, leaning on the doorjamb and crossing her arms over her chest. The part about the rodeo was true. The two-week-long event was a big deal in Antioch.

"Yes. So, since you and I are supposed to be working together, I thought—"

"You thought *wrong*, Agent Lucas."

"Andi, are you going to make me beg?" She said nothing. "Okay, I will beg." Andi almost laughed out loud as Special Agent Cole Lucas got down on one knee on her doormat. Oh, where was her camera when she needed it? "Detective MacLaren, may I sleep on your couch? One night, until I can make other arrangements. Please?"

Andi sighed, and they both knew it was one of acquiescence. Cole flashed a brilliant grin, dimples and all, and she ignored the heat in her body, the rushing of her heart. She *would not* have a reaction to this man. He infuriated her.

Stepping back, she gestured for him to enter the house. He looked around as he stepped into the foyer.

"Do you have your weapon on you?" she asked. Their eyes met, and if Cole's confused expression was any indication, she'd caught him off guard.

"Of course." He opened his jacket, allowing her a view of the butt of his semi-automatic Glock.

She tried to ignore how his tight shirt clung to the muscles of his chest, averting her eyes without trying to be obvious. The last thing she needed was to be caught ogling him.

"Why?" he asked.

Andi opened the closet door and unlocked her gun safe before stepping back. "I need you to put it in here. I will show you how to open it."

"Why?" he repeated.

Heat rushed her cheeks as she met his eyes. "Because I have a child." She berated herself. What did she care about what he thought?

Cole's eyes widened, and Andi had to stop herself from a scathing retort. He definitely wouldn't check her out anymore. He wasn't the kind of man that was interested in women with children. She ignored the pang of regret that rushed her. He was an ass. She didn't care anyway.

"You have a kid?"

Andi glared. "Yes. And he has to live in this house, just like I do. I'd appreciate if it was impossible for him to get his hands on things that could hurt him."

"Okay." He pulled his gun from its holster and handed it to her.

"I'll show you. There's a keypad and a code."

Cole nodded and took a step towards her.

Andi was all too aware of how close his body was to hers as she showed him how to get into the gun safe. Her breath caught when she turned to see if he'd understood the combination as she'd pressed the numbers in and found his face only inches from hers. Cole was looking into her eyes, not at the gun safe. The small closet was claustrophobic. Her stomach roiled and heat crept up her neck. Her face had to be crimson. She took a step back.

She cleared her throat and Cole took a deep breath. The floral fragrance of her hair teased his nose and he had to restrain himself from touching her. She had no patience for him and his hands on her would infuriate her, so he planted his fists at his sides. But she smelt so good. Like fresh flowers mixed with clean linens.

Andi looked great in the jeans that were clinging to her every curve and the tight Green Bay Packers T-shirt that was accentuating the generous bosom her previous shirts had hidden. She looked even better than she had in the khakis and button-down he'd seen her in during the day. He wanted her.

He'd never become involved with a woman he'd worked with, and he wasn't about to start. She was a mother — that'd shocked the hell out of him, and should have been an even further deterrent, but somehow, it wasn't.

"Did you see what I just did?" she asked.

No, Cole hadn't seen a damn thing, except how her jeans and T-shirt clung in all the right places. "Can you do it again? I need to memorise the combo, after all, right?" He tried to keep his tone light so she wouldn't catch on that he'd been watching her body, not her hands.

"Yes." She was already exasperated with him.

He flashed her another grin. Unfortunately, she seemed to be as immune to it as she had been to the others he'd given her. What the hell was with that? Women *always* responded to his grin.

Cole had her show him how to get into the gun safe several more times, then tried it himself so he was sure he could get his gun. When they were both comfortable he'd grasped the technique and memorised the combination, he whispered his thanks. Andi gave him a small smile and nodded. That was all he was going to get from her.

They stepped out of the closet and she closed the door. Her house was nice — spacious and sprawling for a one storey. She guided him into her living room and he looked around. The tan couch, loveseat and recliner all matched and were arranged in a manner that encouraged conversation.

The huge flat panel television on the wall was a guy's dream. There was a fireplace in the corner of the room, the mantel full of family photos. The opposite corner contained a red, blue, green and yellow toy box. Right next to it was a table and four tiny chairs consisting of the same primary colours. The room was practical, decorated simply and, somehow, totally Andi. Lived in, but not messy.

He wandered over to the fireplace, looking at the pictures and knick-knacks that decorated the mantel. There was a small boy with bright red hair in a large picture at its centre. He was dressed like a cowboy, sitting on a bench, a rocking horse in the background, grinning at the camera. Cole smiled.

"Is this him?" he asked, glancing over his shoulder.

Andi stiffened, but nodded. "His name is Ethan."

Cole looked back at the mantel, spotting a picture of Andi

with a handsome, redheaded man. Both were in full police dress uniform, and the man had a big smile on his face. Andi's smile was shy in comparison. There was a medal displayed in a dark wood case standing next to the photo frame.

He sensed more than saw her come to stand next to him, and Cole glanced at her. Andi's expression was pained. His heart ached. What was up? It didn't matter, he wanted to comfort her, but thought better of touching her, though she was not standing as close now as she had been in the closet.

"His name was Iain, and the picture was taken the day I made Detective."

"Was?" Cole probably shouldn't have immediately zoned in on that part of her statement, but it was out of his mouth before he had paused to think.

"He was killed in the line of duty three years ago." Her voice trembled.

Cole wanted to throw his arm around her shoulders, but didn't.

There was a wedding picture of the two of them not far from the picture she'd just discussed. Why that one hadn't caught his eye first was a mystery, because Andi was radiant, more beautiful than he'd ever seen her, as she and Iain gazed at each other in the picture.

"I'm sorry, Andi."

Shrugging, she turned away from him. "Three years…is a long time," Andi whispered, her back to him.

Like she was trying to convince herself. He wasn't about to contradict her, but what could he say, anyway?

She cleared her throat. "I do have a guest room, but it's being used for storage right now, so it's a mess. The bed in there isn't even made up. I'm sorry."

"The couch is fine," Cole said.

"Let me get some blankets for you." Andi disappeared down the hall before he could answer her.

Wife and mother was a new side to her. Of course she had a life outside her job, but her boss had praised her so highly, telling him she was very involved in her career. He'd never imagined she was married — or had been — and was a mother.

His attraction to her didn't diminish — he was glad she was available. But was she seeing someone? What the hell was wrong with him?

Cole needed to be focused on work, on his case, not on Detective Andi MacLaren — at least not *how* he'd like to be focused on her. Her naked beneath him was more like it. *No.* It couldn't happen. Even if she could halfway stand him — which she couldn't — nothing could happen between them.

"Here you go, Agent Lucas," Andi said, plopping a few blankets and a pillow down on her brown couch. She looked so damn good in those jeans he wanted to change his mind...again. Being between the sheets with her might be worth it.

"Cole. Please call me Cole. I know we got off on the wrong foot and continued down that path, but, again, I want to apologise."

"Goodnight, Cole." Obviously, she didn't want to talk to him about anything, let alone his overdue apology.

"So, that's it? You're not going to accept my apology?"

"Not tonight. I'm tired, and we have a long day tomorrow." She turned to go.

"Andi, wait." Why was he calling her back? He could respect that she was still upset with him — she had every right to be. He'd gone a bit overboard with some of the things he'd said.

Keeping Cass' phone call from her had been unnecessary from the start. He hadn't needed to carry it on in the car after they'd left the warehouse. It'd only served to get her so pissed off at him she'd barely uttered a word all day. So much for getting somewhere on the case.

Andi glanced over her shoulder and Cole grabbed her wrist. He yanked her into his arms and covered her mouth with his.

He hadn't intended to kiss her but as her soft, warm lips caressed his, Cole couldn't have changed his mind even if he'd wanted to. Her curves hit his chest with enough impact that should have jarred him back into his head, but he was lost and overheated immediately. He wrapped her in a tight embrace and kissed her harder.

She fought him, but his mouth was demanding over hers, and Andi opened for him, melting against him, surrendering to him. She slipped her arms around his neck and Cole bit back a groan. Her taste, sweeter than he'd imagined, was like ripe berries. He needed more.

Andi whimpered against his mouth, her tongue dancing with his. His cock stood at attention, straining against his zipper. He moaned as her body melded to his, breasts to chest, hips to hips. Cole had to have her.

As he walked them back towards the couch, she pushed hard against his chest, breaking the kiss and shoving him away from her. They both panted hard.

"Don't...don't ever do that...again," she stammered, the gorgeous swell of her breasts lifting and pulling her shirt taut as her chest heaved. He could see peaked nipples. His erection throbbed and he struggled for coherent thought.

Cole dragged his gaze to her face. Blue eyes wide, cheeks rosy, freckles noticeable, her lips swollen from his. Though she'd been appealing before, how she stood before him now blew that out of the water. She was gorgeous.

He needed to say something. Anything. Apologise? He wasn't sorry in the least. *Speechless* just about covered it.

She trembled and rubbed her arm. It took all he was made of not to pull her back to him and kiss her again.

There was no chance to answer. Andi turned on her heel and fled down the hall, slipping into the room farthest away from the living room. She didn't even pause to look at him as she slammed the door.

He winced. What the hell should he make of what had happened? He stared down the hallway for a moment, his heart pounding. Never in his life, not even when he was a teenager, had one kiss stirred him to the point that Andi's had. Then she'd run from him. His body shook with unfulfilled need.

Cole couldn't blame her, really. No way should he have given in to the urge to kiss her. But he had the sinking suspicion he would have to do it again—and more. He wouldn't be able *not* to. And hell, she'd kissed him back.

The voice of reason chided that he didn't get involved with women he worked with, but his cock certainly disagreed. He ignored them both and dragged his hand over his face. The morning would bring complications.

Cole sighed and glanced at the couch. It looked comfortable, but would he be able to sleep?

Chapter Five

Cole jolted awake. Where the hell was he? He swallowed a yawn and blinked. What time was it?

He looked to his left, finding a pair of very blue eyes staring at him. The little boy cocked his head to one side, as if assessing him. The eyes before him were familiar — Andi's eyes.

Sitting up, he glanced over the small kid. The red hair was full of curls. A smattering of freckles covered his cheeks, also like Andi's. He was cute.

Cole adored his sister's two girls. They were seven and nine, although this boy couldn't be more than three or four.

"Hi," he said softly. The little boy smiled at him, then tentatively reached out and touched his arm.

Glancing around, Cole didn't spot Andi, so he looked back at the kid. He was dressed in light blue pyjamas with police cars, German Shepherds and flashlights printed on them. Cole smiled back.

"What's your name?" Andi's son asked.

"Cole. What's yours?" She'd told him his name when she'd mentioned him last night, but it didn't come to mind.

"Ethan. I'm three." He held up his little hand, three fingers proudly presented, and Cole smiled again.

He reached his hand out for a proper handshake, his smile becoming a grin when Ethan slid his tiny hand into Cole's.

"Ethan!" Andi called, her voice shrill. Her son jumped. His big blue eyes were as wide as saucers as she entered the room.

Cole stared, frowning. Her tone suggested she didn't want him talking to her kid.

"Mama?" the little boy asked. He shifted on his bare feet.

Andi's chest heaved as if she'd taken a deep breath. "Go get dressed, buddy," she admonished in a normal tone of voice.

Ethan grinned and nodded, then dashed down the hall.

"Cute PJs," Cole said, after Andi had murmured a somewhat polite morning greeting. He looked her up and down, remembering the feel of her in his arms. Her face reddened, but she remained quiet, avoiding his gaze.

"Thanks. My mom made them," she said after clearing her throat.

Made what? Oh, pyjamas. He'd complimented the kid's sleepwear. Right.

Andi was so put together already, and it wasn't even seven in the morning. He'd give just about anything to see her flushed and pink, her hair messed up again, especially if he was the cause.

"Coffee's almost done brewing." Her tone was tight, telling him she had no desire for small talk. Cole had got to her. He bit back a smartass grin. It would only tick her off.

Andi faced the kitchen without waiting for his answer.

"He can actually dress himself?" he asked.

Andi's shoulders stiffened. "Yes."

Damn. He'd not meant to upset her. Why did she take everything he said as an insult?

Andi needed to check on her son. Ethan had been in his room too long, and it was already six forty-five — she'd left Cole about twenty minutes ago. Ethan had been very proud of himself lately. Each night, he and Andi would pick out his clothes and lay them out, and Ethan would dress in the morning without her watching. She always made sure he'd done a proper job, of course, but even she basked in her son's sense of accomplishment.

She shut off the burner she'd been scrambling eggs on and covered the frying pan to keep them warm. Andi took a sip of coffee and set it on the kitchen island before heading back into the living room with a sigh, praying she could hold onto her sanity.

Cole would probably want to talk about what had happened last night, but she didn't. She just wanted to forget it. She promptly banished all memories of his lips on hers and the sudden tremble that had slid down her spine. She ignored her traitorous body. Andi hadn't felt that way in—well, never, really. Not even Iain had melted her with one kiss.

Iain. His smiling face popped into her head and she was rushed with guilt, just as she had been last night. *Damn Cole.*

Her heart stopped at the sight of Ethan on Cole Lucas' lap. He was tying her son's shoes. As if it was the most natural thing in the world. She wanted to protest, but her voice abandoned her.

When she'd seen the FBI agent and the little boy shake hands earlier, her heart had skipped a beat she didn't quite understand—or have the desire to acknowledge.

Cole Lucas couldn't *possibly* be good with children. As a matter of fact, he couldn't even *like* kids. Somehow it was just…wrong. He was a first class jerk. She suppressed a growl and stepped into the room.

Two sets of eyes, one deep blue and the other steel grey, met hers at the same time. They both smiled at her, Ethan flashing a brilliant grin, Cole's a bit tentative. She berated herself because she liked how her son looked in Cole's arms, just as she had liked being there herself.

Her gaze locked with his. Andi was frozen for a moment until Ethan's voice broke the spell.

"Cole helped me, Mama." His statement kicked her into mommy-mode.

Good. It was what she needed. She couldn't meet Cole's eyes again.

"I see that. Did you say thanks?"

Ethan looked at Cole, then back at her. "Thanks, Cole!" he said obediently, and scrambled off the FBI agent's lap.

"No problem, kiddo." Cole ruffled her son's copper curls

and Ethan giggled.

Andi's heart stuttered. "Are you guys hungry?" she forced out.

"Yeah!"

"Famished," Cole said, speaking at the same time as Ethan's exclamation.

Andi focused on her son, looking away from Cole's grey eyes and dimples. "I made scrambled eggs, bacon and toast," she told Ethan, who beamed and skipped towards the kitchen.

"Thanks, Andi," Cole said, walking beside her.

She acknowledged him with a nod. "Thank you for helping my son."

"I didn't mind in the least. He's a cute kid."

"Thanks." She was polite, handing him a mug for coffee after assisting Ethan into his booster seat. "I would have thought you didn't like kids."

"Oh?" Cole asked, raising an eyebrow at her.

A blush rushed her cheeks. She'd insulted him, but she'd not meant her tone to be snide. "Well…"

"I'm not that guy, Andi," Cole said evenly.

She stared at him, not wanting to admit she knew exactly what he meant. She did think he was *that guy*.

"I see no need to discuss it," she said, concentrating to keep her voice normal. She didn't want Ethan to know anything was wrong, or for Cole to realise how much he'd flustered her.

He didn't answer, just thanked her for the mug and fixed himself some coffee. Andi quickly made plates for all three of them and sat to Ethan's right at the square table in her breakfast nook. Cole took a seat across from her son. She resisted the urge to scoot her chair farther away from him.

"I have two nieces," he said.

"Oh?" Andi asked, looking pointedly at the food on her plate.

"They're seven and nine. My sister's kids. I don't get to see them much, but I adore them."

"What's their names?" Ethan asked.

Andi smiled as he was able to follow the conversation. The little boy looked at Cole before taking a huge bite of toast.

"Kelsey is nine, and Lacey is seven."

"I want to play with them," Ethan announced.

Cole laughed out loud. "They live far away, buddy. In Seattle."

Unfortunately, her son would have no idea where that was.

"Oh," he said, his tone disappointed. "Maybe someday?"

Cole looked at Andi and she gave a slight shrug.

"Maybe," Andi agreed quickly, wiping the crumbs from her son's mouth gently.

Ethan made a face, but let her do so. He took a drink of orange juice, and she admonished him to slow down.

"Good. I like kids," Ethan said.

Cole chuckled. "I like kids, too." He tweaked the little boy's nose.

Andi couldn't look away from him. Cole grinned, dimples flashing, and her face heated. She broke eye contact, cursing herself. *Work*. Focus on work. "What's today's agenda?"

"I'd like to talk to your partner."

She nodded absently, losing her determination again. Cole's ease with Ethan had her heart needing a cardiologist. Andi reminded herself that she didn't like Cole Lucas *at all*, but it wasn't working. She was seeing a different side of him. It only resulted in chaos and confusion.

As a matter of fact, nowhere in sight was the pompous ass from the previous days. Could she actually figure him out, perhaps even get to know him? She shook her head. She didn't want to like him, didn't need to figure him out and most definitely *did not* need to get to know him. He wouldn't be around long enough for it to matter.

It *shouldn't* matter, so it *didn't*.

"Something wrong?" Cole asked, his voice breaking into her thoughts.

"No...why?" Andi stuttered, her cheeks blazing. There was no way he would miss it.

Cole gave a slight smile that confirmed her suspicion. "You got awfully quiet."

"Mama, okay?" Ethan asked.

Great. Her three-year-old was much too smart for his own good. He never failed to surprise and impress her with the extent he was able to follow conversations, and of course the ability was at its height when she was embarrassed. "I'm fine," she told them. Andi forced a smile.

"I know you like to go in early, but I'd like to shower, if it's all right with you," Cole said.

"Oh, of course. I'm sorry I didn't offer. Didn't mean to be rude," Andi rushed her words. She was a complete heel.

Cole smiled again, flashing dimples, and Andi's heart quickened. "No problem."

"Towels are in the cupboard behind the door in the guest bathroom. I'm sure you know where that is?" Cole nodded. "Then...we can head out whenever you're ready."

He put his dish in the sink before disappearing around the corner. Andi gulped, trying to ignore the picture in her head of him naked in her bathroom. She chastised herself and concentrated on what Ethan was trying to ask her.

* * * *

Cole sighed as the hot water ran down his body. It was relief. What the hell was he going to do about Andi? Breakfast had been delicious, and something he hadn't expected from her. The scrambled eggs and bacon had been the first home-cooked meal he'd had in longer than he could remember. He certainly didn't deserve it.

He'd settled on the fact that he owed her another apology, even if he didn't really regret the kiss he'd stolen. Well, not really stolen. She'd kissed him back, after all.

If he didn't try to smooth things out, work today would be a nightmare. They *did* have a case to solve. Regardless,

Andi wouldn't make it easy, and that lessened his already weak desire to offer the olive branch in the first place.

He squirted shampoo into his palm then slapped it onto his dark hair, scrubbing vigorously. He suppressed the urge to yawn. No matter how the day went, it would be a long one.

Cole hadn't fallen asleep until well past midnight. The taste of Andi's lips had haunted him. The feel of her full breasts flattened against his chest, her rounded hips against his...the endless cycle in his mind while he stared at the ceiling of her living room.

When sleep had finally claimed him, he'd dreamt of her. Vivid and erotic. In his dreams, she'd done things to him he would give anything to experience with her in reality.

He'd awoken after two a.m., painfully uncomfortable, his body so taut he was surprised he hadn't had a fricking wet dream, as horrible as that would have been. Was he a thirteen-year-old kid?

The rest of the night, his sleep had been fitful. He'd woken every hour or so, and in worse shape than every previous hour. Damn good thing his body was over the condition by the time Ethan had woken him. But Cole wasn't cured. He wanted Andi.

Rinsing his hair, he ran his fingers through it one last time before reaching for his soap. He tried not to think about her and failed miserably. He rubbed his body down, inhaling the pleasant masculine spice of his body wash.

What would her hands feel like on his chest? Would she touch him all over?

His cock jutted out, the sudden erection throbbing as the hot water sluiced against it. Cole gripped himself, groaning as pleasure and the need for release took him over. He stroked himself from base to tip, squeezing with just the right pressure as he found his rhythm. It wasn't as good as Andi's hands would be, but perhaps he could relieve some tension.

What the hell was he doing jacking off in the shower? He

hadn't done that in ages. Cole cursed and released his grip. He needed to grow up, rinse off and get moving. He had a case to solve, and here he was fantasising about someone he could never have. *That* was all there was to it.

Cole dragged his hand down his face. He wasn't used to the back and forth, even in his own head. When he wanted a woman, he got her. Last night he'd been determined to have her, hadn't he? Now he was going to back off?

He stared at his erection. *Get off* was more like it. He needed a quick orgasm to clear his mind. Cole took care of business, biting his lip to keep from shouting his release as the warm jets shot up and hit his stomach.

Sighing, he rinsed himself off. He'd hoped to feel relieved. Satisfied even. He was sorely disappointed. He still wanted Andi and the confusion because of it swirled in his thoughts.

How the hell was he supposed to make this work?

Chapter Six

The car ride to the hospital was quiet—too quiet. There was no way Andi would bring up the kiss, and, at the moment, Cole didn't have the balls to say a word. If she found out what he'd done in her shower, she would flip.

He shifted in the driver's seat, then shot her a glance. She was looking at him. He bit back a cringe.

"Something wrong?" she asked.

"No." Damn, that had sounded clipped even to his own ears.

Andi raised an eyebrow and looked away, staring out the window. Awkwardness settled over them. Cole preferred her pissed off. At least then she had some spunk and he didn't feel like he'd done something wrong.

"So..." Since when could he not handle a woman? He shook himself just as he noticed she was looking in his direction again.

"What?"

Oh, right. He'd spoken. Cole cleared his throat. "Tell me about your partner."

She smiled and it took his breath away. Jealousy hit him in the gut. Would she ever smile for him like that?

"He's great. A damn good cop, and a good friend." Her expression was wistful. "He's always been there for me."

"That's what partners are for."

"Oh? I wouldn't think you've ever been bothered to have a partner. You're not very good at it."

Cole let her jibe slide. He pulled into the hospital parking lot.

The introductions went all right, Cole giving the blond

man's hand a strong shake. Despite his wounds, Detective Crane stood by his bed to greet them, ignoring Andi's immediate enquiry about how he was feeling. Cole had to admire him for that. He wasn't as tall as Cole, probably six-one, and made of lean muscle. The hospital gown didn't take away his dignity, and a sling around his neck lay unused.

He told Cole to call him Pete and eased back into his bed. Cole didn't miss the slight wince as he resettled himself, but neither he nor Andi mentioned it.

She was rigid, looking around the room, her conversation even to her partner stiff and unnatural, from what he'd known of her so far. Pete studied her and Cole shifted on his feet when his green-eyed stare rested on him. It was like the guy could see through him.

The small talk stopped when Andi's cell phone rang and she glanced at the screen. "I've gotta take this."

Pete nodded and before Cole could acknowledge her, she slipped out of the room into the corridor.

"What did you do to my partner? I haven't seen her like that in ages. It's like you kissed her or something." Pete shook his head, but his gaze was keen.

Cole said nothing, concentrating hard on giving a blank expression.

Unfortunately, understanding dawned on Andi's partner's face. "You *did* kiss her, huh?"

He wanted to be sarcastic and shrug it off. He didn't even know this guy, but he was going to admit it. Why the hell was he going to tell him? "Last night."

Pete's eyes widened, then he cocked his head to the side. "How'd that go for you?"

"It didn't," Cole said.

"Well, you don't have any fresh bullet holes, so I'd say it didn't go as badly as it could have," the detective said, his tone serious.

Cole said nothing for a moment then squared his shoulders. "I don't get involved with women I work with, so don't worry about it. It won't happen again." He was still trying his best to convince himself. Especially after his shower incident.

"Oh, I'm not worried. Andi can hold her own," Pete said, then gave him a long look. "But FBI agent or not, if you hurt her—or that little boy—I will personally hunt you down. They mean the world to me."

Once again, Cole's instinct to lighten the comment with sarcasm or humour fizzled out when he met Pete's eyes. Andi's partner was completely serious. What exactly did the other man feel for Andi? Cole was hit with a wave of possessiveness he had no right to.

"There's nothing to worry about," he repeated. "I've never gotten romantically involved…or otherwise"—Pete gave him a wry grin—"with any woman I've worked with. I'm not about to break that record." Though he'd already kissed her, so did his record still stand? He ignored that train of thought.

Andi's partner studied him, then gave a curt nod. Pete was going to drop it.

They talked for a few moments more, an instant ease between them. Cole genuinely liked the guy. Detective Peter Crane was tall, blond and good-looking. He wasn't married—did that have something to do with Andi?

They were laughing when she walked back into the room. *Laughing.*

Andi's irritation flared and she glared at them both. Pete shot her a curious look, but said nothing. Cole flashed a smile, dimples and all, but Andi ignored it—and the way her stomach jumped—as she took a seat at the end of Pete's bed. Her partner's eyes were dancing. What the hell was so amusing?

"So, when are you getting out of here?" Cole asked Pete.

Her partner shrugged. "Soon, I hope. My arm's fine." He lifted it to prove it, obviously ignoring the empty sling.

Andi shook her head. "But what about your lungs?" What

if Pete wasn't as well as he was trying to convince them?

"Fine." Pete nodded. Andi gave him a long look. "Seriously, partner, I'm fine."

"Can we talk about the night you got shot?" Cole asked. They both looked at him.

"As you saw in the report, I didn't see anyone," Pete said, his tone hard, but full of regret. She knew he was angry at himself more than anything.

Guilt rushed her and Andi studied her shoes. Pete reached for her, squeezing her forearm as if he could read her mind, and she flashed a grateful smile. She caught Cole's intense gaze. He was silent as he watched. Heat crept up her neck and she swallowed hard.

"Why were you there in the first place?" Cole asked.

"Andi and I were helping Sully and Kurt out on a stolen property case. I have a guy who won't talk to anyone but me. He insisted on a meet that night, then the idiot didn't show."

"We heard the shots and headed over," Andi said.

"First on the scene," Pete said.

"And Carlo saw you before you saw him."

"Yeah well, whoever it was led with their gun," Pete grumbled, shaking his head and rubbing his arm.

Andi bit back a wince.

"Your informant, you think he could be in with my guy?"

"Nah, I don't think he's smart enough."

"I talked to him," Andi said. "He was drunk that night, passed out in his girlfriend's apartment."

"Corroborated?" Cole asked.

"Yes," her partner answered before she could. "Tell me about Carlo Maldonado."

Cole nodded and started give him details on Carlo from the year he'd spent with the guy.

Andi grunted. *Nice.* Pete only had to *ask,* and Cole would tell him everything? Perhaps she didn't have the right equipment below the belt to get a straight answer from him.

Jerk.

The reasonable voice that pointed out it'd be good to get her partner's take on things was ignored.

"So, all that's left is to find Maldonado," Pete said.

"That would be a good start." Cole nodded. "He's pretty savvy, but he's no doctor. He's walking around with some holes in him."

"He can't bleed forever," Pete said.

"Not without dying and I need him alive." There was an edge to Cole's tone. He wanted the guy bad. Maybe Andi would be able to get somewhere with him on the case if he was driven by his need to arrest Maldonado. She could convince him to focus on what he wanted most and leave the rest to semantics.

"So far no pharmacies have had any break-ins." Pete glanced at her for confirmation of new information and she nodded. "I almost expected it."

"And I checked all hospitals for a hundred miles every day for a week. But I know him. He wouldn't show up at one."

"Unless he passed out and someone called nine-one-one."

"Yeah. I thought about that. Not so much to date. No John Does I came across had any holes in them." Cole rolled his shoulders and Andi averted her eyes from watching the way his shirt moved over his muscles.

She sat through the exchange in silence. The two men had an instant ease with each other. She was jealous, but of what? The fact that she and Cole hadn't clicked? Or that Cole was talking to *her* partner?

Well, Cole and Andi had clicked in one way. That kiss. Her body warmed and she groaned. Pete shot her a look, and Cole's dark brow arched. *Damn.* It must have been too loud. She shifted on the end of the bed.

"You all right?" Pete asked.

She glared at him but nodded. Her partner's eyes danced and Andi avoided Cole's gaze.

"Well, I'm gonna hit the restroom. I saw one down the hall," Cole announced.

"Okay, man. We'll be here," Pete answered.

Andi's breath exited on a whoosh as soon as Cole had closed the hospital room door. Alone with her partner, she could relax, regroup. Brace herself for dealing with Cole for the rest of the day.

"So, what's the real deal?" Pete asked.

"Meaning?" She raised an eyebrow.

"Agent Lucas?" Pete's tone was amused, but his eyes were serious.

"Like I said, meaning?"

He shook his head and Andi grimaced. Time for the third degree.

"I think you like him."

"What?" Andi sputtered. *Hell no.* "Please. He's a pompous ass. Conceited and arrogant, and…"

Pete laughed. "Methinks the lady doth protest too much."

Andi scowled, and Pete laughed harder. "I don't think so."

"Oh, come on, partner. He's not so bad."

"Not so bad? Okay, Pete," Andi said, her tone patronising. Oh, she should smack the look off his face. He was supposed to be on *her* side.

"He kissed you." His tone was nonchalant, but he was studying her.

What. The. Hell. Cole had told Pete he kissed her? She *would* kill him. Lying to her partner wouldn't work, even if that was her plan. Pete always saw right through her. Andi's cheeks heated and—of course—he noticed. His expression became much too knowing.

Dammit.

"Wow," he whispered.

"Wow *what*?"

"Andi MacLaren, blushing and speechless. A first, I think."

"Shut up, Pete." Andi sighed.

"So it's *true*." He gave a low whistle, and she glared.

"And?"

61

"*And*…you tell me. He doesn't have any bullet holes, and seems to be walking all right, so…"

"So, nothing. Dammit. Just drop it."

Pete laughed, and she narrowed her eyes.

"It's about time, Andi. I've been worried about you," he said.

She shot him a glance. "What do you mean?"

Pete took her hand and looked into her eyes. "Iain's been gone three years…"

Andi yanked away. "Stop. Just stop. I love Iain."

"Love? Why isn't it *loved*?" His tone was low. Tears sprang to her eyes and she blinked them back. "I know you loved Iain. But you can't become a nun."

"This isn't about Cole Lucas…"

"No, it's not. Not really. It's about you, locking yourself away." He gripped her hand again.

"I haven't locked myself away." Andi shook her head.

Cole. She was attracted to him, right? No—she couldn't confess it to her partner, because she hadn't admitted it to herself.

Pete threw his good arm over her shoulders and pulled her against him.

Andi rested her head against him for a moment. "I don't want to talk about it."

"I realise that, darlin'." Pete smoothed her hair and smiled. "But since you won't marry me, I'm worried about you." She pretended not to see the wince as he lowered his injured arm from her face. Obviously his arm still pained him, though her partner would never admit it.

"I would kill you if we got married." When Andi looked at him, his eyes danced, and then they both shared a laugh.

"I have no doubt about it." He winked.

The door opened and Andi looked up. Her gaze collided with Cole's. Something passed through those steel eyes, but he schooled his expression so fast, she'd probably imagined it. He smiled, but his dimples were missing.

She rushed to her feet to help with the three cans of soda

he was balancing precariously as he tried to manage the door to Pete's room. Cole muttered his thanks, but his body was stiff. What exactly had she missed?

Andi handed Pete a can, and he inclined his head as he opened the tab then drank. Cole stared at her partner, but said nothing. He plopped down in the seat next to Pete's bed, his brow furrowed. What could he possibly be so broody about?

"How long have you two been partners?" Cole asked, his light tone belying his expression.

Andi looked at Pete, then back at Cole.

"About five years," Pete said, and she nodded. "I was her best man when she married Iain."

Cole laughed, but his eyes were flat. "Somehow it doesn't surprise me that Andi had a best man."

Pete grinned.

Andi harrumphed, but smiled because the grin on her partner's face was infectious. "Well, Pete was friends with Iain, too, so it doesn't count."

Pete chuckled and shook his head. "How about you, Agent Lucas? Any partner of note? Been at the bureau long?"

"Ah, partnering up isn't for me." Cole ran his hand through his dark hair. Andi smirked. Not a shocker she'd been right about him. "But call me Cole."

Pete nodded.

"Been with the bureau since I was twenty-five. It's all I've ever wanted to do."

"Yeah, me too. Joined the force at twenty-one," Pete said.

Conversation between the two men flowed naturally, and once again all Andi could do was watch. And envy them. *Men.* She was used to being in a mostly male profession, so why she let Cole and Pete's apparent ease get to her was irritating.

"What's next, you two?" Pete asked. "Any promising leads?"

"Finding Maldonado," Cole and Andi spoke at the same

time. She glanced at him, a small look that locked with his. His eyes were intense. Andi swallowed hard and ignored how her body warmed up.

Pete broke the spell with yet another laugh. "Would you look at that? Y'all are already in sync."

"Shut up, Pete," Andi muttered. She slapped his good arm, but her partner only beamed. Cole shook his head and gave a small laugh.

"I suppose that'll come in handy," Cole put in. He grinned, flashing dimples this time, and her heart went into overdrive.

"We should probably go," Andi said. Her words were rushed and she scrambled off Pete's bed. Wait…what was wrong with her? She wanted to *leave* with Cole? Be *alone* with him? Jealous or not, Pete was a nice buffer.

"Well, don't forget about me, partner. I might be missing prom, but my head ain't broke. If you guys get stuck, I can always put in a good two cents."

"Thanks, I'll keep that in mind," Cole said.

Andi quirked an eyebrow. *That* from him?

"Three heads are better than two," Pete said.

"Sure wouldn't hurt."

"You want *help* all of a sudden?" Andi snapped.

Pete's eyes widened, but he said nothing.

Cole had the nerve to just shrug. "Can't hurt," he repeated.

"Let's go." Andi clenched her jaw. She headed for the door, not saying goodbye to her partner and ignoring his final bellow of laughter.

Every time Cole redeemed himself a little, he had to piss her off and ruin it, damn him. And damn Pete for liking him, too.

Chapter Seven

Carlo woke and rubbed his eyes. It took him a moment to orient to the room. Ah, yes, he was still in the ranch house. The couch spun when he tried to sit so he gave up and sank back down. His side burned. Shifting slightly, he moaned as the pain in his leg radiated outward.

He was going to die. If he didn't get his ass up and out of this house, he was going to die. He needed to find some antibiotics. *How* was going to be fun, because he couldn't draw attention to himself. That was why he'd nixed the original plan to break into a pharmacy or some shit. As of right now, all he could manage was bleeding all over the place.

Antioch wasn't large, and if he could make it to the rodeo, he could find Berto. Or whatever he was calling himself these days. Supposedly, his old buddy had got out of the life, but Carlo didn't buy it. Rumour had it that Caselli was branching out and Berto was the boss down south. The bastard was dark enough to pass for Hispanic, so who knew?

There was some stupid big deal rodeo in town. Berto's ranch was supposed to have a major part in it. No wonder his former boss had been able to track him to Texas if the rumours about Berto were true. But if that *was* the case, why was it that Gains and Reese were the first to come after him? If Caselli had resources in the south, he'd have used them. He was a cheap-ass, and it took funds to send two guys in a big black Escalade after Carlo.

He sucked in a breath and pushed his body up and off the couch. "Fuuuuuck!" Carlo's yell echoed in the large, empty living room, but at least he was up.

His bladder throbbed as much as his wounds, so he headed to the bathroom. Carlo's fingers trembled as he yanked his zipper down. He shook his hand before he made a grab for his dick. He didn't want to piss all over his hand.

"That went well," he said, zipping up. "I'm *still* talking to myself. Jesus."

His reflection in the large mirror was a blur of messy dark hair in need of a cut and thick bags under his brown eyes. His normally olive skin was a shade or two paler than normal. He was sweaty, his limbs heavy.

Carlo lumbered out of the bathroom. Checking his temperature was an afterthought, but he didn't feel as weak as he had, so he didn't go back for the thermometer. The fever had broken for now, but all sorts of bad things were headed his way if he didn't get some meds. No other options.

He looked down as he limped along the hallway. His leg wasn't seeping anymore — at least his pants appeared to have dried — for now. The pain still radiated with every step he took, but it wasn't as bad as before. He needed to move on. Now.

Reaching for his forty, he checked it, even though he knew damn well it was locked and loaded. He smiled and tucked it into the small of his back. Too bad he didn't have a holster handy. Last thing he needed was to shoot himself in the ass. Carlo took one last look over his shoulder and winced. He couldn't clean the blood off the couch cushions, but right now he needed to look out for his own ass. Hopefully the local police weren't the brightest crayons in the box. Either that, or he was fucked.

He slipped out the back door, kicking the glass he'd broken in the lowest windowpane out of the way so he didn't have to step on it.

If more of Caselli's goons found him in this condition, there was no doubt he wouldn't get away again. Berto... that was his ticket. He had to make it to the rodeo. There had to be medical supplies there, even if they were meant for horses or bulls.

He slipped into the sleek black BMW in the driveway. The keys had been in the kitchen, so Carlo didn't have to break in or hot-wire it. He'd have to ditch it in a few, but first he had to get out of the neighbourhood unnoticed. A stranger limping down the street would be conspicuous.

"Here's to hoping there's no nosy neighbour who knows when Mr Beemer will be back in town."

That would just be his fucking luck.

Rounding the corner, he kept the luxury sedan at exactly twenty-five miles per hour, as the speed limit signs posted. He was in a stolen car, in a residential area, and even though the police would likely be scarce, Carlo wouldn't chance it. No ID, a gun and an *acquired* vehicle wouldn't go over well. And there was that little federal fugitive problem to consider, too.

Two streets over from where he'd been staying, and well on his way to a main thoroughfare, he saw a blue, modern-day hot rod in a driveway, one house from the corner of the street. The car itself wasn't what caught his eye. The tall, dark-haired guy who got out of it was. Carlo's heart took a dive for his stomach. Mike Amato — no, Cole Lucas.

An attractive woman with her hair in a ponytail got out of the passenger seat. Carlo winced as he passed them, but neither looked up from their conversation to notice the black BMW driving by.

So the FBI agent had figured out where he was and given chase. But who the hell was the woman?

Well, well, well. Didn't things just get interesting?

* * * *

"Who is that?" Bella whispered loudly to Andi as Cole walked into the kitchen with Ethan on his hip. Her son's infatuation with Cole was firmly in place, and Ethan had actually greeted him before Andi.

After working with Cole all day and not bickering with him, she could maybe see what Pete and Ethan had noticed. As much as she tried to deny it to herself, she was drawn to him. Her partner's words in the hospital about locking herself away echoed through her mind. She didn't want to admit how that sentiment had hit home.

Andi shot her seventeen-year-old babysitter an amused look. Subtlety was lost on the girl. She was obviously ogling Cole, but to his credit, he didn't react. He was probably used to it—no one was born with that ego.

"Cole, this is Bella. She takes care of Ethan for me after school," Andi said.

Cole flashed a dimpled smile as he set Ethan to his feet. Andi grinned, imagining what that smile was doing to the teen. He put his hand out to shake Bella's hand, and she took it—shyly, for her—cheeks crimson.

"Nice to meet you, Bella," Cole said, giving her a wink.

Damn, was Bella about to swoon?

"Nice...nice...to...meet you."

Stuttering? That was new.

"Cole, Cole, I have to show you!" Ethan jumped up and down, tugging on Cole's jeans.

Andi was about to admonish him to mind his manners, but Cole squatted down in front of her son. "What is it, buddy?" he asked, his tone amused.

"See what I made!" Ethan announced. "In there." The little boy pointed to the living room.

Cole smiled and took his hand. "Show me what you made." He let Ethan lead him into the other room.

"Oh my God, Andi, he is *so* hot," Bella gushed.

Andi laughed, but shook her head. She wasn't going there with Bella. At. All.

"Who is he?" The girl's tone was distracted as she peered into the living room.

"He's working with me on a case."

"He's not a...*criminal*...is he? *Please* say he's not," Bella said, locking her wide-eyed gaze with Andi's.

68

Andi smiled. "No, he's not a criminal, Bells. But I am sure he's too old for you."

"Duh. He's not too old for *you*," Bella said, flashing a huge grin, her dark eyes twinkling.

What the hell was she supposed to say to that? *God, please don't let me blush in front of my babysitter.* Bella was too sharp for her own good. Andi would never live it down, either. The girl was as bad as Pete.

"Besides, I can always look. Brad Pitt's still hot, and he's over forty," Bella said. Andi laughed. How could she argue with that logic? "I mean Pete's hot, too, after all."

Did Bella know how old Pete was? Her partner would be upset at being compared to a man over forty — almost fifty, actually. Pete was only thirty-four, but didn't even look that. She chuckled.

"I'll be sure to tell him you said that," Andi teased.

Bella's expression became horrified. "Oh, please don't."

"I was teasing, silly. I wouldn't rat you out. I'll tell you a secret." Andi let her voice drop to a whisper. "I think Pete's pretty good-looking myself."

"Hmmm…" Bella cocked her head to the side. "Not as hot as Cole." The girl winked, and Andi laughed again, grateful for Bella. She hadn't been so lighthearted in days.

"How was school today?" Andi asked. Steering the conversation away from Cole was prudent. No telling what would pop out of Bella's mouth. *Plausible deniability,* Andi chanted. *Coward,* a voice whispered, but she ignored it.

The girl made a face, obviously not approving of the subject matter. "Fine, I guess. You know, just school."

"Ah," Andi said. "Anything interesting going on?"

"Not really. Doing good, all around. AP English is killing me, though."

"I loved English when I was in school."

"Oh, me too, but it's more of a struggle than I thought it was gonna be. Listen, I should run. I do have a paper to write. Ethan's bathed and fed, like always." She looked down for a moment, shifting her feet. "Not complaining since you're paying extra, but any idea if you're going to be late on Friday? I kinda have...a date..."

"Sure. I'll make sure we're not in late... A *date*, Bells? Who's the boy? I need to do a background check."

"Andi!" Bella grinned. Beamed was more like it. "Hey, you said *we*..."

"Yeah... Cole is staying here while we work on this case."

"Ohhhhh...and you're worried about *me*?" Bella said, her tone sly. She winked.

Andi laughed. "Don't get any ideas, kiddo, it's not like that."

"It should be."

"Isabella Marie," Andi exclaimed. Heat crept up her neck and she bit back a groan. Cole's mouth moving over hers popped into her mind, but she pushed it away, ignoring the warming of her traitorous body. Bella giggled and shrugged. Andi fought for control. Damn Cole and his effect on her. "Anyway, no subject changes. Tell me about this boy," she managed, trying to focus on her young friend.

"His name is Matt. He's a senior, and this'll be the second time we're going out." Bella's face glowed.

Cole's dimpled grin came to mind, along with its appeal. *Stop it. Get a hold of yourself.* "Good kid?" Andi asked, trying to sound stern.

"Yes, Andi." Bella gave an overdramatic sigh. "I swear, you're worse than Mom. She met him, she likes him."

Ah, good. Bella's mother Natalie was a great judge of character. "All right, then. Do me a favour and bring him over."

"Bring who over?" Cole asked, coming back into the room, Ethan on his heels.

"I'm not sure I will—you'll drill him and scare him off," the girl said quickly before Andi could answer Cole.

"Bella's got a boyfriend."

Bella's expression was a mix of pleasure and exasperation, face bright red. Andi couldn't help but grin. "He's not my boyfriend...yet. If I introduce him to you, promise not to ruin things?"

"I don't know, Andi's pretty scary sometimes," Cole said playfully.

Andi glared at him.

"I know, that's what I'm afraid of," Bella said, grinning.

"Hey! I *am* standing right here."

Neither Cole nor the teen looked repentant in the least.

"I just want to meet him, Bells, I won't eat him. And you"—she pointed at Cole—"are supposed to be on *my* side."

Cole put both palms up in surrender. "I know better than to take sides between two women." He looked from Andi to Bella.

"See? Smart man." Bella winked and both she and Cole laughed.

"Anyway, Bells, I am serious, I want to meet Matt."

Bella rolled her eyes and swung her backpack up onto her shoulder. "Okay, okay. Promise you won't be overbearing and I'll bring him."

"I promise. What time's your date?"

"Seven."

"Okay." Andi looked at Cole. "We'll be back by six-fifteen at the latest." Cole nodded in agreement.

Bella rewarded them both with a wide smile. "Thanks, I appreciate it. I really like him."

"I hope I do, too." Andi winked.

"See you later. Nice to meet you, Cole," Bella said, waving.

"Bye, squirt. See you tomorrow."

"Bye!" Ethan jumped twice, holding onto Cole's hand. Andi winced at his loud tone, but Cole laughed again and Bella slipped out of the front door.

"Be right back. Gonna put him to bed," she said, scooping Ethan up and propping him on a hip.

"No problem. See you in the morning, little man," Cole told Ethan.

Ethan put his palm up for a high-five with his enthusiastic goodnight, and Andi had to smile despite her sudden nerves when Cole returned the gesture. Her son would soon be asleep and she'd be alone with the FBI agent.

After a short read of Ethan's favourite story and a kiss on the forehead, she met Cole in the kitchen, her heart giving a tiny flutter as he stood at her coffee pot. The rich scent of freshly ground beans tickled her nose.

"Thank God I don't have to deal with teenage girls on a regular basis," Cole said over his shoulder.

"She's pretty great, actually. I've known her since she was seven years old."

"Ah. So, you weren't kidding about the background check?" Cole asked.

She cringed and put two bowls of spaghetti into the microwave. "You heard that?" she asked.

"Oh yeah, your voices carried," he said, laughter in his tone.

Andi racked her brain to try to remember if she'd said anything embarrassing. She gulped. "What else did you hear?" She strove for normal and met Cole's grey eyes.

"Hmmm, well I'm hot, Pete's hot and Brad's hot, for a guy over forty." He grinned, flashing dimples.

"Yes, well…" The microwave beeped and she jumped, but the distraction was welcome. She turned her back on him without hesitation and forced a breath. Her heart pounded in her ears.

"She's right, you know," Cole said. Andi looked like she was about to jump out of her skin. Her lack of comfort was good—he was going to push a little and see how far it got him.

He noticed the hesitation when she turned to face him, two dishes of pasta in her hands. His stomach rumbled and he thanked her as she set one down in front of him. Cole made a grab for his fork, making sure their hands brushed. Andi yanked away. He let it slide.

"About what?" she asked, her blue eyes widening.

Cole met her gaze and smiled. "I'm not too old for you."

Andi stared at him for a moment, and his smile slid into a grin when he noticed the pink tinge of her cheeks. Damn, he wanted to kiss her. He'd fantasised of little else since the other night.

Muttering something he didn't catch, she looked away from him. Cole held back his laugh so he wouldn't irritate her. Obviously, Andi wasn't ready to admit that she wanted him. She'd kissed him back just as fervently as he'd kissed her. "Want some coffee?" Andi asked as she rushed back to the counter after setting down her spaghetti.

"Sure," Cole answered. She fiddled at the cupboard and with the carafe for longer than necessary. He wanted her to join him at the table. Talking to her settled him.

Finally, she took a seat, handing him a steamy mug. Cole cleared his throat and muttered thanks. After a short pause, he said, "So, what's the deal with you and Pete?"

"What do you mean?" Andi asked.

"Well, you two were pretty cosy at the hospital." Cole tried to keep his tone light. He was still more jealous than he wanted to acknowledge, but he would never admit it to Andi.

She laughed and Cole quirked an eyebrow. "Pete and I are very close, but there's never been anything there."

"Oh?" Cole asked, going for nonchalance. She gave him a long look—he'd missed the mark.

"Honestly. We've been through a lot together, and he was there for me when I was lower than rock bottom, but we've never been more than friends."

Cole locked his gaze with hers and he smiled when Andi's face reddened. She was thinking about the kiss they had shared, no doubt. He needed to kiss her again. He reached for her hand and, surprisingly, Andi didn't pull away from him.

"So, never wanted anything with him outside of work?" Cole asked, cursing the words as they came out of his mouth. Where the hell had that come from? He intertwined their fingers and ignored how his heart skipped a beat.

73

Andi shook her head. "Pete's not my type."

"Oh?" *Interesting.* "What exactly is your type?"

"Certainly not cocky FBI agents," she said. The grin on her face took his breath away.

Cole leaned closer. Her lips parted.

A cell phone's shrill demand sounded and she shot to her feet, sprinting to the counter to grab it. Cole bit back a curse and released a breath, shifting in his seat to ease the tightness in his jeans. He'd been so close. She would have let him kiss her this time.

"MacLaren," she said, her tone ragged. Avoiding his gaze, she leaned against the counter, facing him. Her flushed cheeks gave him some hope. Andi was as affected as he by what had passed between them moments ago. He couldn't—wouldn't—put a name to it, but Cole wanted her even more. "Ah, yeah. Sure. Let me look at my notebook."

He didn't ask who was on the phone, but it sounded work related. Andi met his gaze for a split second, then her eyes darted away.

Without acknowledgement of any kind, she left the kitchen. Cole shoved his hand through his dark hair. He wanted to talk to her about something—anything, but what could he say?

"How's it feel to want?" he whispered, then cursed.

He waited for her to disappear around the corner and down the hall, then he cleaned up the kitchen, even loaded the dishwasher. Why he was being all domestic, he'd no clue, but Andi had fed him for the past few days, there was no reason she had to clean up after him as well.

Cole settled onto Andi's couch, reaching for the remote. The volume on the TV was low, and her bedroom door ajar. He could hear the steady hum of her voice though he couldn't make out her words. Was the call about his case? About Maldonado? He found it hard to give a shit at the moment. *That's new.*

Ethan's laughter drifted into his thoughts. He hadn't seen the kid much today. He'd have liked to have spent more time with him. Andi's son was asleep right down the hall — he could check on him. Might be good to make sure he was okay, right?

He'd never considered himself a coward, but he didn't move from his seat. Longing hit him in the gut, but for what? Andi, yes, he wanted her...but Ethan? Cole had never desired a family of his own. Besides, Cass and her kids had always been enough. He even liked her husband Dale, though the electrical engineer was a bit of a geek. They were family. The only family he'd ever have. Or need.

They'd married when he'd been in college, then they'd had Kelsey soon after. Cole had already been pulling away, choosing a college two states from the Seattle home Cass had raised him in from the age of twelve. She'd only been eighteen, and proving to the courts she could keep him clothed and fed after their parents had died in a car accident had been a bitch. But she'd done it, making sure his sorry juvenile delinquent ass finished high school and pushing him through college. His anger at the world had run through his blood his whole teen years. He'd done things he'd be embarrassed to admit.

Cass was the only family he had — and Cole had fled, although he hadn't faced that until years later. Seeing her happy should have been satisfying after all he'd put her through, but it hadn't changed his decision to leave. She'd married and he'd managed to graduate, then had gone right into the FBI academy as soon as they would take him.

He'd thrived in the anonymity of undercover work.

No connections. At that moment, his undercover mantra, drilled into his head by many experienced training agents from as far back as his FBI academy days, popped into his head.

No shit. He didn't need the complications. The risk. The problems.

"It's not a problem now," he said aloud. But was it? Even after only a few days, that little redheaded kid made him... what? Want to be a father? No way.

"No." Cole shook his head, holding onto as much denial as he could manage. He'd never shirked responsibility, but parenthood was firmly in the *hell no* category. That hadn't changed. That *wouldn't* change, not even for a roll in the hay with his new partner.

Chapter Eight

The pickup truck he'd stolen was a good choice. Carlo looked around the vast dirt parking lot—field, really—of the rodeo. Trucks and horse trailers for miles. Damn Texans and their big trucks. Conceited, too. The Chevy he was driving was even a *Texas Edition*. No one would ever hear of a *New York Edition* Chevy truck. Nope, only in Texas.

Too bad he'd had to lose the Beemer, it was more his style. But the owner should be grateful. Carlo had simply left it in a grocery store parking lot and cleaned it up as best he could, wiping it down with bleach wipes and praying the slight bloodstains on the black interior weren't visible. Unless someone took a black light to it, he should be fine.

He pulled the truck into the first parking gate he saw, stopping at the little attendant hut like a good patron. After that ordeal was over, he followed the instructions given by the handlebar-moustached geezer. The old man had had the nerve to lecture him about tardiness, stating that most of the cowboys were already in the arena.

Pulling in next to a semi-length horse trailer with a Circle Bar B logo, Carlo glanced around. He stalled out the truck, thanking God it was a five-speed and the engine shut off so he would be able to hot-wire it again.

"Fuck," Carlo muttered as his feet hit the uneven dirt ground. His leg screamed. He took a deep breath, then two. "Get a hold of your fucking self."

Inside the building that'd been marked 'Participant Lodging and Offices', Carlo wandered, encountering no one. Where the hell was Berto?

Just when he was about to give up, the last closed door on

the left of the empty hallway had a handwritten, taped-up paper sign that shouted 'Circle Bar B'.

Carlo reached for the doorknob. The room wasn't locked. The wooden door creaked as he pushed it open and stepped inside. It was dark, but some light leaked through the curtains at the far end of the room. A couch with Southwestern patterned upholstery took up the left side of the room and on the right was a desk, some shelves and a computer that had seen better days.

The gun hammer being cocked sounded in his ears at the same time that a muzzle pressed into the back of his head. Carlo froze.

"You have some fucking nerve coming here."

He put his palms up in surrender, and as far away from the forty in his waistband as possible. Berto sounded *pissed*. He needed help, not another bullet wound.

"Berto…"

"Do *not* call me that," the other man spat. "Turn around very slowly, keep those hands up and I might refrain from putting a hole in you."

Carlo did what he was told. Berto flipped the light on and stared him down. Carlo backed up a few steps, keeping his hands where his old friend could see them.

"You always did have balls bigger than your brain," Berto said, shaking his head. "What the fuck do you want?"

"Just some help."

Gun still trained on him, Berto's eyes narrowed. "I heard about Big Rod and Jim. Didn't think you had it in you."

"How'd ya know it was me? I thought you were out of the life?" Carlo stared into Berto's dark eyes. Would he lie? Was he really out, or working for Caselli from a new venue?

"I am. I don't like getting calls about losers like you. Caselli promised me I was done. I paid my dues. I'm out. I've *been* out."

"Calls?"

"Gains called me a few days before he died to see if I'd seen your sorry ass. Figured you'd show up sooner or later."

Berto had changed. Wearing dark jeans, cowboy boots and a western shirt, his outfit even included a huge belt buckle and a black cowboy hat. He looked like a born Texan, not the transplanted northerner he was. The glare on his face was familiar, though.

"Sorry for showing up."

"Seriously? You can go to hell, Carlo. Get the fuck out of here before I shoot your ass. You're jeopardising my life. I have acres and acres I could bury your body on. Caselli wouldn't weep, that's for sure. By the way, he's *pissed* about Reese and Gains."

"What, no police, even FBI for you? You'd rather kill me? Maybe you're not *that* out of the life, after all."

Berto growled, the gun pointed directly at Carlo's chest. "For all you've done to me over the years, it's nothing less than you deserve."

"But I saved your ass a time or two…"

"Fuck you."

"Look, I just want some medical supplies and a loan."

The other man threw his head back and laughed. His smile didn't reach his dark eyes. "A loan?" He lowered the nickel-plated Ruger .375 Magnum and pulled out his wallet. Carlo stayed put. Berto had always been a fast draw and a fantastic shot. He could kill him in seconds. "Get yourself a fucking first aid kit."

"Tried that. I need antibiotics." Carlo winced with the admission.

Berto arched a dark eyebrow and laid the gun on the desk. "You're hit?"

"Times two." He shrugged. "Get me what I need and I'll get out of your hair. I don't even give a fuck if you call the cops."

"Huh, how about that? The coward isn't afraid of the police."

"Cole Lucas is in town."

Since he'd been out of the life for a few years, Berto could only know of Lucas by reputation, but Carlo's old friend wasn't stupid.

Berto put his palm up, wallet in the other hand. "Do me a favour and keep your plans to yourself. You can have the money." He threw some bills.

They floated to the ground and Carlo cursed Berto to hell and back for forcing him to show weakness as he scrambled to pick up the money. He glanced at the three Benjamins before tucking them into his pocket.

He banished the memory of the suitcase he'd had to leave behind the night he'd got shot. It had contained twenty-five thousand dollars—Carlo had nicked it from his old boss. It was now in the custody of the Antioch PD, lost to him forever.

"All the meds I've got are for horses," Berto said. "I don't know if I can get anything else from EMS."

A knock at the door made Carlo jump. *Son of a bitch.* Berto noticed—a satisfied smile spread across his lips. "Uh, not so brave, are we?"

"Mateo? Boss? You in there? First round's about to start," a male voice called.

"Thanks, Brody, I'll be there in a minute," Berto called back.

"Mateo, huh?" Carlo asked, quirking an eyebrow.

"Shut the fuck up. You don't call me shit. I'll get you what you need and you *will* get the fuck out of my life."

"Thanks, I mean it."

"I don't give a fuck what you mean."

Carlo nodded. Berto wouldn't call the police—he didn't want the questions that would inevitably come up. Digging into Berto's background would be as detrimental to his new life as Carlo's appearance. But would his old friend contact Caselli, or one of their former colleagues?

* * * *

"This rodeo is a big deal, right? Championship or something?" Cole asked, throwing a rodeo flyer down on her desk. Andi looked up at him, then at the full-colour mini-poster. He'd gone to the kitchen to get some coffee, where the heck had he found the poster? She must have missed it on the events bulletin board.

His T-shirt was dark grey today, and just as tight as all the others in his wardrobe. His expression was serious, and his grip on the Styrofoam cup appeared tight. He was still hot as sin. Andi ignored that train of thought.

"Something like that, yeah. It's for two weeks, and people come from all over the country," she said.

"Ever heard of the Circle Bar B?"

"Should I have?" Andi stared into his grey eyes. Her stomach fluttered, but she concentrated on his words. Cole's tone suggested he thought he was on to something.

He tapped the poster. The handsome, dark-haired man on horseback was looking over his shoulder, his face with an expression of utter focus. 'Champion Owner of the Circle Bar B, Mateo Mata' was the caption.

"Alberto Carbone — Berto," Cole said.

"Who?"

"Used to be Caselli's right hand. He up and quit a few years ago. I only know him from pictures and what I've heard about him Never met the guy."

"I wasn't under the impression one *could* quit in their line of work." Andi glanced at the picture again. Confidence. Control. What the hell else, though?

"Yeah, me either. Normally you *quit* six feet under."

"So what happened?"

Cole shrugged and took a sip of coffee. "Never did find out. Rumour mill — he had something big on Caselli."

"Does this have anything to do with Maldonado?"

"I never could figure out why he picked Texas. But now, I think it was Berto. He — Mateo Mata — owns a ranch. Maybe Carlo thought it was an opportunity to hide, but stay in the loop, provided Berto still has contacts with Caselli or his people."

"You think he does?" Andi asked.

"Well, I find it hard to believe Tony Caselli would *let* someone go."

"And this guy, Berto, is here in town?"

"Bingo."

"All right." Andi shot to her feet and reached for her jacket.

"Let's go calf roping." Cole's twang wasn't half bad.

Andi grinned. She didn't jerk away as his warm hand settled at the small of her back and she let him lead her down the hallway.

* * * *

Boy, the Challenger's out of place around here. Cole got out of the car and glanced around. Nothing but trucks and horse trailers. The hundred-year-old attendant had directed them to Building C, but said most of the cowboys would be at the arena. Competition had started for the day.

One corner of Andi's mouth lifted as he met her blue gaze. "What?" he asked.

"I don't believe I've ever seen you so out of place, Agent Lucas."

Cole stared. She was teasing him? His stomach somersaulted. Was she finally comfortable with him? Normally the *Agent Lucas* would have made him feel distanced, but Andi's eyes were dancing. God, he wanted to kiss her. "I'm a city boy, no doubt. How about you?" He bit back the urge to gulp.

"Haven't been to the rodeo since I was a kid, actually."

"Oh, then let's make sure to have a good time," Cole said, winking. Andi laughed and he was mesmerised. It was the second greatest sound in the world, next to her son's giggle.

They headed into the building and Cole planted his arms at his sides. He ached to touch her. *Focus, you're working, dammit.* But all his attention was on how her ass moved in the tan pants she wore. Hiding, teasing him with only a glimpse of the shape that was there. Shame she didn't have on jeans. Andi's ass was made for tight denim.

"Where to? Did he say a right at the end of the hall or a left?" He jumped. "You okay?" Andi asked, one delicate brow arched.

Cole cleared his throat. "Yeah. Fine. Right, he said to the right."

The look she shot him said she thought he was nuts, but she nodded and rounded the corner, leading them down the empty hallway. He resisted the urge to adjust his pants. His cock was at half-mast. *Get it together, for real, before you embarrass yourself.* As if her catching him ogling her ass wasn't enough. He was working. That meant professional. *See why we don't mix work and play, dumbass?*

Thankfully they reached the end of the hall and the door with the 'Circle Bar B' handwritten sign taped to it. Cole ended his inner turmoil with a firm knock on the door.

Andi made eye contact with him for a split second and squared her shoulders. She was going to let him lead. Good.

The door swung open, but no one was in the doorway to greet them.

"Gun," Andi yelled.

Her Sig was drawn and aimed before he could drop his stance and even think about drawing his Glock. Dammit. *Dangerous.* Cole reached for her, his fingertips brushing her forearm.

She glared at him without losing her focus. "What are you doing?" Andi snapped.

Cole jolted and unholstered his gun. He'd been about to grab Andi and shove her behind him. She was a *cop*—she knew what the hell she was doing. *Son of a bitch*, his reckless instinct could get them hurt or killed. Where the hell had the need to protect her come from? He cleared his throat and trained his gun at the guy pointing a big Ruger .357 Magnum back at them.

"Federal Agent! Drop your weapon," Cole ordered.

Berto stepped forward, but didn't lower the revolver. "Son of a bitch." He shook his head and set the gun on the desk on the right side of the room, then backed away, both hands raised, palms out.

Without a word, Andi reholstered, slid forward and cuffed the bastard. He didn't fight her—which saved Cole from pounding the shit out of him—but he wore a scowl the size of Texas.

"Are the handcuffs necessary?" he grumbled.

"Well, for all intents and purposes, you threatened to shoot me and my partner as a hello so, hell yeah, I think so," Cole said, leaning on the edge of the desk as Andi pushed Berto towards a hideous, Southwestern style couch. The guy took a seat. *Good choice.*

"I wouldn't have shot you. I just want to be left alone."

Andi snorted and moved to stand on Berto's other side. He wouldn't be able to get away from them if he tried something stupid—they had him blocked in.

"I know why you're here," Berto said, sighing. "He's long gone."

Cole's heart sped and he made a fist before he schooled his expression. He didn't want to give Berto any indication of how much missing Carlo—again—made his blood boil.

"He was in bad shape, actually," the gangster-turned-ranch owner said.

"Couldn't have happened to a nicer guy," Cole answered.

"Where was he headed?" Andi asked.

"Look, lady, I—"

"Watch your tone with my partner," Cole snapped.

Andi's eyes widened and their gazes held for a second. Cole gave her a curt nod then looked away. Berto glared up at him.

"I don't know his plans. I didn't fucking want to. I just wanted him—and you—*out* of my life."

"Do you have contact with Caselli?" Cole asked.

"Fuck you."

"No thanks, you're not my type."

The conversation went downhill from there. Berto didn't tip the scales of Cole's bullshit meter. He was telling the truth. *Damn it.* The scum-turned-rancher had no idea where Carlo was, or what the bastard had planned.

Berto had given him medical supplies — legal drugs — and had sent him on his merry way. He didn't even know what the asshole had been driving.

"So you and yours want to be left alone?" Cole asked.

Andi pulled the guy to his feet and started to remove the handcuffs.

"Yes, that's what I've been trying to tell you. I'm straight. I have been for three years."

"If you want to stay that way, you'll call me if the bastard shows up again."

Berto nodded. "You'll be my first call."

"And I better be your last," Cole growled. He didn't need Berto giving Caselli a heads-up.

"I don't contact my old boss."

Cole exchanged a look with Andi. "But he does call you," she said. So she'd caught his distinction, too.

"Tried to entice me to hunt Maldonado when he offed Big Rod and Jim. I told him to go to hell."

"Well, you call me if you get intel on any new visitors, too," Cole said.

"He'll come after me."

"I'll handle it. After all, I bet you have some interesting financials concerning the purchase of the Circle Bar B, not to mention that gun right there. We could haul you in on that right now."

Berto's shoulders slumped. He must have recognised that Cole was the lesser of two evils. "Bastard," he whispered.

Cole flashed a grin. "Nice talking with you, Berto — I mean, Mateo. Good luck with the competition."

The one-finger salute was all the answer he got. Cole laughed.

When they got back out to the Challenger, Andi shook her head. Cole paused, his hand on the door. "What?" he asked.

"Blackmail for information. Nice."

"Ah, c'mon, you have to deal with guys like Berto on their level. Besides, it's true, the IRS would have a field day. You know all his assets were bought with money obtained by crime. We're talking about selling little girls here, Andi. For sex. He's just like Carlo. Scum from the womb to the tomb."

She winced. "All right."

"And now he'll call me. Problem solved, and we both get what we wanted."

"If he's so bad, why's he not in prison?"

"Berto's smart. He's been a suspect in various crimes from time to time, but nothing's ever stuck. I think he's even smarter than Caselli, or he would have never managed to get out."

"And why is that? Why the change of heart, desire for a change of life?" Andi asked.

"The downfall of many a man, from what I hear," Cole said.

"What's that?"

"The love of a good woman." Cole shook his head, frowning, and Andi punched his shoulder hard.

He stared at the glare marring her gorgeous face for only a moment before throwing his head back and laughing. She was glaring even harder when he met her eyes.

Cole rubbed his shoulder as it smarted. "Damn, you have quite an arm on you. That hurt."

"Let's just go, *partner*," Andi said. "We need to see if the attendant saw Maldonado and can remember what he was driving."

He grinned and put the car in drive.

Chapter Nine

Andi tossed and turned. Cole was sleeping on her couch down the hall, and unfortunately, he'd invaded her mind. He was so close...

So much for one night, then making other arrangements. It was a comfort to know he was there, though she wasn't about to delve into what the hell that meant.

Yesterday they had worked well together, *really worked*, and had even got something accomplished, though Berto—Mateo Mata—hadn't been much help. Cole had called her *partner* more than once. It'd been the first time Andi had *felt* like his partner. The first time she'd had confidence they would find Maldonado and arrest his ass. The end was in sight. She didn't dwell on the fact that Cole would leave when the case concluded.

She couldn't get their kiss out of her mind, though neither of them had brought it up since it'd happened. The other night at the table, he'd leaned in as if he was going to kiss her again. Andi's heart had sped up. Sully's interruption had been perfectly timed. What would she have done if her colleague hadn't needed info on Pete's CI and Cole's mouth had landed on hers?

If she closed her eyes, she could feel his warm, full lips moving over hers. She wanted that. To be in his arms, the heat of his body pressing against her. She wanted Cole to kiss her again, to hold her again.

Confusion and guilt warred with the desire that warmed her body. *Dammit.* What was wrong with her?

Letting her eyes slip closed, she was determined to sleep. Cole popped into her mind again. *Leave me alone.* Andi didn't *want* to remember, didn't *want* to feel the way she was already starting to. She still loved Iain. *But Iain is gone,* a voice reminded her. She ignored it and squeezed her eyes tight, her heart heavy.

Cole had...awakened her in ways she'd assumed were a part of her past. She'd always been practical. It was just a part of her makeup. Iain had been her love, her husband, her chance at happiness. A one-time thing.

The more time she spent with Cole, the more she... wondered. What if there was such a thing as a second chance...

What the *hell* was she thinking?

He made her feel like a woman, yes. But physical desire, need and sex—that was one thing. The fact that Cole could stir her with only a look didn't mean there was ever a chance for more.

She didn't want any of it anyway. Sleeping with Cole— *God, did I really just go there? No. Way.* Sleeping with Cole would only bring complications. Even if sex after three years might be fantastic.

Who was she kidding—he would be fantastic.

Men like Cole didn't do relationships. Women like Andi didn't do *without* them. They'd be at an impasse before they could start.

Andi groaned aloud and punched her pillow. It couldn't happen. It *couldn't* happen. It just...

"Andi?" Cole called her name, and knocked firmly on her bedroom door.

She froze, then slapped the touch lamp on her nightstand, grabbing the book she had started reading ages ago. Too late, it occurred to her he would have been able to tell her light had been off.

"Nice," she whispered.

Yanking the errant spaghetti strap of her light-blue tank top back up, she bit back a gulp. She fidgeted in her bed, moving her comforter to make sure her midriff wasn't exposed. *Calm down.* He hadn't come to pounce on her, after all. "Come in," she called.

"Reading in the dark?" Cole asked, a half-smile playing at his kissable lips. He looked at her, then did a double take.

Heat crept up her neck. "Busted," she whispered, looking everywhere but at his face.

Cole chuckled and Andi smiled. What was this man doing to her?

He sat on the edge of the bed without asking permission. Andi's stomach somersaulted. He was close enough to touch, but she maintained her grip on the paperback until her fingertips went numb. "Did you need something?" she asked, cringing internally at the rush of her words.

"Well, I just finished brushing my teeth, and I heard you...groan, or something. It sounded like you were in pain." Cole's tone and expression were concerned. Her cheeks burned even more. Oh, he had *no* idea. "I wanted to make sure you were okay."

"Um... I... I'm fine," Andi managed. So much for an *internal* struggle. *God, please* don't let him mention how red her face must be.

She glanced at him, going for nonchalance. He was wearing a white, ribbed sleeveless T-shirt that clung to every muscle of his chest and stomach, and dark grey sweatpants that rode low on his hips. *Don't stare,* she chanted in her head. What would Cole do if he realised how seriously attracted to him she was?

"I wouldn't think you read those," he said, gesturing to her book.

Thank God she had something else to focus on. The paperback was a historic Scottish Highlander romance novel that Andi didn't let leave the house. The guys at work would never let her hear the end of it.

"It's about history." She cringed at her defensive tone. *Ouch.*

Cole laughed, his dimples flashing. "It's about sex."

She looked down at the cover. A kilt-clad warrior with long dark hair brandished a sword, displaying an impossibly muscled naked chest. Andi made eye contact with Cole before letting her eyes graze over his chest. He seemed just as impossibly muscled as the model depicting the hero of her book.

"It's about love," she said finally.

Cole laughed again. "Regardless, I wouldn't think you'd read something like that."

"I've always loved romance novels, and Scotland, to be honest." Why the hell had she admitted her addiction to romance novels? Cole wouldn't let her live *anything* down.

Thinking of Scotland reminded Andi of Iain. She sighed. "It's all Iain's fault, really," she whispered.

Cole held her gaze silently and she flashed a smile. She braced herself for the tell-tale heartache that always hit when she thought about Iain, but instead, Andi's stomach fluttered.

"Iain read romance novels?" Cole's grey eyes were wide.

"No," Andi said, shaking her head and laughing at the disbelief in his expression. "We met at the bookstore."

"Ah..."

"Iain was from Scotland, accent and everything, even though he'd lived in the US since he was about twelve. One day, I was looking at the new releases in romance paperbacks, and one caught my eye like this one, a Highlander romance. I was scanning the back when I heard a voice in my ear." He'd startled her, really. When she'd turned around, she had been confronted with a tall, extremely good-looking redheaded man with deep brown eyes.

Andi hadn't known what to say. She didn't often get hit on, especially at the *bookstore.* And Iain was so handsome.

"What did he say?" Cole asked. He leant forward.

"He told me if I wanted to experience a real Scot, to put the book down and go to dinner with him."

Cole grinned. "Did you say yes?"

"Hell no. I told him he was pompous and presumptuous, and walked away. I don't know why, really. He'd shocked me, I guess. Iain only laughed and told me I didn't know what I was missing."

Cole shook his head, his eyes dancing. "Obviously, you changed your mind."

"Well, when I got to work the next morning—I wasn't a detective then, I was a patrol officer on the day shift—I got the surprise of my life during briefing." Andi smiled. God, she'd been so mortified. But she was enjoying the time with Cole. Talking about Iain didn't hurt at all. Sharing a lighter memory warmed her heart.

"What happened?" He inched closer and Andi's heart stuttered.

She had to concentrate on his question. "Chief Martin introduced two new patrol officers. One of whom was Officer Iain MacLaren. I wanted to melt into my seat. He recognised me immediately, of course, and winked. He *winked* at me." Andi shook her head, grinning.

"Then the rest fell into place," Cole said softly, a statement not a question.

Her smile faded. "It was supposed to be happily ever after…" She bit her lip, swallowing hard against the sudden lump in her throat. Why had she said that?

Cole tried not to stare at her, but she was so stunning it took his breath away. When her expression faltered, his chest tightened.

He pulled her into his arms. She came to him, wrapping hers around his waist. Her skin was soft as his palms brushed her shoulders, bare except for the thin straps of her tank top, and he almost shuddered.

She was so beautiful talking about the man she'd loved. Andi's blue eyes had been bright, even in the dimness of the room. The jealousy that grabbed his gut made no sense. He wanted her to look at him like that, but he couldn't compete with a ghost.

"You still love him," he whispered into her hair. She smelt like strawberries. Cole let his eyes slip closed and rested his cheek against her silken locks.

When he'd walked into the room to see her skimpy tank top and her long chestnut hair loose, falling in waves around her shoulders, his heart had skipped into overdrive. He'd wanted to bury his fingers in it and caress her all over.

He'd sat on her bed without thought. Why hadn't she kicked him out, or at least demanded he move away from her? She'd done neither, and he'd been so mesmerised by her beauty and candour while she'd told the story about meeting Iain, he'd had to restrain himself from touching her.

Andi looked up and Cole expected her to push him away, but she didn't. She met his eyes. "I do. Part of me will always love him, I suppose. He gave me Ethan."

His heart thumped. He needed to kiss her. Andi had just admitted to loving another man, but it didn't matter. He had to taste her. He lowered his head and captured her lips with his.

She kissed him back, opening for him and rubbing her tongue against his. He moaned and pulled her closer to his chest. She slipped her arms around his neck and he deepened the kiss, moving his mouth hungrily over hers.

His cock stood at attention, pressing against the soft cotton of his sweats. Cole lowered her to the bed. Andi moaned against his mouth and tugged him closer.

Slipping his hand between them, Cole yanked the blankets away. He cupped her breasts through the thin fabric of her shirt and her nipples peaked under his fingertips.

More.

He needed bare skin.

Trailing hot kisses down her neck, he slid a hand under her top, teasing her nipple with his thumb. Andi writhed and crushed her mouth into his. Cole took control of the kiss and groaned against her heated lips.

His hand travelled downward. Warm, soft and supple, she was driving him crazy. She moaned again as he dragged his fingers across her taut belly. Her muscles shivered under his touch and she moved into his hand, demanding he continue his ministrations.

Kissing her again and again, he devoured her mouth and she clung to him, kissing him back with a fervour that surprised and aroused him to the point of pain.

Cole parted her thighs with his knee and settled into the cradle of her body. He bit back a cry—she was exquisite beneath him, chest to breasts, hips to hips. He pushed his pelvis into hers, rocking against her.

Tracing a path down her hip and around the curve of her buttocks, he squeezed the firm roundness before yanking her against him. Andi gasped as he ground into her, breaking their latest kiss. She undulated under him and Cole almost lost control. They had too many clothes on. He needed to be inside her.

He fused their mouths again and slipped his hand inside her boxer shorts. She wiggled at the first brush of her slick hot flesh. His cock threatened to blow—God, she was perfect. Cole needed to see her, taste her. He tugged, wanting the shorts off her. He needed her naked in his arms, he wanted to watch her as he slipped into her wet core.

"I want you so much," Cole breathed.

He trailed kisses along her jaw line, stopping to nibble on her earlobe, then down her neck. She trembled in his arms.

"No. Cole, we have to stop." Andi's chest heaved as she pushed him away, both palms flat on his chest. Her voice was thick and ragged with need. He hesitated. She couldn't know what she was saying.

Cole shook his head, pulling away from her completely and rising to his feet. He made a fist, his body screaming a protest. "I never meant it to go that far," he choked out.

Liar. He'd have been inside her in less than a minute.

Andi scrambled for the comforter and yanked it up to her chin. She was gorgeous, even though pain raged in her sapphire eyes. She was flushed pink, her hair mussed and lips swollen, her freckles prominent. But the look on her face, hurt and guilt, made his heart drop to his stomach.

God, he wanted to crawl back into her bed, to touch her,

hold her and wipe that look away. He wanted her, but that expression was *his* fault.

"Just go, Cole," Andi begged. Tears began to roll down her cheeks.

Oh, hell no. He'd made her cry. Cole's heart stuttered, his stomach roiling.

He took a step forward, but she put her palm up to stop him from coming back to her.

"Just go...please... Just go..."

"Andi... I'm really sorry." Cole ran his hand through his hair and shut his eyes. There was so much he needed to say to her, but words deserted him. He gave up, slipping from the room and closing her bedroom door behind him.

He went straight out of the front door, resisting the urge to slam it. Why couldn't the temperature outside be twenty degrees cooler? His cock was as hard as rock, no change in sight. He throbbed with a need that could only be assuaged by the woman he'd just left.

Cole wasn't angry with Andi — hell, she'd just admitted how she felt about her husband, dead or not. Why had he kissed her? Something about Andi MacLaren made him lose control. She affected him like no woman ever had before.

God, how she'd responded to him. Her kiss branded him. Cole licked his lips and tasted her there. Her hands on him had been better than anything he'd dreamed up or imagined about her touch. The shower incident paled in comparison to the real thing.

Andi had been hot and wet, and damn... He had never *wanted* so badly in his life.

He'd been torn between comforting her and pushing her down onto the bed, taking what he wanted, what they both wanted. Even though she'd pushed him way, there was no doubt she wanted him. The way she'd kissed him back wasn't a lie.

But the guilt on her face and her tears? What the *hell* did she have to feel guilty for? Her husband had been dead for three years.

It smarted...no, *more* than smarted to be passed over for a dead guy.

Cole growled. No. She *couldn't*. Nothing had ever been so right for him. Cole didn't just want her body, he wanted more.

More? No *way*. A sexual relationship was all he wanted, all he had ever needed. It was the same with her...like it had been for years. Nothing had changed.

"I need to go for a run," he muttered to the empty porch.

He stretched quickly, then shook his limbs out, jogged down the three steps, and jumped up and down. Physical activity would get his head back in the game. Maybe it would get rid of his hard-on, too.

"A run will do it," he whispered.

Talking to himself, really? Maybe he was going nuts.

He was the same Cole Lucas he'd always been. He wanted Andi, yes, and he'd have her. But even after he had her, he would be the same man. That chestnut hair, those freckles and those big blue eyes wouldn't change him.

She was the same as every other woman he'd ever lusted after. He'd get into her pants a few times then she would be out of his system.

Cole repeated those words like a mantra as he took off down the street, starting with a jog before settling into a comfortable run.

Maybe by the time he got back to her house he'd have even convinced himself.

Chapter Ten

Andi peered around the door to her bedroom, her gaze darting down the hallway. She paused, listening hard. The guest bathroom shower was running. Good—she didn't have to face Cole just yet. *Coward.*

After scooting into Ethan's room, she woke him. He rubbed his eyes and yawned with his morning greeting. She grinned at her son in spite of herself. She was tempted to snatch him up, stuff him into clothes, rush out of the house in her own vehicle and feed him a fast food breakfast on the way to day care.

"Damn, all that to avoid Cole? I really *am* a coward," she muttered, shaking her head.

"Mama?" Ethan asked as he hopped off his toddler bed.

"Get dressed, buddy. You want pancakes for breakfast?"

"Yeah!" He jumped up and down and she laughed.

Ethan would keep her *normal*. She would make sure he stayed between her and Cole at all times. But what would Andi do when he was safely at preschool and she was stuck with a certain FBI agent *all day long?*

She gulped and bit her bottom lip, trying to forget him and the previous night as memories danced through her mind. His lips on hers. His weight on her body. His hands caressing her bare skin, brushing over her most private places. Andi shivered, made a fist and clenched her thighs.

No. She wouldn't remember. She couldn't. And she *did not* want it—or more—to happen again. *Damn him.*

Making breakfast helped her focus on routine and she didn't think about Cole...much. But she did dread his arrival in the kitchen. Ethan was already in his booster seat, talking about colouring with Bella after school yesterday, so Andi concentrated on that, commenting when it was required and smiling at the picture affixed to the refrigerator. Unfortunately, its childish perfection displayed three figures holding hands. One was labelled 'me', another 'Mama' and the last 'Cole'. Bella had no doubt helped him form the letters. She groaned.

"Cole!" Ethan's shout made her jump. She dropped the spatula and bit back a curse.

Andi ignored Cole's greeting to her three-year-old and released a breath she'd not realised she'd been holding.

"Morning," Cole said, beating her to the spatula as she bent to retrieve it. He headed to the sink and washed it before handing it over.

"Thanks," Andi said. His steel eyes were heated as she met his gaze. She ignored how her body warmed, turning away from him. He didn't move. His body heat radiated, caressing her back as if they were touching. "Hope you like pancakes." Rushing her words, she was glad she couldn't read his face.

"I do."

"I'm hungry," Ethan said.

"Almost ready, baby," Andi said, glancing over her shoulder.

"I'll get him a plate," Cole said, grabbing Ethan's favourite plastic dish with Mater, from Disney's *Cars*, on it.

Before she could protest, Cole forked two pancakes from her done pile onto her son's plate. He cut them up and poured just enough syrup before heading to the table. A wave of emotion took her by surprise and she swallowed back a lump in her throat.

She blinked away tears and concentrated on the contents of her griddle. Cole and Ethan were talking as Ethan ate. The mix of Cole's deep voice with her little boy's much higher one was almost too much to take. Cole laughed at something Ethan said and Andi let her eyes close. Iain would never have the chance to sit and chat with their son at breakfast—or any meal. But Cole was here right now. What was the bigger crime? Her chest ached.

Guilt over the encounter with Cole settled over her. She clutched the spatula until her knuckles whitened. She'd *enjoyed* herself. She *wanted* him, wanted more. He'd made her blood sing, her body throb. Never had she reacted to a man like that. What the hell was she going to do?

"Andi?"

She jumped. She couldn't look at him. "What?" Her voice cracked and she cleared her throat.

"Do you need some help?"

Not with breakfast. "No." Forcing a deep breath, she slapped the warmest pancakes onto the nearest plate in a neat pile before fixing her own plate.

Andi didn't turn around until she'd got herself together and plastered on a smile. From the expression on Cole's face, he didn't buy it. Ignoring him, she dropped a kiss on Ethan's cheek and took her seat.

"Looks great," Cole said, his tone friendly. His smile didn't reach his eyes, his dimples nowhere in sight.

"Thanks," Andi said.

"More, Mama, please."

Once again, before Andi could act, Cole cut one of his own pancakes in half and put it on Ethan's plate. "Here, buddy. Are you sure you can eat all that?"

Ethan nodded and shoved a big morsel into his mouth, holding his small fork backwards. Cole chuckled and admonished him to slow down. Something else that was *her* job. Andi gulped. She stared at the contents of her plate, her stomach in knots.

"You should eat, we have a long day," Cole said.

Andi made the mistake of looking into his eyes. Tenderness and heat...and promises she wouldn't acknowledge. She told herself she wanted none of it. A scathing retort died on her tongue and she nodded. Cole gave her a long look but said nothing, just took a bite of his own breakfast.

* * * *

The ride to the station sans Ethan was awkward. Andi's stomach would never be normal again. It was currently rebelling against the three pancakes she'd stuffed down and the thought of coffee — usually the delight of her morning — was a definite ticket to vomiting.

Cole put the Challenger in park and paused, his hand on the door. "I won't apologise."

Her face warmed and she looked away.

"And I won't lie to you, either. It will happen again." The promise in his words brought her gaze around.

"No, it won't. It can't."

He said nothing, just stared into her eyes before settling his gaze on her lips. Cole leaned towards her and brushed his mouth against hers. It was a tease, and not nearly enough. Andi gasped and her body flushed.

Cole was up and out of the car before she had a chance to react. She was at *work*. How *dare* he? But the protest died. Bringing it to his attention would solve nothing. She swallowed hard, chiding herself.

"C'mon, Andi. We have a case to solve." Cole beckoned with his arm and Andi flexed her fingers, anger boiling up. But she clutched at the feeling, needing it.

With a breath, she rushed past him with jerky movements and ignored his chuckle.

He should *not* have kissed her in the car — or at all — but he couldn't help himself. She'd been stuck with him and Cole couldn't stand it. He needed another look on her face, something other than the doe ready to bolt at any second. He didn't regret the slight touch of their mouths, but it had left him wanting more.

Work was a necessity that would help Andi ignore him, no doubt, and he'd do his best to keep his hands to himself — be professional. They did have a case to solve, after all. Later…tonight…he would focus on her and what was between them—whether she wanted to or not.

Andi beat him to her desk. She turned the dial of her handheld radio on, pulling it from the charger, then pushed the start button to boot up her computer. She was striving for normal, ignoring him. Cole watched her, saying nothing. He took up residence at his normal spot, leaning on the corner of her desk as she slid into her chair. His lips twitched as he fought a smile.

Cole raised an eyebrow as she shot to her feet after sitting for only a moment.

"I'm getting coffee," she said, her words rushed.

"I'll go with you. I could use some, too." Something flickered across her eyes and her cheeks reddened. Wow, she was frazzled. "Is that a problem?"

"No." Andi shook her head and turned on her heel.

He let her make it all the way to the door before pushing off her desk and following. Cole gave a heavy sigh. It was going to be a *long* day.

Their hands brushed as she handed him a Styrofoam cup and she yanked away as if he'd burnt her. Cole winced. He grabbed her wrist and tugged gently until she met his gaze. "Relax. I'm sorry I upset you."

"You didn't upset me." Her denial was fast and she averted her eyes.

"Bullshit, Andi," Cole whispered. "I'm not going to jump on you."

She looked around the break room frantically, but there was no one in sight. "I'm not talking about this here." Her chest heaved and Cole released her with a sigh.

"Fine. But we have to get through the day. You pick how we do that."

The hum of two male voices drifted down the hallway and Andi jumped away from him, reaching for the coffee pot. Her hand shook as she lifted it. She blew out a breath and Cole grabbed for the sugar, shaking his head. Pushing her got him nowhere.

"Sonoma Street, yeah, I know," a uniformed cop said as

100

he headed into the room.

"That's a good neighbourhood," the other officer answered.

They were both young and dark-haired. The guy on the right looked Hispanic. Cole nodded to them as one took a seat and the other waited not far from him, in line for coffee.

"Morning, MacLaren," the seated guy called.

Andi smiled over her shoulder and stirred her coffee as she scooted out of Cole's way. "Morning, Shannon, how's it going?"

"Pretty good."

"How're ya, Rodriguez?" Andi asked the guy now pouring himself a steaming cup.

"Good, good. We were in your neighbourhood this morning, though. Manning made his way over there before we left."

"My neighbourhood?"

"Yeah, seventy-six fifty-one Sonoma. Family was on vacation. Got back this morning. Someone broke the window in the back door and made themselves at home. Nothing but medical supplies and a bottle of Jack Daniel's missing. Blood all over the place."

Cole straightened and Andi shot him a look. She quickly introduced him to the two cops, Shannon Crowley and Mark Rodriguez.

"Any prints?" Cole asked.

"Well, there were blood smears on the counter, so probably. Even a partial handprint. Like I said, Detective Manning met us over there. Dunno if he'll call in Crime Scene or gather the stuff himself," Rodriguez said. "Car was missing, too, a black 2010 BMW 320. We haven't found it yet."

"Andi?" Cole asked.

"Yeah, let's go," she said. The two cops exchanged a confused look, and Andi flashed a smile. "Thanks, guys, see ya later."

"So much for coffee, huh?" Cole asked, falling into step

with her as they headed back out.

"I guess so. Let me grab my radio. Meet you by the car."

"Sure." Cole shoved his hands into his pockets and headed out of the building.

"You think it's Maldonado?" Andi asked as she got into the Challenger.

"It's gotta be."

She swallowed hard and gripped her radio until her knuckles whitened. "It makes too much sense to end up being someone else."

"That's what I was thinking, too," Cole said. Her expression looked even graver, her eyebrows drawn tight. "What is it?"

"Sonoma is only two streets over from mine. Maldonado was in *my* neighbourhood, not far from my house...my kid...Bella."

Cole grabbed her hand and squeezed. "We'll get the bastard."

"We have to," she agreed.

He looked at their joined hands and his heart missed a beat. Holding her, comforting her was right. "Besides" — Cole met her eyes — "I'm at your house now. *I* will keep you and Ethan safe."

Andi stared at him, saying nothing, and it took all he was made of not to lean in and kiss her again.

Work. They had work to do.

Cole broke away, starting the car and shoving the shifter into gear.

Chapter Eleven

Andi looked out of the window as the Challenger sped down the road. She couldn't spare Cole a glance. *I'm at your house now. I will keep you and Ethan safe* reverberated between her ears over and over.

She didn't need someone to keep her and her son safe. She was a cop. Had an alarm system, training, guns. Everything was covered. So why did those words tear through her like a vow? And why was it so appealing? She didn't need Cole Lucas and all the feelings he dredged up.

Get it together, Andi. Cole was here for this case. As soon as they got his guy, he'd move on and her life would return to normal. Pete would come back to work, and everything would be as it always had been. She needed to believe that.

Cole sighed and Andi straightened in her seat. She peered out of the corner of her eye. Her tongue was frozen, but what could she say anyway? He reached down to shift the car, his biceps contracting against the sleeve of his T-shirt as he moved. She followed the defined line of his forearm down to his wrist, her gaze settling on the steering wheel where he'd returned his grip.

Every glance at his hands flamed her cheeks. She didn't want to remember what they felt like on her bare flesh. Especially *down there*. Andi averted her eyes again and swallowed hard, ignoring the tremble that slid down her spine. *Damn* him.

They turned into her neighbourhood, and she clung to the distraction as Cole navigated onto Sonoma Street, heading to seventy-six fifty-one. Her skin crawled. Carlo Maldonado had been *close* to her home.

"We'll get him, Andi," Cole said, as if he could read her mind.

She nodded, not trusting her voice.

Pulling into the driveway, Cole parked behind a white, unmarked Ford Crown Victoria. Jared Manning's car.

Andi hadn't seen her fellow detective since he'd left for vacation the week before. She was glad he was back, but he wouldn't like them bumping him from a case. And this was their case. She had no doubt whose blood they would find in the house.

She followed Cole up the sidewalk and onto the porch of the house. The whole subdivision had been built in the late eighties by the same builder. Floor plans and square footage varied, but other than that, the houses were cookie cutter.

An older woman with worry heavy in her hazel eyes met them at the door after Cole's knock.

Andi scooted forward and put her hand out. The woman looked at it, but didn't take it.

"I'm Detective MacLaren, this is Agent Lucas. May we come in?"

"There's already a detective here," she said, her short silver hair shifting as she glanced over her shoulder.

"Yes, ma'am, we're here to help," Cole said, smiling.

The woman's expression softened and she offered a slight smile in return, her cheeks tinged pink.

Jesus, it figures. The man could melt a nun. Andi shook her head and Cole shot her a look that said 'What?'

She followed the woman before he could go in front of her. He said nothing, but she could sense him close behind. She suppressed a shiver. *Focus. On. Work.*

Jared towered over the tiny balding man he was listening to, his dark head bent. The youngest detective at the PD, he was a nice guy in Andi's experience, but he went through partners like water—he was in need of one now. He had a stubborn streak with a side of cocky. She bit back a snort. Not unlike someone *else* she knew.

Andi glanced at Cole, but he was charming the woman who'd introduced herself as Sarah Reynolds. She was telling him that her husband, Tom, was a former banker, and she used to be an elementary school principal. They were retired and had just got back from a cruise where they'd celebrated their thirtieth wedding anniversary.

She took a moment to make a mental catalogue of the room, drowning out their voices. As Rodriguez had mentioned, there were spots of dried blood on the floor and a bloody handprint smeared on the counter. Why would someone on the run be so sloppy? Maldonado had been in the game long enough to know better than to leave so much behind. He must be in *bad* shape — no wonder he'd sought out Berto for help.

"If you'll excuse me," Jared Manning told Mr Reynolds, making a beeline for Andi. "MacLaren, what's up?"

He looked her up and down — wanted to know why she'd impeded his territory. Cole appeared at her side before she could answer her colleague, standing much too close. Jared raised an eyebrow.

Andi took a step away from Cole, noticing his clenched jaw.

"Jared, this is Cole Lucas, he's with the FBI. We're working a case together."

"FBI?" Jared asked, but he thrust his hand out to shake Cole's. "Jared Manning."

Cole hesitated and Andi glared at him until he shoved his hand into the other detective's. What the *hell* was wrong with her *partner*?

"Yeah, looks like this is tied in," Cole said, giving Jared a shake that jarred his shoulder.

Jared pulled away, shooting Andi a puzzled look. She shrugged. Even at his gruffest, Cole hadn't acted like this before. It was as if he was jealous. *Wait — no way.*

She cocked her head to the side and studied him for a minute, but he wasn't looking at her. Her belly fluttered.

"Well, then I'll tell you what I got," her fellow detective

said.

The two men talked and Andi listened, watching as Cole's shoulders finally loosened and his chest heaved as if he'd released a breath.

She glanced at Jared. He was handsome, but he'd never tempted her. He'd been with the department about six years, a detective just over three, and was a few years younger than she. Nope—not her type. Jared was a flavour-of-the-week kind of guy when it came to women, and not shy about it.

Andi harrumphed. And Cole wasn't? A laugh bubbled up, but she swallowed it back. They were two peas in a pod, these guys. Jared, almost as tall as Cole and just as muscular, but with dark brown eyes, instead of grey ones. Attitude the same.

"What happens next?" Mr Reynolds broke into their conversation.

"We'll dust for prints and take samples of what appears to be blood so we can catch the person who broke in, Mr Reynolds," Jared answered.

"And then I can clean up this mess?" Mrs Reynolds wanted to know. "Our restroom is in horrible condition, too."

"We'll send someone to handle that, Mrs Reynolds," Andi said.

"Oh, no. I don't want to wait. It's my house, I want to do it myself," the older woman insisted.

"Then go right ahead, ma'am," Cole answered, flashing dimples at her.

Andi wanted to roll her eyes when the woman, who had to be in her sixties, practically swooned.

"I have an evidence kit," Jared said.

"Good, then we can get to the lab," Cole said.

Jared processed the scene while Cole continued to speak to the wife. Mr Reynolds asked Andi a few more questions.

"What about my car?" Mr Reynolds rubbed his face, then skimmed the top of his balding head with his palm.

"As soon as we find it, we'll let you know, Mr Reynolds. I'm sorry about all this," Andi said, offering a smile. His wife took a step closer to him, and the older man pulled her to his side with an arm around her thin shoulders, dropping a kiss on her cheek.

She tried not to stare, and tried not to dwell on what Mrs Reynolds had told Cole. Married thirty years and still adoring each other? It was a miracle. Andi ignored the beat her heart missed and refused to look at Cole. Jealous or not, the FBI agent wasn't for her. She'd better get that straight.

Jared presented the homeowners with his business card as soon as he'd sealed up his kit. "We'll keep you informed as best we can about your case. Call me if you have any questions, or can think of anything else," the detective told them.

Mr Reynolds nodded and rubbed up and down his wife's arm.

They jogged down the steps, leaving the Reynolds inside their home, and stopping between their two vehicles.

"Our lab might not be as techy as yours," Andi said as she took the catalogued and bagged evidence, making eye contact with Cole. "But it's probably faster. If we take it over there in person, I bet Max will have it back to me in a few days."

Cole shot Jared a look when he laughed. "That's only because a certain assistant to the medical examiner has a fancy for some MacLaren."

Andi shook her head, her stomach fluttering at the scowl on Cole's face. "Nah, he's just efficient."

Jared didn't disagree, but his expression said it all.

"I don't care where we send it," Cole said, standing much too close for the second time that day. Andi shifted on her feet but didn't scoot away. The radiating heat from his body warmed her.

The flow of Jared's and Cole's deep voices faded as they chatted about the case.

Physical attraction alone had never been enough for

Andi, no matter what they'd shared the night before and how he'd made her feel. And with Cole, no matter how much she wanted him, she could never have more than a hop in the sack.

She'd never been so turned on in her life as she had last night. Guilt washed over her in a wave, almost as strong as it had then, and she swayed. *Iain.* What was wrong with her, thinking about Cole like that? *Wanting* Cole. Sex with Cole. Making love to him—whatever she called it.

Iain had never melted her like Cole had. If she closed her eyes, she could feel the burn of his touch against her skin... taste his kiss on her tongue. Iain... *No.* Andi would *not* compare them. That was wrong on every level. She shook her head.

"Andi, you all right?" Cole's warm hand settled on her forearm, steadying her. His heat spread up her arm and across her chest and she almost shivered.

She looked into his steel gaze and ignored the jump of her stomach. "Yes." She tried to discreetly tug away, but he didn't release her, and Jared watched them. A blush rushed her cheeks. *Not here. Work. Work. Work.* "I'm great. We'll go to the lab." Andi stepped away, and his hand fell to his side.

Cole nodded and headed to the Challenger's driver door.

Andi's forearm tingled from Cole's touch. She needed to get away from him.

Being with him the rest of the day was going to be a test her resolve wouldn't pass.

Chapter Twelve

Andi's resolve definitely was beyond *tested* over the next two days. Avoiding Cole's touch was a mission. She'd failed miserably as far as wanting him — his kiss, the feel of him against her — was concerned. She'd ventured into *craved* some time ago.

Resisting his draw was killing her. Every time she saw him with Ethan she melted a little more. Every time they accomplished something on the case, no matter how small, she saw him in an ever clearing light.

Cole Lucas was a good man.

He did care about something other than himself. Maybe he cared about Ethan...and her?

She was starting to like him. No, she *already* liked him — maybe even cared about him. Andi shook her head. She couldn't think like that. That would only lead to temptation.

"Hey, Andi. I was just talking to Manning. Someone called in the black Beemer. It was in a grocery store parking lot, no damage. Looks like he just parked it there," Cole said, striding over to her work area. "And he was smart enough not to jack something from the same location. So who knows what he's driving now."

Andi jumped, cursing when she jammed her knee into her top drawer. Cole stopped in his tracks. Heat crept up her neck.

"You okay?"

"Yeah, you just startled me." She made a dismissive gesture with her hand. She ploughed on before he had a chance to answer her. "We need to head over there?"

Cole paused, giving her a long look before he spoke.

"Nah, it was wiped clean. Manning processed it. Not so much as a print, but I *know* it was Maldonado. Now we just have to be on the lookout for that truck, and keep an eye on the stolen reports."

"Yeah, the rodeo parking attendant said it was a late model, tan, Texas Edition Chevy. Hope he didn't damage it."

"Texans get sticky about their trucks," Cole said, flashing dimples.

Despite his stereotype, Andi's heart skipped a beat and she smiled back. The owner of the truck had been frantic when he'd reported it stolen—like he'd lost his child.

"Looks like our rash of stolen vehicles is all your guy. At last count, what are we at, four? Five?"

"Sounds right, according to your lieutenant. Maldonado has a bad habit of shooting up the crime rate wherever he lays his head."

"I suppose we could thank him for not wrecking or ruining the cars."

Cole shrugged, settling on the edge of her desk. He was close enough to touch. Andi averted her gaze. If she looked at him, she was likely to move closer and beg him to put his hands on her. *Damn, so much for remembering I'm at work.*

"Did Berto's phone records give you anything?" Cole asked, leaning down to look at her computer screen.

Oh, right. That's what she'd been doing. Andi took a breath and ignored his scent—clean, masculine spice—as it tickled her nose.

"Uh, no. Nothing." Damn, had her voice shaken? She was a mess.

He ran a hand through his hair and sighed. Andi wanted to reach out to him but managed to control herself.

"Oh, well. It was worth a shot," he said.

"Yeah, bummer. I was hoping something would jump out at me."

"I hate dead ends," Cole said, shaking his head.

"Me too." Andi gave a sigh of her own, glancing at the

clock on the wall. Her stomach growled.

"Wanna grab some lunch?" Cole asked as he followed her gaze.

"Sure." Andi stood and stretched. She'd been sitting at her desk for longer than planned.

She jumped as Cole's warm hand settled at the small of her back to guide her from the CID room, but she didn't pull away. She wanted to burrow into him, to beg him to hold her, kiss her. She groaned.

"You all right?" Cole asked, for the third or fourth time that day.

She *really* needed to get it together. "I'm fine, just hungry."

"Me, too. Breakfast seems like days ago."

Andi refused to think of their morning meal. Together, with Ethan. How *normal* it was. Sharing their morning with him had worked its way into her routine in such a short time, it was hard to imagine a time before him.

She shivered. Cole felt it and rubbed her back. It was automatic comfort and she leaned closer to him without thought. Did he know what he was doing to her? Heat from his hand and his side next to hers radiated into her, warming her in more than one way. Desire settled over her and she bit her bottom lip as a slow burn settled low in her belly.

"Cold?" he asked.

"No. I'm good." Andi stepped away from him. Her body screamed a protest. "Thanks, though. Let's go to Dixie's." His gaze was hot when it met hers. Cole Lucas could see right through her. *Dammit.*

"Dixie's is good for me. I checked it out the night I got into town. I like that place."

Nodding, she widened the gap between them as they walked down the hall. The locally famous mom and pop restaurant was a popular lunch stop for the force. Hopefully, some of the guys—anyone would be acceptable—would be there and they wouldn't be able to avoid company for lunch. God knew she needed some distance from him.

Andi spared one last look at him and her heart sped up.
He was looking right back at her. *I'm so screwed.*

Chapter Thirteen

"He's down. I tucked him in. Do you need to check on him?" Cole asked as he slid onto the couch next to her.

Andi smiled and shook her head. "No. Thanks for indulging him, I appreciate it. Especially since he didn't want me in there."

She trusted him with Ethan. His heart thumped. Cole wanted to pull her to him and kiss her. "I enjoyed myself, but he didn't make it through the whole book."

Shaking her head, Andi reached for the remote. "He rarely does."

Cole grabbed her hand and tugged. "Andi," he whispered.

It was a while before she met his gaze. "Cole, I—"

He ignored her words and leaned in. He needed to kiss her again.

Andi's phone sounding from the coffee table made them both jump. Cole cursed when she yanked her hand away and grabbed the cell.

Son of a bitch. That was the second time that stupid phone had stopped him from kissing her. He needed to toss it into the dishwasher or something.

"MacLaren," she said as she hopped off the couch. She started to pace in front of the fireplace.

Cole tracked her with his gaze and forced a breath. Was she constantly going to run from him? The day had gone okay, even though she'd shot away from him like he was a leper every time he'd touched her. He'd seen something hot and aching in her eyes before they'd headed to lunch, but it had been fleeting, much to his chagrin. How much longer could Andi avoid what was between them?

"Pete, hi!" she said, a bit too loudly.

The hum of Pete's voice was steady, but Cole couldn't make out the words. She rubbed her neck as she walked back and forth, not looking his way once. It was as if she were alone in the room.

"That's great," Andi said. "Yeah, I agree. It's been too long. Dinner tomorrow night? Sure. Yeah, I can cook." She finally glanced Cole's way, but her gaze didn't linger. "I'd say about seven. Yeah, Pete, I miss you too."

Miss him? She missed him and he missed her? She was going to cook for him? What the hell? Cole scowled. Despite what she'd told him, he had a niggling doubt that Pete was just a friend.

"Yeah, we can sure have a tell-all about the case. That's the real reason you want to see us, huh?" A pause, then she laughed. It sounded like heaven.

Cole's scowl deepened. He crossed the room in two strides, folding his arms as he stood in front of her. She shot him a look, eyes wide.

Ripping the phone from her hand would be rude, and she'd get mad at him, but he was tempted.

"How's the little guy?" Pete asked.

At least proximity would let him eavesdrop.

"Uh, he's good. Asleep."

So, Pete wanted to chit-chat. Cole didn't have time for that. He reached out and caressed her cheek. Her eyes went even wider and she stepped away from him.

Undeterred, he flashed a smile and leaned in, pressing his mouth to hers in a quick kiss. Andi gasped.

"Andi? Everything okay?" Pete's voice held concern.

"Yes…it's fine… I'm fine, I mean."

"You sure? You sound like you're out of breath."

She cleared her throat and pushed Cole away, a hand to his chest. He grinned. Let her shove him from her, it wouldn't last.

"I'm good. Gonna shower and hit the sack."

Not alone, she wasn't. Cole itched to touch her, but he

114

stayed where he was, their gazes locked.

Pete continued to talk about everything and nothing, and the more Andi answered, the steadier her voice got, and she squared her shoulders. Then, with a final look that could have killed him, she turned on her heel.

"Will do. Do you need a ride home from the hospital?"

"Nah, Nate's gonna pick me up. You know my mom, she insisted," Pete told her, his voice fading as Andi headed away from Cole.

"Ah, tell your brother I said hello. See you tomorrow, looking forward to it."

Her bedroom door closed without sound, but it was like a shout to him. She'd shut him out. Cole sighed. Tonight was supposed to be different—she was supposed to finally let herself go.

When would he get through to her?

She wanted him as much as he wanted her.

They'd shared a meal, played with Ethan...together. It had been *right* and...normal. Then the little boy had requested Cole read to him before bed. Cuddling with a child on a toddler bed, a book in his lap, was like nothing he'd experienced, not even with his nieces. He...wanted more.

Why didn't that unsettle him? He should be rejecting that desire, not embracing it, aching for it. What the hell was wrong with him...and just how many times would he have to ask himself *that* question?

There was no *more* for him in Antioch. He'd work this case then move on. He still had Caselli to bag. Nothing would force him off that course, especially unobtainables.

The only acceptable desire was to be between Andi's legs, her naked body beneath him while he plunged into her.

He cursed and flopped onto the couch. Cole looked at the TV and whipped the remote off the coffee table.

Flipping through channels held no desire. Nothing caught his eye, even the news. Two-hundred-options-and-nothing-on syndrome. He switched off the television and lay down, staring at the ceiling. Silence descended.

Images of them together, the other night in her room, plagued him. Her feel, the taste of her kiss, it was too much. His cock stirred with interest and Cole's hand drifted down his stomach, then slid into his sweats, brushing under the waistband of his boxer briefs. Just as he gripped himself, he sat up, shaking his head.

Jacking off in her shower was one thing. But on her *couch*, with her kid asleep down the hallway? Damn, he was a bastard.

"Screw it," Cole muttered. He swung his legs over the edge of the couch and stood. He slipped his hand into the pocket of his grey sweats, fingering the condom he'd grabbed from his wallet earlier.

His bare feet padded soundlessly on the carpet. Cole paused at Ethan's room and peered inside. The little boy was as he'd left him, sleeping deeply. His copper curls were prominent against the pale dinosaur-print sheets. The matching comforter was pulled up to his shoulder, his little arm over the top as he lay on his side. God, he was cute. And smart. Andi's son had already staked a claim on a sizable chunk of his heart.

When he reached the end of the hallway, he tapped on her bedroom door and waited. "Andi?" he called as loudly as he risked.

No answer.

Cole waited a few more moments then knocked a second time.

There was no way she was asleep already. She'd told him she was a light sleeper ever since she'd had Ethan, and besides, it'd only been about fifteen minutes since she'd left him, still on the phone with her partner.

He listened at the door, letting his police instincts kick in. He couldn't hear anything, not her voice, not even the water running in the shower—she'd told Pete she was going to take one...

Cole knocked again, but didn't wait. "I'm coming in," he

called.

He opened the door. The room was dim, lit by the lamp on her nightstand. Another glow peaked out from the open bathroom door of her master suite. Andi was there, staring at him, her eyes wide and face crimson, freckles noticeable, wearing nothing but a towel. Her chestnut hair was wet and loose, appearing black.

"Cole...what...?" she sputtered.

"I called your name and knocked. I thought..." She was fine, no tragedy had struck. Anything he could say would sound lame or worse...like a lie.

He looked her up and down, his heart thundering. He was in so much trouble now. Bursting into her room was a good idea, right? His cock certainly thought so. It sprang to attention, already aching for freedom.

"You...thought...what?"

Cole took a step closer, and she clutched the towel to her breasts with white knuckles. He swallowed hard. He needed her in his arms, needed her to lose the towel so he could toss her on the bed and get inside her.

"I just..." Cole whispered. What could he say? His hands itched to whip the terry cloth from her body.

"Cole..." Andi's voice shook, but his name was the sweetest sound he'd ever heard.

He stopped in front of her. She would scoot back now, demand he leave her room. Cole sucked in a breath and waited for her rejection. His stomach twisted.

But instead of taking a step away from him, Andi leant forward. His heart leapt, and he yanked her into his arms, the strawberry scent of her shampoo tickling his nose.

Cole crushed his mouth into hers, driving his tongue deep inside. The towel hit the carpet as Andi snaked her arms around his neck and shimmied closer. His cock throbbed, pressing into her belly through his sweats as he splayed his hands on the shower-damp skin of her naked back, smooth as satin.

Skimming his fingers lower, he cupped her firm bottom,

lifting her against him and rocking. The pressure was torture. Pleasure and depravation. *Not enough.* He needed to lose his clothes.

Andi moaned into his mouth, rubbing her tongue against his, and Cole answered by holding her tighter.

She buried her fingertips in the hair at the back of his neck and Cole groaned. He had to have her. *Now.*

But she had to want this too. She had to be sure.

"Tell me to stop," Cole breathed, breaking the kiss and meeting her eyes.

He still cupped her bare bottom, her pelvis tight to his. On her tiptoes, she wiggled against him and a moan fell from his lips. She was already killing him.

"Andi...don't do that unless you're aware of the consequences." He kissed her again, his mouth demanding and hard. "If you're going to stop me, do it now," he begged, spreading hot kisses along her jaw line.

"No," Andi whispered.

Cole pulled back, staring into those blue eyes. His heart stuttered. "No?"

"No, I'm not going to stop you, Cole," she whispered. She tugged on his black tee.

He froze. "You sure?"

After wanting her so badly for so long, why the *hell* was he giving her an out?

"Yes." She yanked his shirt up over his stomach, her fingers brushing his abs. Cole quivered. Her touch was addictive.

"I don't want to be a regret." He gripped her face lightly. She smiled and leaned up, kissing him in answer.

Cole shed his shirt and pulled her back into his arms. When her breasts touched his bare chest, he almost came undone. His body shook. Andi beneath him the other night had nothing on now. There was no stopping tonight.

He melded her body to his and crushed her mouth. She kissed him back just as urgently and soon they were both trembling with need.

"I want you so badly," he breathed.

Andi nibbled his bottom lip, sending a shiver down his spine.

"I want you too," she admitted. "Take your pants off."

Cole didn't have to hear the order twice. He pulled away from her and ripped his sweats and boxer briefs down. He kicked out of them as they hit the carpet, his erection jutting as it sprang free.

She gasped. Her eyes were glued to his body, and Cole was hit with an unfamiliar wave of self-consciousness. He wanted her to be pleased by what she saw.

Her nudity jarred him as well, his gaze trailing her body. Andi's blush spread all the way to her toes.

She was perfection. Large breasts he ached to cup and taste. Rounded hips, the ideal edge of softness to a flat stomach, heaven in the dark, trimmed curls that guarded her core. Long legs that were made to wrap around his waist.

She enfolded her arms around her slender body, but Cole shook his head. "You're gorgeous, don't hide from me," he whispered.

Her blush deepened and she averted her gaze, but her breasts lifted as she took a breath, then Andi took a step towards him. She reached for him, dragging her fingertips across his hard pecs. His nipples tightened and he bit back a gasp.

"No hair, huh?" she whispered as her caress became firmer, and she traced his defined lines with her fingertips.

Concentrating on her words was a chore. "Never had much, no." Cole let his eyes slip closed.

Every sweep of her hands set him on fire. When her touch dipped lower, he groaned. Her teasing fingers continued downward, skimming his cock. She caressed his tip, then his entire length, exploring him until he ached.

Cole bit his lip to keep from crying out. Andi gripped him, stroking from tip to base several times. He swayed on his feet and gently encircled her wrist.

"If you do that much more, this will be over before it starts," he admitted. He panted, his erection throbbing.

Andi smiled. "You like it?"

"To put it mildly."

Cole yanked her to him again and took her mouth. He swept her up into his arms then deposited her on the centre of her bed. Cradling her body, he followed her down.

"God, you're perfect," he breathed, closing his eyes as the sensation of her naked body touching his washed over him. She was warm, lush and supple, but more than that, she was *right* against him.

Andi caressed his stubbled cheek, then settled her hand at the back of his neck. He obliged, slanting his mouth against hers again as he caressed her breasts.

Her nipples peaked against his palms, and he teased them with both thumbs as he cupped and kneaded her. Moaning, she arched into him and rubbed her tongue against his. Burying her fingertips in his short hair, she held him closer as Cole deepened the kiss, devouring her mouth.

He slipped a hand between them, parting the dark curls between her legs. Writhing under him, Andi begged for more.

Cole spread kisses down her jaw line and neck. She cried out when he closed his mouth around her nipple and teased the other with his thumb.

The taste of her clean, hot skin burst in his mouth. He ran his tongue around her nipple before lavishing the other with the same treatment. Andi yelped as his warm wet kisses continued down her belly and he planted a kiss on her inner thigh, urging her legs apart.

"Relax," Cole whispered, teasing her with his thumb and dropping a kiss above her most sensitive place. "Let me in, babe." She wiggled against his grip.

Their eyes locked and she panted, but she opened for him and he settled between her legs. Her swollen, ready flesh glistened and his cock pulsated. Tasting her was going to take him past his limits, but it was something he had to do.

Andi cried his name, burying her hands in his hair with the first brush of his tongue against her sex, and Cole moaned. She was perfect in every way. He gave her no mercy, sucking her into his mouth and pushing his tongue inside her, plunging in and out.

Her hips came up off the bed until he held her down with both hands. She thrashed and moaned, moving her head back and forth on her pillow.

Cole slipped a finger inside and she screamed, her thighs shaking. Her inner muscles clenched him and he froze. She was close, but he didn't want her to come that way. He needed to be inside her when she shattered, clutching his cock tight.

He shot up her body, fusing his mouth to hers. She gripped his shoulders, arching into him and kissing him back frantically. Andi quivered in his arms, but he held her tight to him.

Cole was trying to kill her. Andi didn't have time to contemplate his bringing her to the edge with his mouth then impeding her orgasm. Before frustration could settle over her, he was on her, holding her close, kissing her into oblivion. His taste this time was a mixture of her essence as well, and desire made her a rippling puddle.

The hot length of his erection burned her hip and she throbbed from head to toe. Never had she been this aroused. She *wanted* him, needed friction and pressure from him.

She thrust her pelvis into him and Cole groaned against her mouth, rocking against her.

"Cole... I need you inside me," Andi whimpered, pulling away from their kiss. "Please... I...need...you..."

He nodded, pressing a quick, hard kiss to her lips, then turning away. She trembled at the loss of his warmth against her.

Relief poured over her as she heard the tell-tale crinkle of the condom wrapper. Her eyes devoured his gorgeous, muscled body as he rolled it on. God, she'd never had this much fire for someone in her life. Her blood was boiling. She wanted to touch and taste him all over.

"Looking at me like that...you're killin' me," he breathed. He sat on the edge of the bed and Andi reached for him. She had to touch him.

He whispered her name and she dragged her hand down his chest. She tugged on his hand. "Come to me, Cole. Please."

Andi wiggled under him as soon as Cole covered her body again, his erection brushing her core. Heat bloomed, making her ache. She lifted up and Cole gripped her with both hands. He leant down and kissed her gently. Her stomach somersaulted at the tenderness in his steel eyes.

They both cried out as he slid into her. Andi tilted her hips, taking him deeper, and his name fell from her lips.

She writhed, begging him to move, but he stilled above her, looking down, his gaze intense, unreadable. Her heart thundered. The rightness of the moment overwhelmed her.

Move. She needed him to move. The pleasure would chase those dangerous thoughts from her head.

Cole pulled out then plunged forward, eliciting another cry from Andi. She gripped his biceps and urged him on, meeting him thrust for thrust. She wrapped her legs around his waist, demanding even more. He gave her what she wanted, fast and frenzied. She panted against him as they moved together.

Sweat covered them both, but she wouldn't have it any other way. He took her higher and higher, pressure building steadily until it consumed her. Her head spun and she screamed. Release hit hard. She arched into him, her whole body contracting. Throwing her head back, she called his name, her nails digging into his shoulders as she clutched him to brace herself. Her thighs shook and she wrapped herself more tightly around him as she fought to breathe.

He was right there with her, pulling almost all the way out before thrusting hard. Cole stilled, buried deep, and moaned her name as he pulsed inside her. He kissed her throat and Andi shivered with an aftershock of passion that he soon echoed, squeezing her in his arms.

Cole collapsed on top of her, but she liked his weight. They both panted, chest heaving against breasts.

Coherent thought was impossible. Emotion and pleasure warred, hitting her in a wave.

He tugged against her tight grip and she reluctantly loosened her arms and legs. Moving away gently, Cole slipped out of her body and Andi involuntarily shook.

Before she could speak, he leant down and kissed her. It was a deep, languorous kiss that melted her already sated form. She snuggled into his warmth. The kiss went on for what felt like forever, and Andi moaned.

"Wow," she whispered, taking a breath as he broke the seal of their lips.

Cole met her eyes. "Understatement."

"No one has ever made me feel like that," Andi confessed. Her stomach roiled. Why the *hell* had she said that? She'd never intended to say it aloud.

He rewarded her with a brilliant smile, dimples and all. Her heart sped into overdrive.

"Me either," he whispered.

She leaned into him, staring and holding her breath. "You're not just saying that?" Andi didn't want the answer, so it didn't matter. Or so she tried to convince herself. As she fought to maintain his gaze, everything in her demanded she look away.

Cole cupped her face, teasing her cheek with his thumb. "I wouldn't lie to you."

Throwing her arms around his neck, she crushed her mouth into his. He groaned, kissing her back without hesitation. Their tongues danced and Andi nestled into his chest as he pulled her closer, sighing against his mouth.

She uttered a protest when he pulled away.

Cole chuckled. "Relax, babe, just going to clean up. I'll be right back." He kissed her forehead then slid into the bathroom.

Andi admired the way his muscles moved as he headed back to her bed.

"You're looking at me like that again, Andi," Cole growled. "You're asking for trouble." He pressed a warm, wet washcloth between her legs, staving off her retort.

She bit the inside of her cheek to keep from yelping and her face burned. Cole was so gentle with her. After what they'd just shared, her embarrassment was ridiculous. Chiding herself, Andi shook her head as he tossed the cloth into her laundry basket in the corner.

He smiled, flashing his dimples, and slipped back into her bed. Pulling her into his arms, he kissed her. "Can I sleep with you?" Cole whispered against her lips.

Andi pulled back and met his eyes. Words deserted her and her chest tightened.

"I mean sleep here, with you," he whispered, caressing her cheek.

"Oh..."

"I wasn't sure how you felt about Ethan seeing me in your bed."

"Oh." Andi's heart dropped to her stomach. Her son had never seen a man in her bed, because there had never *been* one.

Guilt rushed her and she had to blink back sudden tears. Cole studied her, saying nothing. Should she kick him out? *No.* She *wanted* to sleep in his arms. It had been so long since she'd felt the comfort of being held by a man who'd just made love to her.

Iain. She paused, waiting for guilt to overtake her. She licked her lips, tasting Cole there, and held her breath. No assault of guilt or remorse. Andi wouldn't question it now.

She met Cole's eyes and her chest constricted. He paused, his jaw tight. His Adam's apple bobbed as he swallowed hard.

Cole and Iain. Iain and Cole.

She still loved Iain, but...somehow... It was odd to think about Iain while Cole held her. What the hell was happening to her?

"I'll just go," Cole whispered. He sat up and shot to the edge of the bed.

"No." Andi gripped his forearm. His muscles rippled under her fingertips. "Stay. Please."

The hesitation in his body made her heart thud. His eyes asked, *Are you sure?*

"He never wakes before six. I want you to stay." She rested her palm on his chest and cuddled closer to him. "I don't want you to go," she repeated.

He slid his arm around her shoulders and settled beside her, pulling up the comforter. Cole smiled and kissed her with a tenderness that made her stomach somersault all over again.

That smile…that kiss…mean nothing. His words meant nothing. There was no deeper insight to his assurance that no one had ever made him feel like she had.

They'd shared some incredible sex. End of story.

The intensity she'd experienced had to be because Iain had been her last lover, a lifetime ago.

Even as he held her, her head on his muscled chest, her body nestled close to his, Andi repeated those words like a mantra. She had to.

Otherwise, she would fall in love with Cole Lucas.

125

Chapter Fourteen

Andi studied the heat swirls of her coffee, her tongue thick and sour. Her cheeks warmed as she tried not to watch Cole fixing himself a mug. His back muscles rippled under his tight shirt as he reached for a spoon then the sugar.

Her gaze trailed down, following the curve of his tight buttocks. The dark, clinging jeans didn't leave much to wonder about. She closed her eyes against the rush of memories...his body on hers, his mouth, his hands...them moving together, shattering together. A shiver slid down her spine. Then...sleeping in his arms... When was the last time she'd slept as well?

Ethan babbled away about day care, but Andi wasn't paying much attention. *No mother of the year award for me.*

It was a good thing her son didn't notice as he shovelled eggs into his mouth, offering a bright smile and further chatter between bites.

Cowardice had made her sneak out of bed and into the bathroom to shower. Heaven forbid she wait for Cole to wake so they could have a much needed adult conversation. But chiding herself didn't change how she dreaded — well, everything.

Looking at him, talking to him, *working* with him. They'd crossed a line they couldn't step back over.

What was she supposed to do if he tried to kiss her, touch her? Melt into him, most likely.

Avoiding Cole's touch now that she knew what it was like to be with him would be a hundred times harder than before.

When she'd finished her shower, her bed had been empty.

The shower in the other bathroom had been running. Cole hadn't even tried to come into her bathroom—she didn't know whether to be disappointed or relieved.

Andi had shoved herself into clothes and hurried down to her son's room, leaving the question unanswered. She needed an Ethan buffer in a big way. She gulped, shifting on her seat as Cole fixed himself a plate of the food she'd made.

It was natural, her new normal. Something she craved every morning. God, she was losing it.

One night in his arms and she could visualise the point of no return.

It couldn't happen. He was leaving after they arrested Maldonado. The day they'd met he'd told her how he felt about small towns. Besides, he had a bigger case to wrap up, federal stuff that would take him back into dangerous territory, and for some reason that scared her. Why did that scare her?

Before, Andi would have rejoiced at the thought of him leaving. Now...well... Her heart ached. Not seeing him every day?

Oh. Shit.

She was so screwed. For her own protection, she would have to pull back. Andi would tell him how things were going to be.

As soon as they dropped Ethan off, she'd explain that last night had been a one-time thing. A weakness she couldn't repeat. She *wouldn't* sleep with him again.

Andi didn't regret being with him but, for both their sakes, it couldn't happen again. Cole would understand. He was a professional. She'd seen him be professional, and would just have to get him to focus on that—the case, Maldonado. End of story.

Remaining his lover would be...messy. Andi didn't *do* messy.

"Are you okay?" Cole asked as he slid onto the seat across from her. His gaze was intense and she swallowed hard.

Sit still. She forced a breath and nodded. If she tried to speak, she'd stumble over her words.

Cole ruffled Ethan's hair, causing her son to giggle.

"You're awfully quiet," Cole said slowly.

How the heck could he be so *normal*?

Andi cleared her throat, shooting a meaningful glance at Ethan before meeting Cole's grey eyes. He nodded slightly and one corner of his delectable mouth lifted. So, he'd understood. But it didn't make her feel any better.

"We should probably talk about it," he said, sipping his coffee and holding her gaze.

Heat crept up her neck and she shifted in her chair. Maybe he hadn't caught her subtlety after all. Or — more like Cole — he didn't care. "Not now."

"I know. But it'll happen." The promise in his tone made her heart skip.

She ignored the tenderness in his eyes. Andi *would not* cave. She'd made the right choice. Being firm with him was the only thing that would save her heart.

"We'll talk, *later*."

Cole nodded and took a bite of toast. He gave her a once-over that made her squirm. Her cheeks burned.

"Andi," he whispered, but she looked down.

"Pete's coming over for dinner tonight," she said a bit too loudly.

"Unca' Pete!" Ethan's exclamation made her breath exit on a whoosh.

Saved by the kid. *Thank God.*

Cole sighed and leant back in his chair, but said nothing.

"Yeah, Uncle Pete. It's been too long since he's been over. But he hurt his arm, so no jumping on him, okay, buddy?"

Ethan nodded and flashed a grin. Wiping the grape jelly off his cheek with a napkin, Andi ignored the face he made.

"Okay, Mama. Cole, you know my Unca' Pete?"

Cole chuckled. "Yes, I do. It'll be good to see him again."

"We can play!"

"Sure thing, kiddo."

Andi bit her lip. She'd always been transparent when it came to Pete. How would she deal with both men in the same room? They'd hit it off at the hospital, but Cole might act differently now that they'd had sex. And she'd have trouble avoiding Pete's third degree. No doubt her partner would jump for joy when he figured it out. Andi had zero desire to hear it, and she certainly wasn't about to volunteer information. She'd *kill* Cole if he told Pete.

"Something wrong?" Cole asked.

She shook her head. "No. Wrap up your breakfast, we need to go."

Irritation flared across his handsome face. His full lips were set in a hard line, his eyebrows drawn tight. "You and I are not done."

Ignoring him, she reached for her coffee. That was exactly what she was afraid of.

* * * *

"Thanks, Max." Andi hung up the phone and Cole stepped towards her.

He planted his hands at his sides. Touching her at work was out of the question—he'd had to tell himself that about a thousand times in the two hours they'd been at the station. So far it'd been working, but Cole was dying to grab and kiss her into oblivion. To touch her, make love to her again. Hold her like he had the night before.

Their eyes met and she reddened. It was adorable the way a blush lit up the freckles across the bridge of her nose, but he admired the way she looked at him head on, for once, not glancing away. "Well?" he prompted.

Her discomfort at breakfast had led to a *very* silent ride to work. Andi hadn't said one word to him after she'd come out of Ethan's school. Was she going to ignore him all day?

Cole wasn't about to let the subject drop. And he wasn't about to let her get away from him now that he'd had her. He was going to be in her bed tonight—and every night—

until they got Maldonado. He'd worry about *after* later.

"That was Max, from the ME's office. The blood at the Reynolds' was a match for the fourth, unknown type at the scene of the warehouse."

"Of course it was," Cole said.

Andi nodded and one corner of her mouth lifted. "Not often you're wrong, huh, Agent Lucas?"

Whenever she called him *Agent Lucas* in that tone of voice, he wanted to laugh. It was endearing, not distancing.

Cole shook his head, grinning. "You doubted me? I'm hurt." He clutched at his chest and she laughed. God, he loved that sound. This was the first time all morning she had some semblance of *normal* with him. It was a start.

"What now?" she asked

"Well, we're up to five stolen cars, all used, not abused. Still no idea where the hell he's staying." He sighed.

"I've thought about that..." Andi said, head tilted to one side.

"Oh yeah?"

"Yeah. There are two or three abandoned buildings not far from the warehouse this all started in. We've had to kick people out of them from time to time. I think Kurt and Sully caught a drug case there, too. Last year, someone was cooking meth."

"Carlo would want to be left alone," Cole said.

"Right. The place is private. The hotels are all full because of the rodeo. Besides, the three hundred dollars Berto gave him won't go that far. And I really doubt he headed to the next town over to find a vacancy."

"I thought about that, too. Bet he's kicking the shit out of himself for losing the twenty-five K he stole from Caselli."

Andi grinned. "Poor guy. And it's not doing a damn thing but sitting in the evidence room. And that nice black Escalade in impound. No wheels for Carlo."

Cole chuckled. "Caselli's probably pissed about the cash and the car on principle. It's not like he's hurting."

Wincing, she leant back in her chair. "All that from trading little girls for sex?"

"Among other things. He's got his hands in drugs, too. And suspected to be behind a huge gambling ring. He's a multi-tasker."

"Nice."

"Before I got involved, the Bureau was building a case on some major gambling, embezzlement stuff, under RICO. Unfortunately, it turned out to be a bust. The two agents undercover were discovered and barely managed to get out."

"Did they get hurt?" Andi asked, concern evident in her expression.

Cole ignored his stomach somersaulting. Did she care about him like that? "No. But that's when we turned our focus to the human trafficking. It was a miracle I could get in with him."

"You did, though. You're good at your job. You care about this case."

He bit back a gulp. A compliment from Andi? He stared into her blue eyes, unable to speak right away. "Andi…" Her name was little more than a croak. He wanted to reach for her hand, connect with her, touch her somehow.

She broke eye contact, her face red all over again. "Not at work, Cole."

"I'm not going to let it drop, like I told you at home."

Andi looked up sharply, her eyes wide. "Home…" she whispered.

He cleared his throat. *Home.* The word had significance to her, but he didn't know why the idea appealed to him so much. Andi's home, his home? Cole shook his head. "Your house. You knew what I meant." He shifted at his post on the edge of her desk.

They fell silent. He wasn't used to the awkwardness of *the morning after*. Precisely why he didn't get involved with women from work. But Andi wasn't *just* someone from work. She meant more to Cole.

"Do you want to check out the place I mentioned? Flash

Maldonado's picture around?"

Cole jumped. Andi raised an eyebrow, but the distraction was welcome.

He pushed away the much too serious thoughts about her. They'd had sex. It was the best sex he'd had in a long time. He banished the word *ever* as it tacked itself onto the end of his last thought. *No way.*

"Sure." His voice cracked and he bit back a wince. "Couldn't hurt."

Rising from her seat, Andi threw an unsure glance over her shoulder. Cole straightened. Instinct screamed at him to settle his hand at the small of her back, like he'd done a dozen times. However, today was different.

Don't touch her. If he started, he wouldn't be able to stop.

"What's wrong?" Andi asked, looking him up and down. *I need you.* "Nothing. Let's go."

She nodded and turned on her heel.

The walk down the long hallway was silent. Sounds of life were amplified. Footsteps, voices in the offices along their path, phones ringing, radio chatter, doors opening and closing. Even the water fountain, where a uniformed cop was bending to have a drink. Cole's ears rang with the obvious lack of Andi's voice.

Still nothing as she opened the car door and got in. The click of Andi's seatbelt made him sigh.

"Is it just going to be like this from now on?" Cole asked.

"Like what?" she asked, eyes wide. A pretty good impression of innocence, but he had no doubt she knew *exactly* what he was talking about.

"Shutting me out."

"I haven't...shut you out." Her voice shook with the lie neither of them bought.

He gave her a long look. Andi's statement didn't deserve a contradiction. "You and me. Now. Let's have it."

"I don't want to talk about this." She shook her head.

"Of course you don't." Cole made a fist and tapped the steering wheel with his knuckles.

"I told you inside, not at work."

"We're not at work. We're *outside* of work. Only you and me here. No one else to worry about. Let's have it."

She swallowed hard, her face red. Cole wanted to reach for her, comfort her in some manner. But he stayed frozen, waiting for her to speak.

"We have work to do," she said.

"I'm not going anywhere until we talk."

Andi sighed, and closed her eyes. "Last night…was…"

God, please don't let her say a 'mistake'. Cole's heart thudded. He jolted in his seat. Good thing she didn't see. "Fantastic," he said.

She opened her eyes and their gazes locked.

Cole wouldn't let her go, wouldn't let her shut him out. The idea…hurt.

She looked torn, pained. Andi bit her full bottom lip and he wanted to lean over and take her mouth with his.

"It can't happen again," she whispered. Her words were shaky, and she planted her hands on her knees, her knuckles white.

"I'm not letting you go." Cole's voice was low but firm.

Andi gasped, but didn't look away from him. "I…"

"You needed last night as much as I did."

She shook her head, her expression shouting denial. Her fingers flexed and her knuckles blanched.

Desperation clawed at him and Cole forced a breath. His heart pounded. *Calm the hell down.* "The truth is… I need you." *Shit. Oh. Shit.* He'd actually said it out loud.

"N-n-need me?" Andi croaked.

"Yes." He nodded and concentrated hard on portraying confidence. His stomach was in knots. When was the last time he'd allowed a woman to do this to him? That would be a big, fat *never*.

"I…"

Yeah, Cole didn't know what to say, either. "Let's just go."

Since when was cowardice a part of his makeup? He

wasn't weak.

He shook his head and fought the urge to break away from her gaze.

Andi was staring at him, her expression—for the first time *ever*—unreadable. She probably thought he was a coward, too.

He turned the key with more force than necessary and the Challenger roared to life. "Is this place far?" he asked, cursing his shaky tone.

"No. Do you remember how to get to the warehouse district? It's one street over."

"I do. Hope we have some luck."

Andi cleared her throat and adjusted the volume on her portable radio. "Me too."

Chapter Fifteen

Damn, it had taken him almost an hour to catch up with the bright blue Dodge Challenger. But he'd got lucky just cruising the main streets, not even having to hop on the freeway.

The FBI agent was near the warehouse where Carlo had taken out Gains and Reese. And the woman was with him in the car. What the hell?

They drove around the block a few times, moving slower than necessary. What were they looking for? Why was the woman in the car? They pulled over once or twice, motioning homeless-looking people over to the driver's side. The talking—or questioning or whatever it was— didn't last long. Then they would move on. Carlo watched, keeping his distance.

After a few hours, he followed them back into town, and to the grocery store where he'd dumped the Beemer. He waited for them to walk into the store, boredom settling over him. Never had had the patience for stakeouts.

The radio in the red Cavalier he'd jacked was broken, so he didn't even have that to distract him.

Cole Lucas and his woman came back out about a half an hour later, both carrying plastic bags. What was the FBI agent doing, playing house? He watched them chatting as they put the bags in the trunk of the car.

It'd be dark in less than an hour. He could observe them at the house with less worry of being caught. Not that Cole Lucas would notice him—the FBI agent was so far up her ass it wasn't even funny.

Blending in with traffic was easy as he followed them,

and he pulled behind a sleek silver sedan across the street and close to the corner.

Carlo watched them as they got out of the car. She shook her head, and though he couldn't see the look on Lucas' face, his shoulders were tight — the FBI agent wasn't happy.

After dropping the grocery bags he had in both hands, he grabbed the woman's arm. She resisted, but Cole Lucas had her pinned between his body and the car in seconds. His dark head bent low, and he kissed her. Didn't stop kissing her. Whatever argument they were having was lost as the bag in her hand slipped to the ground and her arms went around his neck. Lucas' woman certainly didn't look upset.

"Who woulda thunk it?" he whispered.

The couple broke apart and retrieved what they'd bought at the store, the woman swaying on her feet until the FBI agent put his arm around her shoulders.

Lucas didn't even look away from his chick as he escorted her up the walkway, porch steps, and into the house. He'd always been sharp, but now the guy was lost to her.

What the hell had happened to the badass Carlo had known for more than a year? He'd considered Mike Amato, Lucas' alias, his good friend. He couldn't see Mike anywhere in the pussy-whipped man headed into the house. But it'd been lies, a game.

Cole Lucas would get what was coming to him.

Carlo had been watching them almost daily for over a week. Not once had he been spotted. Testament to the fact the FBI agent was slipping. To Carlo's advantage, of course.

The front door opened and he froze, his gaze intent. A girl, sixteen or seventeen, sauntered down the porch steps, throwing her dark hair over a shoulder. She had a purple book bag on one arm and paused behind the blue car, pulling a cell phone from her pocket.

"Well, well, what do we have here?" he whispered.

Light from the device illuminated her cheeks as she read the screen, a smile splitting her face. She didn't even look up as she crossed the driveway of the house next door, then the lawn, before tucking the phone back into her jeans.

She had one hand on the railing and a foot on the bottom step of the porch before changing directions and heading towards the sidewalk. He watched her lithe, slender body as she went to the mailbox on the corner. She reached in, her hair falling forward like a curtain as she leaned. The kid was appealing, no doubt.

Carlo grinned. "Hello, opportunity. Why yes, I hear you knocking."

Heart pounding, an idea bloomed. He glanced at the burner phone he'd picked up from Wally-world a few nights before. Lucas was a big draw...but a girl... A pretty one... Dollar signs danced through his head. He'd grieved for the twenty-five K he'd lost long enough. Time for some steel balls.

Calling anyone within his former boss's organisation was a big risk. They knew where he was...sort of. But if he grabbed the girl, Lucas would come after her. He'd promise Caselli first crack at the FBI agent and sweeten the deal with the girl.

She was a bit too old to bring into the life, but her looks would still get him a good deal, or at least tempt his old boss.

Swallowing the nerves creeping up his throat, he made his fingers dial the cell.

Ring. Then two more.

Shit, maybe voicemail would save his coward ass for now.

"Yo," the deep voice barked.

Well, not so much.

"Bruno?"

The pause was so long Carlo's heart skipped two beats. Was Caselli's right hand still on the phone? Bruno Gallo — Bruno G or just G to most — had risen in the ranks when Berto had gone straight. He'd never liked Carlo, but the feeling was mutual.

"No shit." The tone held equal parts anger and wonder. "Maldonado, I'm gonna kill your ass."

Tension forced a humourless laugh from Carlo's mouth. His stomach jumped. "I have something Caselli wants."

Again the silence on the other end of the phone just about killed him. Bruno Gallo was a bastard.

"Caselli wants you dead. End. Of."

"He'll change his mind when he hears what I have to offer."

"You really do have balls bigger than your brain, don'cha?"

Carlo ploughed on, gripping the phone tighter to his ear. "Cole Lucas."

This time the pause didn't shock him.

"Define *have*," Bruno demanded.

"He's here, and I have a plan."

Bruno laughed. "You're mostly useless, Maldonado, and you always have been."

"I got rid of Big Rod and Jim, did I not?"

His former colleague growled and Carlo was hit with a wave of satisfaction. *Fuck Bruno Gallo.*

"You *will* die."

"Why don't you run that by the boss first? Something tells me he'd be interested. He wants Cole Lucas more than he wants little ol' me."

"I'd prefer a twofer," Bruno said.

"You don't get to choose," Carlo snapped.

"We'll just see about that."

Carlo paused, chest tight. Good fucking thing he was an excellent bluffer. "Since when do you run the show?"

"Fuck you, Maldonado."

"That's what I thought." He released a breath. "Let me talk to Caselli."

"*I'll* talk to the boss," Bruno said.

He could see the scowl on the other man's scarred face in his mind. But Carlo had won for now. Caselli wouldn't pass up a chance at the traitor FBI agent.

Dangle, dangle. His former boss would bite.

"What do you want?" Bruno asked.

Carlo jumped in his seat in the shitty Chevy. "Back-up. More specifically, a way out. Money. And I'll go away forever. Caselli won't ever have to worry about me again."

Caselli's right hand growled again. "I'll see what I can do."

"Will you? Or will you stab me in the back?"

"I said I'll talk to Caselli and I *will*." Bruno sounded insulted.

Smirking, he shook his head even though Bruno couldn't see him. "I have a plan."

"I'm sure you do. I'll be in contact."

"You do that," Carlo answered.

Click. The line went dead as Bruno ended the call.

Satisfaction hit Carlo in a wave. Finally, something was going to go his way.

* * * *

Pete raised his eyebrow as he gave Cole a once-over at Andi's front door. The tall blond had a wine bottle in one hand and thrust the other out—as an afterthought?

A navy blue sling hung unused around his neck, as it had in the hospital, but the detective's injured arm didn't look any worse for the wear.

"Hey," Cole said, giving his hand a firm shake as Andi's partner stepped into the house.

"Howdy." Pete's smile was wide, but Cole was a little uneasy. Hadn't Pete known Cole was joining them for dinner? The man knew he was staying at her house, after all.

"Looking good, man. How's the arm?" Cole said.

"Good, good. Glad to be out," Pete said, as if the hospital was jail. "Raring to get back to work, though."

One corner of Cole's mouth lifted and he nodded. "When's that happening?"

"Damn doc wants me to take it easy. She won't release me yet." Pete shook his head, his fair brow furrowed.

"I bet that's—"

"Unca' Pete! Unca' Pete!" Ethan's shout cut off Cole's statement, but he grinned at Andi's son.

The little boy barrelled into Pete, throwing both small arms around him. The detective hauled him up on his right hip, but Cole didn't miss his wince.

Andi appeared in the kitchen doorway, hand on one shapely hip, and slotted spoon in the other. "Ethan, what did I tell you?" The admonition made the child's smile fade.

"Aww, don't yell at him, partner," Pete said, grinning. "He's fine. How're ya?" He tickled Ethan's tummy.

"Good," the little boy giggled.

"We're good," Andi said at the same time, her eyes sweeping all three of them.

She smiled and Cole's heart jumped.

Pete made it to Andi's side in two strides. She took the wine and thanked him. Her partner leant down to press a kiss onto her cheek.

A wave of possessiveness washed over Cole. He bit back a glare, forcing himself not to move. Who exactly was he upset with—Pete for his action, or himself for his...feelings? Why was he letting this happen? Women *never* got to him. Andi was no different. *But she is different,* a voice chided.

His words in the car floated into his mind. He'd told her he needed her. *Dammit,* it was true.

"Dinner's almost ready," Andi said, taking his attention.

Pete nodded and set Ethan to his feet, grimacing and rotating his shoulder.

"You okay?" Andi asked, her eyebrows knitting.

"Yeah, just a bit stiff."

Her expression shouted that she didn't believe a word, even though he plastered on a smile.

"Hey, man, want a beer?" Cole asked, stepping forward. Poor guy was gonna get nagged at.

Pete shot him a look, but nodded. "Sure, sounds good. Wine is for dinner, anyway."

They headed into the kitchen, Ethan jumping up and

down to punctuate his conversation with Andi's partner. Pete laughed, but took the little boy's hand and hung on his every word.

Cole watched the natural way they interacted. They were one hundred per cent comfortable with each other, and his gut tightened. Did Ethan feel the same way about him?

Wait, was he actually...envious? Worried the kid didn't like him?

Cursing under his breath, he shook his head. Pete's eyes narrowed and Cole pretended not to notice.

After meandering to the refrigerator, he grabbed two beers. Andi smiled at him from the counter where she stood tending an electric skillet. Whatever she was making smelt fantastic. She'd explained it was her secret speciality when they'd been at the store. *You'll love it,* she'd promised.

"Want a beer, babe?" The word slipped out without thought.

Andi shot a look to Pete and Ethan, but they were too involved in conversation to notice. Her cheeks pinkened and she shook her head. Cole didn't want to upset her, but he wouldn't apologise, either. Pete should know about them.

Them? They were a *them* after one night? *Damn straight.*

She'd really flip if he kissed her, but he wanted to. Pull her into his arms right then and there and plant one on her. Pete would have no doubt what was going on between them. But that was a guaranteed one-way ticket out of her bed.

Cole scowled. He headed to the table and handed a bottle to Pete.

"Thanks," Pete said, flashing a smile.

There was no reason to be rude to the guy, but he had to force a smile in return. He took a long pull after cracking open his bottle, then a deep breath. He set the beer down afterwards, lifting Ethan into his booster seat to keep his hands busy, then slid onto the chair next to the little boy, across from Andi's partner.

Ethan gave him a high-five and Cole ruffled his hair, smiling genuinely at the grin on the kid's face.

Pete was staring at them. The open appraisal made Cole want to grunt in satisfaction. He had an easy relationship with Andi's son, too.

"So, how goes it?" Pete asked.

"It's good. We'll talk about the case after little man goes to bed," Andi said.

"Of course," Pete said.

"Anything you need help with, Andi?" Cole asked.

Her partner's eyebrows shot up, but Cole ignored him.

"You can get plates, if you want," she answered. "Glasses for the wine are over here, and too high for me to reach." Andi gestured to the cupboard on her right.

He shot to his feet, feeling Pete's eyes following his every move. If he wanted something, the guy should just open his mouth.

Cole got everything required for their meal, including Ethan's cartoon character dish and cup. Pete helped him set the table in an awkward silence, his perceptive gaze never far away. Cole wanted to squirm.

"You two have been...getting along better?" he asked as Cole returned to his seat.

Reaching for his beer and fighting the urge to chug it, he nodded. "You could say that."

"Ah," Pete answered, leaning back in his chair, appraising him again.

Cole's stomach knotted. Hadn't he wanted all the cards on the table—for Pete to know about him and Andi? "Dinner smells great, Andi." Words rushed, he looked away from her partner.

Coward. Is it for her sake or yours?

"Andi's chicken magic," Pete said.

She grinned. "You weren't supposed to tell him, Pete. It was *supposed* to be a surprise."

"Sorry," he answered, an unabashed grin on his face.

"Chicken magic?" Cole asked.

"It's awesome. My favourite thing she makes," her partner said.

Favourite thing? As in, he was over for dinner a lot? Cole scowled. He didn't like that. At. All.

"Can't tell you what's in it, though," Andi said. "Or I'd hafta kill ya." She grinned again.

Cole glanced at her, but their gazes locked. He sucked in a breath as her cheeks reddened and her freckles brightened. Damn, he needed to kiss her. Touch her, anything.

When he finally broke away, Pete's eyes on him made him freeze in the chair. The guy hadn't missed their little visual rendezvous, that was for sure.

Andi shifted on her feet, and tucked a non-existent lock of hair behind her ear.

Clearing his throat, Cole straightened in his seat. "I'm sure I'll love it. You're a great cook."

"Thanks." Her appreciation warmed him.

If Cole looked at her like that again in front of Pete, Andi would kill him. And he'd called her *babe*. No way Pete had missed that. God, she'd never hear the end of it later. Her partner was one of the most perceptive people she knew. It made him a damn good cop, and a damn nosy friend.

She bit back a sigh. What the hell was she going to do? She'd made up her mind and had told Cole they wouldn't make love again.

Then he'd told her he *needed* her. A tingle raced up her spine.

Her resolve had been shot to hell, as well as her concentration for the rest of the work day. She'd tried to shoot him down again when they'd got home that evening. Cole wouldn't hear of it, of course. She'd found it difficult to be mad at him when she'd been pinned between his hard body and the Challenger. He'd kissed her until her toes had curled.

They'd end up back in her bed tonight.

Andi bit her bottom lip. She needed to say no. She needed

143

to stay away from him. But…she needed to have him kiss her, have him inside her then sleep in his arms.

She needed Cole, too.

Her heart dropped to her stomach. What was she doing?

Pete watched them still, cataloguing everything he saw, no doubt to bring it up to her later. Where was her fun-loving, jokester partner? This *observer* was much too serious.

It wasn't like she could avoid him for very long, either. Pete was a pusher, like Cole. He'd get her to spill her guts, no matter how much it *wasn't* his business. Plausible deniability was long gone.

Andi didn't have a leg to stand on after the look that had passed between her and Cole moments ago.

It's about you, locking yourself away. Pete's words from the hospital echoed in her mind. Is that what she'd done? *No.* She'd lost the first man she'd truly loved. Ethan had been *six weeks* old. Andi had done what she'd had to do. Dating hadn't been on the table, even long after Iain had died. She'd been a mess.

As a matter of fact, her partner had seen her through it when she'd been at rock bottom. Pete had stayed over, changed diapers, handled two a.m. feedings and held her when she'd fallen apart.

"Mama, I'm thirsty," Ethan called from his seat at the table.

"I got it," Cole said, grabbing the colourful cup and heading to the fridge before she could react. "Milk, buddy?"

Her little boy nodded. Things like that evaporated her resistance to Cole. He was so perfect with Ethan. She wanted to sidle up to him, have him pull her against him and kiss her. Even Pete and Ethan's joint presence didn't dim the desire.

Andi swallowed hard, ignoring the questions in Pete's eyes. She looked away from the man who'd been her partner for the last five years, reaching for the Creole spices and sprinkling her creation with a heavy dose. Dinner was almost ready. Hopefully it would keep the reins on Pete's tongue.

Despite Cole's chair being much too close to hers—a fact Pete didn't miss, though he said nothing—their meal was a pleasant affair. Under the table, Cole managed to brush her thigh with his, and even rested his hand on her knee a few times. Each touch melted her a bit more, and Andi had to stop herself from leaning into him.

She planned a short escape to put Ethan to bed, though her son whined until Pete agreed to carry him to his room. Andi didn't miss Cole's clenched jaw. The night before, her little boy had insisted he read to him before bed, but tonight Ethan was all about Pete. That was obviously bothering him. But why was he jealous? Why would he be? Ethan hadn't seen Pete in a long while. Cole was his new constant. They were both great with him, but only seeing Cole with Ethan tugged at her heart.

Andi put it out of her mind as Pete retreated from her son's room and she went in to get him into pyjamas and tucked in.

"Mama, I love Cole and Unca' Pete," Ethan muttered, giving into a huge yawn.

Her heart flipped. Pete loved him, no doubt. But did Cole? She dropped a kiss on her little boy's forehead and caressed his soft cheek. "I love you, little man."

He smiled and blew her a noisy kiss with his small palm. "Love you, Mama!"

Chuckling, Andi gave him one last caress and slipped from his room, closing the door halfway.

The hum of Pete's and Cole's deep voices made her smile. At least they were getting along as well as they had in the hospital. If Cole had noticed Pete's speculative looks, he hadn't acknowledged them.

"Hmmm, interesting," Pete was saying as Andi joined them in the living room.

She declined the dewy bottle of beer Cole offered and didn't dare slide onto the couch next to him. Andi sat on the edge of her oversized recliner and Pete pulled her ottoman forward and sat next to the glass-topped coffee table, facing them both.

"What's interesting?" Andi asked.

"That Maldonado is up to about five cars and hasn't damaged them," Cole said.

"What the hell could he be up to?" Pete mused, his head cocked to one side.

"I thought he might be staying in Homeless Row," Andi started.

"So we checked it out today, but nada," Cole said, slicing the air with his hand.

Glancing at him, her heart sped up. He'd finished her sentence. Pete stared, a fair eyebrow raised and a smile playing at his lips.

Great, her partner hadn't missed it.

"Where else have you checked?"

"For possible residences? Nowhere." Cole looked at her.

"Well, there's the old trailer park. They've cleaned it out pretty well, but there are about eight or nine junkers still on the property," Pete said.

"Ah. Yeah, I suppose we can go look tomorrow," Andi said.

"Good deal," Cole said. "Hope it's the place, and we catch him sleeping."

Pete chuckled. "This guy is one slippery bastard, huh?"

"Seems that way," Andi said.

"I never thought he had in it him to evade me this long," Cole said, his tone thoughtful.

"Well, I know y'all will get him."

Andi smiled. "Thanks, partner."

After Pete's third degree and several more investigation suggestions, she excused herself to clean up her kitchen. The ticking clock above the sink caught her attention. Wow, already after nine.

The guys were still deep in conversation, but work and case talk had come and gone. It turned out Cole was a Dallas Cowboys fan. Pete's face lit up with that admission,

146

so the two had turned to stat and player talk Andi had no interest in.

Hockey and baseball were the two sports she claimed as favourites, but she didn't really follow either closely. Iain had been into rugby and what he called football — soccer — and had had no use for American football. But he and Pete had got into some lively debates.

Andi shook her head. Instead of the normal wave of sadness, she was overwhelmed with loving memories. She rubbed her chest. Her eyes welled with tears she didn't understand, but she swallowed them back. What was wrong with her?

The dishwasher had already been loaded, the table, counter and cutting board wiped down. Pete and Cole had both contributed, so all that was left was her electric skillet. She ran the water over it, grabbing her new sponge.

"Hey, Andi, I'm gonna take off." Pete popped his head into the kitchen.

She jumped.

"Oh, sorry, partner, I didn't mean to startle you." He stopped by the sink and pulled her into a quick hug.

"Thanks for coming," Andi said, smiling and meeting his green eyes.

"I can't miss out on chicken magic." He grinned. "You and I have a lot to talk about, partner."

Her gaze slid away as she squirmed and she shut the hot water off.

"Ah, there's that avoidance," Pete said, amusement in his tone.

"I don't know what you're talking about," Andi said, her voice shaky.

Pete laughed. He cupped her face and tilted her chin up. "I'm happy for you," he whispered.

Heat rushed her cheeks, but she couldn't look away. She scowled. "Pete —"

"Goodnight, partner." He pressed a kiss to her cheek. "Turns out Mr Fed isn't so bad, after all?"

Andi pulled away and flung hot water at him. Pete darted out of the way and chuckled. "I'll call you tomorrow."

"Where's Cole?" the question was out of her mouth before she paused to think about it.

Her partner smiled, warm and approving. "Checking on Ethan."

She swallowed hard, ignoring the beat her heart missed. *Do not show your reaction.* "I'll call you tomorrow if we find anything at the trailer park," Andi said quickly.

Pete's smile widened to a grin, but he said nothing.

"Good. Night. Pete." She spaced the words and forced a breath.

He only laughed again and offered a wave. "I'll see myself out." He winked.

Andi rolled her eyes, but her whole body tingled.

She and Cole were alone in her house. Again.

148

Chapter Sixteen

She was at the sink scrubbing her electric skillet. Cole pressed a kiss to the back of her neck, then nuzzled the hollow of her ear, nipping her earlobe. He watched the shiver travel down her spine and slipped a hand around her waist, settling it low on her stomach. He pulled her bottom against him.

His cock shot from six o'clock to *midnight* in two seconds flat.

"I thought he would never leave," he whispered against the baby hairs at the back of her neck. Her ponytail brushed his cheek.

"Cole..."

"Stop thinking, Andi." He nuzzled her again, rocking against her firm bottom. "That's half your problem."

Cole whirled her around and covered her mouth with his. She yelped, but he smothered it with his tongue, exploring her sweetness. Kissing him back, she moaned after only a moment, shooting her arms around him.

He pulled back, staring into her half-lidded sapphire eyes. Warm, probably soapy water sank into the fabric of his pale blue button-down shirt—the only non-tee with him in Texas.

"You got me wet," Cole said, his lips hovering over hers.

Andi bit her bottom lip, but she couldn't hold back her giggle. "You grabbed me. It wasn't my fault."

After pressing a quick kiss into her lips, he took a step back. "Then I guess I just have to take it off."

"You won't need it," she whispered. Her tongue shot out to moisten her kiss-swollen lips, and Cole bit back a groan.

She reached for a dish towel and dried her damp hands. After tossing it back on the counter, she stepped towards him, leaning up and touching her lips to his while her deft fingers worked his buttons.

He took control, cupping the back of her head to bring her closer. She whimpered, but he deepened the kiss.

Andi pulled away, face already flushed pink. "You're distracting me from getting you naked."

He laughed, caressing her cheek with his thumb, tracing the freckles along the bridge of her nose. *Thank God she quit thinking.*

"By all means, continue. We can't have that."

She flashed a smile that made his heart thud and his cock throb. When she got his shirt open, Andi placed both palms flat to the hard planes of his chest. She stroked him, following his defined lines. Cole gasped. Her touch made his blood boil.

He had an intense need to throw her down on any surface, strip her and *take* her. How much had he had to drink? Control wavered. Swallowing hard, he groaned as her thumbs teased his nipples to hard peaks. He shifted back and forth on his feet.

Smiling, she slipped her hands onto his shoulders, pushing his shirt back to expose more skin. Andi explored him, taking much more time than he'd allowed her last night. He craved her touch. But at the same time, Cole burned to be inside her.

She reached for the fly of his jeans and he jumped. Andi froze. Big blue eyes met his gaze. "You okay?"

"You're killing me."

Andi grinned and kissed him. The little vixen knew *exactly* what she was doing, and liked it.

He devoured her, taking control and shoving into her mouth with his tongue. Cole yanked her into his arms. Sliding his hands down her back, he cupped her bottom and rocked into her, pushing his hard cock into her softness, but it wasn't enough.

She snaked her arms around his neck. Cole lifted her higher and Andi wrapped her legs around his waist.

Cole pushed her against the kitchen wall. She clung to him before pulling away to take a breath. They panted against each other.

"Sorry, that was rough," Cole said, working his fingers under her shirt, brushing the soft skin of her stomach.

"Bedroom?" she gasped.

Nodding, he fused their mouths. If he could run as he carried her, he would have. Her hands were hot on his back, her lips on his throat, his cheeks, his neck. Nipping, kissing, driving him crazy.

He plopped her down at the centre of her bed without finesse. They both laughed. Cole paused, looking down into her gorgeous smiling face. When was the last time he'd had fun with a lover?

She lifted her hips and he helped her shimmy out of her jeans and panties, tossing them over his shoulder, no care for where they landed. Andi laughed again and reached for him.

Cole kissed her, shooting his hand between her legs. He groaned, moving his fingers over her slick folds, taking a moment to tease her clit. She was already ready for him and pushed up into his hand.

He parted their mouths. "Looks like I wasn't the only one wet." He grinned.

Andi turned scarlet, but didn't look away. "Something's wrong with this picture."

"What's that?"

"You have no top, I have no bottoms."

Cole chuckled and stood at the edge of her bed.

"Lose the jeans, Agent Lucas," she breathed, eyes devouring him.

He bit his lip to keep from making a sound. God, the look on her face made him burn. Something was wrong with him to have this much desire for her. Two beers screwed his head up more than normal.

Unzipping his fly, Cole did her bidding, banishing all thought. He needed to follow his own advice. *Stop thinking, you idiot. She's ripe and ready, in a bed. She wants you. So take her. Make her scream your name just like last night.*

He forced a curt nod and stomped out of his jeans and boxer briefs. Turning back to the bed, he froze. Andi had lost the shirt, bra and ponytail. Her dark hair teased her shoulders. "God, you're gorgeous," he whispered, crawling up to her from the end of the bed. His cock pounded.

One look at her full nakedness and he was about to lose it like a teenager. He'd already seen her, had her, last night. Tonight should be no different. But lust thundered through his blood. He ignored it and focused on her.

Andi's cheeks were pink again, freckles standing out, and a smile played at his lips. If he pointed out how hot the blush looked on her she'd throttle him, so Cole kept his thoughts in his head.

He leant down and placed a tender kiss to her mouth. Trailing his lips along her neck and collarbone, she buried her hands in his dark hair and let him taste her. Cole continued on, lavishing each nipple with attention until she writhed beneath him, whimpering like before. He could get used to the little sounds she made. He'd taste her all over, but he needed her kiss again, so he headed back up, pressing his lips to her cheek, her forehead and finally her lips. She opened for him from head to foot, her mouth, her arms, her thighs.

An unmanly shiver went down his spine, but Cole disregarded it and lowered himself over her. Their skin touched as Andi arched into him, breasts to chest, hips to hips. She wrapped her legs around his waist and pulled him closer.

His heart pounded in his ears as her mouth seared his. Letting her lead the kiss, he mated his tongue to hers as she explored his mouth. Her heart echoed his, thumping hard against his chest.

Cole *needed* to be inside her.

As if she'd read his mind, Andi cupped and squeezed his ass, yanking him flush against her sex. He bit back a yelp as the tip of his cock parted her folds without guidance from his hand. Pleasure shot into him.

She pressed her pelvis to his — he was lost. He fell into her, kissing her harder. Andi was right there with him, meeting his first thrust.

He cried out, but the sound was lost in the heated kiss as they started to move together. Grabbing her hips, he propelled forward over and over, thrusting to the hilt. Andi arched into him, flattening her breasts against his chest and gripping his shoulders, nails digging in. Cole didn't care. She could make him bleed.

Andi ran her hands all over the wide expanse of his back, but settled on his biceps as he moved even faster. She writhed under him. *God*, she was killing him, moving with him and clinging when his thrusts took him away.

Her inner muscles clutched him, her sudden orgasm making the pressure in his lower back too much to bear. He was close...so close.

Cole swallowed her scream of his name by taking her mouth desperately. He thrust hard once, twice and, devouring her in rhythm, he grunted as his cock jerked and he spilled himself inside her. Her core contracted against him in waves and he moaned into her mouth, struggling for control as the intensity clouded his brain.

Andi clung to him as Cole rocked against her. He wasn't ready to pull out, to part himself from her luscious body.

Aftershocks of their shared pleasure rolled over him. He crushed her against his chest to stave off the tremble that threatened his legs...arms...everything.

What the hell had she done to him?

Cole lifted his head. Her skin glistened, lips kiss-swollen, chestnut locks mussed and whole body flushed pink. She was the most beautiful woman he'd ever seen.

Half-lidded blue eyes met his. "Cole?" she whispered.

They both panted hard, her breasts heaving against his

chest.

He flashed a smile and took her mouth. The kiss he'd intended to be tender quickly became more, her fingers slipping down his back and cupping his ass again. He shifted against her, wishing his cock was ready for round two.

Ending the kiss, he tried to pull away, but she held him tight. He couldn't think. His thoughts spun, chaos that made no sense. "Did you feel it, Andi? The magic between us?" The words tumbled from his lips, and he froze.

What did he just say? Out loud? *Shit.*

Cole held his breath and waited.

"Yes," she whispered, holding his gaze.

His heart thumped. Damn, her answer...mattered. What the *fuck* was wrong with him?

"Let's get cleaned up," he croaked.

She nodded and loosened her hold. Cole had no desire to pull away from her. Loss hit him as his now flaccid cock slipped from her body.

Wait. His *naked* cock.

No condom. No protection? *Shit.*

Andi noticed where his gaze landed. She sat up and their eyes met.

"I'm sorry."

She reached for his hand and entwined their fingers, pressing a kiss into his knuckles. "It...felt wonderful." Her cheeks reddened, but she didn't look away. "I'm not sorry."

"But... I finished inside..."

"One time won't matter," Andi answered, leaning in to kiss him.

Cole cupped her face and nodded. What the hell else could he say? She had him so wadded up, he didn't know if he was coming or going.

He slipped from the bed, needing a moment alone. He told her he'd get something to clean her up and closed the bathroom door. Cole sank his hand into his hair and dragged it down his face over the stubble on his cheek.

It took fifteen minutes to shut his head off and calm his racing heart. When he went back to her, Andi was curled on her side, looking magnificent as she slept.

Damn, he'd taken so long she'd passed out on him.

Sitting on the edge of her bed, Cole kissed the crown of her head. Her breathing was a deep, even rhythm. She didn't stir as he grabbed her comforter and sheet and covered them, pulling her into his arms.

Andi nestled close, as if she'd done it hundreds of times. He could hold her forever. Contentment settled over him and scared the shit out of him. He caressed her hair, running his fingers through the thick locks, brushing her shoulders, her back, as she nestled closer. She sighed in her sleep and Cole smiled as he pressed another kiss to her forehead.

One time won't matter, she'd said. What would happen if it *did* matter?

A picture popped into his head, Andi caressing a tummy rounded with…his baby.

Cole jolted and he glanced down at the woman in his arms.

Never, *ever* had he planned on kids.

He'd never even had a relationship that'd lasted more than a month.

Ethan was great, but the little boy was hers. *Not* his. Would never *be* his, and that was fine. It was *great*. He'd didn't want more. So why did that bother him?

What if he'd knocked her up tonight?

"Jesus, something's wrong with you," he whispered.

What happened to a few fucks then she was out of his system?

Andi was the same as all the others, right?

Right?

She shifted against him as if she could read his mind and didn't like his thoughts. He was so full of shit she knew it in her sleep.

God, Cole was *screwed*.

"Well, Andi… I promise I'll be there for you, if one time

does matter," Cole whispered against her temple, cursing the *rightness* of that statement. He crushed his eyes shut and ignored the pounding of his heart.

"Just go to sleep, asshole," he told himself, shaking his head.

Andi sighed and smiled in her sleep. Cole pulled her closer.

He was *so* screwed.

Chapter Seventeen

Carlo watched the house for hours. Cars came and went. Mothers with baby carriages took strolls down the sidewalk. He sat unnoticed in the late model sedan he'd jacked from the mall parking lot. The grey Camry wasn't too old, wasn't too new. He was practically invisible. He'd chosen well, and the tinted windows were a Godsend.

It had taken the bastard two days to get back to him, and three more to finalise his plan, but Bruno would be in town soon. Until then, Carlo would handle this shit himself. He'd get the girl, Cole Lucas would come after her and he'd have his former boss's attention.

It would be easy, too.

That stupid ass Lucas was so into his woman he hadn't even seen Carlo once, as many times as he'd watched them go into that house. *Fool*. He *never* would have thought it possible the bastard would be cowed for a woman. No pussy was that good. No doubt Lucas was hittin' that.

Finally a green Honda Civic pulled into the driveway next to Cole's woman's house. He knew from watching that the girl lived next door with only her mother.

"Dammit."

Two teens got out of the car, a sandy-haired boy, seventeen or eighteen. The girl stood by, swinging a purple backpack to her shoulder while he opened the back passenger door. They chatted, but he couldn't hear their conversation.

The kid helped Cole's woman's boy out of the back seat, and he hopped up and down in place as soon as his small feet hit the pavement. The girl laughed, taking the little boy's hand. The elder male leaned in and kissed her.

"Oh, Jesus," Carlo muttered.

Then the kid grabbed his own backpack from the car and waved. Both the girl and the little boy waved back as the teen jogged down the street.

"See you later," the girl yelled. That Carlo heard, even with the window open only a crack. He threw another gesture over his shoulder and she flashed a starry-eyed grin before he disappeared around the corner.

Carlo shook his head. "Too bad she won't be here when you get back, loverboy."

He waited for them to get into the house. The little boy had to jump up each step. She was patient with him, holding his hand, but Carlo cursed each leap until they made it to the top. Why the hell did kids do those things? It was three fucking stairs. No need for it to take ten minutes to hit the porch.

The door closed and he took a deep breath. This was it. Nice and easy, like a smash and grab. He would get her to his car and tie her up, then he was in business. Caselli would give him money and a ride and get the traitor as a bonus.

Carlo crossed the street with minimal protest from his healing wounds — antibiotics and pain meds did wonders. His limp wasn't even that pronounced.

The butt of his gun inside his jacket firmly grasped, he reached for the doorbell with the other.

Ding dong. He waited.

Just before he was going to press it again, she wrenched the door open.

"Matt, did you forg—" The grin on the girl's face faded a bit when she saw him, but her expression was still pleasant. "Oh, sorry I thought you were someone else. Can I help you?"

The little redheaded kid was standing about ten feet away in the doorway of another room. *Damn.* Oh well, the kid was what — two? Not like he would be able to tell the cops anything. Carlo plastered a smile on his face and gripped his gun tighter.

She looked him up and down but said nothing. The girl was stunning up close. Not short, not tall—about five and a half feet, mahogany hair hanging loose about her shoulders, big, expressive brown eyes. High cheekbones, creamy olive skin. Italian. Exquisitely expensive.

Her age wouldn't matter. Carlo would have no trouble selling her. Maybe he could sample the goods first. Quality control and all that. Unless she was a virgin—they always went for more. But he could still play a little.

Carlo cleared his throat. "Is the man of the house at home?"

Her brow furrowed and she shook her head, hair swishing with the movement. "No, um... Is there something you need?"

"You."

He grabbed her arm and spun her, slamming her against his chest and sliding one arm around her waist, pressing his gun into her side.

The tiny boy stood frozen in the doorway, his blue eyes wide. "Bad man!" He pointed at Carlo. "Gun!"

How the fuck did he know what a gun was?

"Ethan, run! Run now," the girl urged.

Carlo jarred her against his chest and she struggled. She stomped on his foot.

"Fuck! Stop fighting me right now, or I'll pop the kid."

The girl froze in his arms. "Ethan, please run!"

Carlo followed as the little boy's eyes darted to a panel on the wall of the foyer, and the plush wingback chair underneath it. An alarm? No fucking way the kid knew how to— He rushed to the chair.

Raising his gun, he trained it on the toddler. The girl screamed and Carlo clamped his hand down on her mouth, cupping her jaw to prevent any biting ideas. Her sharp intake of breath gave him a little satisfaction.

* * * *

159

"MacLaren."

Andi looked over her shoulder from the computer and rubbed her eyes.

Cole, who'd been bent over staring at the screen as well, straightened and they turned collectively.

Lieutenant Nick Wells had an odd expression on his face as he approached her cubicle. "Andi, you need to go home. Now."

Cole shot her a look, jaw clenched. Something was wrong. He sensed it, too.

"Tell me." She had to restrain herself from reaching for Cole's hand. Dammit, she was a cop. She didn't need comfort. Digging for professionalism, she stood and squared her shoulders.

Nick hedged, shifting back and forth on his feet. In full uniform, his navy tie swayed. Andi met his dark eyes.

"Just head home. Ricketts and Crowley are on their way."

"Dammit, Nick. Tell me what I'm walking into." Shit, her voice wavered. Cole took a step towards her, but didn't touch her. Still, his closeness helped.

"Your alarm went off. Your son pressed the panic button. The company dispatcher couldn't make much out, other than 'gun' and 'bad man'. Dispatch got guys on the way in less than three min—"

Andi sprinted down the hall, away from Nick and Cole. It was either that or pass out. *Ethan. Bella.* Her heart dropped to her stomach.

"Andi, wait!"

She didn't pause with Cole's shout. She just headed around the corner and out of the building. Wrenching the door open to the Challenger didn't get her far. Cole's hand on her upper arm yanked her to a stop, preventing her from climbing inside.

"Stop. Take a deep breath. It's gonna be okay."

Cole pulled her into his arms and she didn't fight him, despite their very public location. The strength of his muscles, his body, his arms around her grounded her. He caressed her cheek, guiding her face up. "Take a breath," he repeated, his steel eyes soft as he cupped her face. "I'll drive."

Andi nodded. She couldn't manage a sentence. Worry burned her from the inside out, ate at her heart, her stomach. Cole pressed a quick kiss to her lips and helped her into the passenger seat before slipping behind the wheel in seconds.

When she didn't belt up, he reached across her body to do it for her, but she grabbed his wrist. "I got it. Just get us home."

He nodded, his full lips a hard line, and eyes narrowed as he faced forward. So, he was worried too. Andi swallowed hard.

The drive to her house was only nine minutes, but it felt more like an hour in her head. Two cruisers were in the driveway and one was in front of the house on the street. The siren of a fourth was cut off mid wail as it pulled up. Pete's truck was there, too. He wasn't allowed to come back to work for a few weeks, but still had his radio. No shocker he'd been listening.

There were cops everywhere, on her lawn, front porch and driveway. Her fellow detectives would likely show up next. Everyone must have answered when they'd heard the call go out.

Why had she left the handheld on her desk on minute volume?

She was out of the car before Cole had it fully stopped, and Andi ignored his shout to wait. Composure was gone. The strong police detective was gone. She was all mother, and nothing would keep her from her son.

Sprinting up the three steps to her front porch, she dashed into the open front door. Pete was talking to one of the uniformed officers, Nina Ricketts.

Why the hell wasn't Pete with Ethan?

"Andi, wait." Pete stepped towards her, hand up. As his grip landed on her upper arm, she yanked away from the worry in his green eyes.

161

Gaze darting over the scene—her house, yard, porch, even her foyer—her blood ran cold. Her co-workers were organising a search grid.

"We'll find them." His words were tight, sling hanging around his neck, unused as usual, and he had both hands on his lean hips. He looked tired, and was dressed much too casually for work, in denim shorts and a plain grey T-shirt.

"Find them?" Her words cracked.

Get it together, Andi, you're a frickin' cop.

Then Cole was there, hovering in the doorway. Silent, assessing. Her eyes shot to him and back to Pete. Her partner settled both hands on her shoulders and squeezed. "I know you taught Ethan how to use the alarm panel, but if he could, where would he go from there?"

"Ethan, alone?" Again her words were strained. She forced them out through the pain in her chest.

"It's likely Bella is gone." Pete's tone was even, police-like. His manner was as hers should have been. She clung to that sentiment and took a deep breath.

"Where have you looked for him?" Cole asked, stepping forward.

"Officer Crowley is in charge of the search outside. We're going to handle the house. Now." Pete stared at Cole. Some sort of non-verbal communication passed between her partner and her FBI agent.

Cole nodded.

Ordering herself to calm the hell down, Andi reached for the detached police professional she was and failed, mostly. A missing child always got her right in the chest, but that feeling was nothing compared to now. This was *her kid* they were talking about. She shifted on her feet and looked at Pete, then Cole.

"Let's go." The determination in Cole's voice put her even more in check. She *would* find Ethan...and Bella. And they would both be fine. There was no other option.

They split up and called his name. The longer they failed to locate him, the more 'not here's that were called out, the more Andi's legs shook, gut tightened, heart threatened to exit her chest. Her eyes burned, but she ignored it and pushed through. Her baby was lost.

Logical places yielded nothing.

Then she heard a male voice outside call, "MacLaren!"

Pete beat her to the door and outside. Cole was on his heels, both broad backs blocking her view as they ran down the porch steps and around to her back yard.

"Over here," Officer Shannon Crowley hollered from Natalie and Bella's backyard.

Her partner hopped the four foot chain-link fence and crouched by the blue baby swimming pool that was upside down on Natalie's covered patio.

"Squirt, it's Uncle Pete," he said.

A flash of red curls, and her son was in her partner's arms. The empty plastic mould rocked as he slipped out from under it.

Cole ran through the open gate, Andi on his heels.

Face buried in her partner's neck, Ethan repeated, "My Bells," over and over.

She hurried to them, ignoring Cole, who bee-lined for Shannon. The officer was talking into his radio, no doubt letting dispatch and everyone listening know they'd found Ethan.

Wide blue eyes locked onto hers as she reached Pete and her son. Andi's heart plummeted. He was so scared.

"Mama!"

She practically ripped him from her partner's arms and held him as close as she could. Small arms shot around her neck and she tugged him closer. He buried his face against her neck, his tears wetting her skin and the collar of her shirt. Rubbing his back, she whispered reassurances until he quieted. Ethan lifted his head and met her gaze. Andi wiped the tears from his cheeks.

"Bell Bell, Mama. The bad man took my Bells."

Andi's stomach somersaulted with her three-year-old's confirmation that the teen was indeed gone.

Kidnapped. Innocent, sweet Bella.

"Someone call Natalie." Her voice cracked, her chest ached. So close. What if Ethan had been hurt? Taken? Shot?

"I'm gonna kill that bastard," Cole spat.

"Cole," Ethan exclaimed before Andi or Pete could answer.

Her son scrambled to get loose, so she set him down and he darted to Cole. Her temporary partner and lover swung him up into his arms and held him close. Andi watched them together. Cole soothed Ethan as she had. The little boy kept nodding his head as her man talked in a low even voice, and Andi bit back a gulp. She could *not* lose it. Her chest tightened, she struggled for breath. Tears hovered, but she shut them down. *Not now.*

Pete shot a comforting arm around her shoulders and she leaned into him for only a moment before stepping away.

She was stronger than that.

"What happened?" Andi asked, a tremble shooting down her spine.

Shannon Crowley cleared his throat. She met his whisky-coloured eyes. "The alarm company told us that he kept saying a bad man had a gun and took his 'bells'. He kept asking for his mom and Cole. He told the operator that you and Cole had guns, but you were the good guys. After that, I'm guessing he ran. He didn't stay on the phone with dispatch."

"Ethan said the bad man rang the doorbell and pointed a gun at him. He said he hurt Bella," Cole said, striding forward.

Andi bit back a wince.

"Squirt, can you remember, did the bad man have hair like mine, or like Cole's?" Pete asked.

Necessary as it was, interrogating any child was difficult, but this was *her* kid. Andi's mind screamed a protest. However, her son answered before she could comment.

"Like Cole's," Ethan answered, his face contorted as he remembered. "He walked funny."

164

She and Cole exchanged a glance. "Maldonado," they said at the same time.

"A gun. A big gun, too," Ethan added, laying his head on Cole's shoulder.

"Baby, you did so good. You climbed up and pushed the button just like we practised." She stroked his cheek.

"I told the lady everything."

"Good job, Ethan," Cole said. Her son beamed.

Ethan reached for her, and Andi pulled him from Cole's arms, propping him on a hip. Pete stepped away, his phone to his ear. His voice was low, calm, as he asked for Bella's mother. She ignored the guilt and worry as it skittered across her body, squeezing Ethan tighter in her arms.

"Natalie's coming home," Pete said, slipping his cell back into his pocket.

How could she tell her close friend and neighbour she'd found her child, when Nat's was still missing?

"I'll talk to her," her partner said, as if he could read her mind.

Andi nodded, voice gone. Pete had always been better at those things than her.

The walk back to the house was filled with dread. Bella... gone. Ethan too close to danger, and Carlo Maldonado on the loose and holding all the cards.

"Detective MacLaren," Officer Nina Ricketts called from near the front door. "Does there seem to be anything out of place, or missing?"

Andi looked around, taking a few calming breaths. No, everything in the foyer was in order, down to the potted plant she always forgot to water on the table she threw her keys on every day. "Nothing," she answered.

Ricketts nodded, jotting a few notes on her pocket spiral, her blonde updo bouncing with the movement.

"I didn't think so," Pete murmured "But I told her to ask you anyway."

She set Ethan to his feet, but he didn't go far, looping his arms above her knee.

"It's like a smash and grab, so Maldonado," Cole said.

"Do you think he'll hurt her?" Pete asked.

"No. He's needs her in one piece if he plans to sell her."

Andi swallowed hard. Natalie would never forgive her. She would never forgive herself. How the *hell* had he found out where she lived? And why Bella?

"He's after me," Cole answered, as if he'd read her mind. "Leverage. I would bet money on it."

"So now what?" Andi asked.

"We wait." His jaw was a hard line.

"No. We need to find her," she said.

"We won't have to wait long. He wants me. He'll contact us."

"But we don't—" Andi's statement was cut off by Bella's mother's appearance in the doorway. Her brown eyes—a match for her daughter's—were bloodshot and her scrubs a mess. She'd rushed right from the hospital.

"Andi?" Natalie's voice shook. Her friend was all mother, like Andi had been. Nat's persona of the strong trauma RN was in the background.

Andi rushed forward and pulled Nat into her arms. Her long-time friend trembled from head to foot. She soothed her as best she could, smoothing her short dark hair and whispering to her.

As a mother, she had empathy. The moments before they'd got home, her worry for Ethan had been paramount, only to worsen when they'd failed to locate him right away. She wouldn't be able to cope without him. But Nat wouldn't be without Bella for very long. As a cop, Andi *would* get Maldonado.

"Where's Bella?" she asked. Tears cascaded down her cheeks.

Pete appeared at her side with a tissue box. Natalie snatched one, but did nothing more than hold it. "We'll find her," Andi's partner said.

"How could this have happened?" Natalie asked through a new sob.

Andi stared. What could she say?

"I got this, partner. Go be with Ethan and Cole," Pete whispered in the vicinity of her ear.

She nodded numbly and watched Pete gently guide her neighbour into the living room and sit her down on the loveseat. He dragged the ottoman from the other side of the room and took a seat in front of her. Their low tones didn't carry, but Natalie's crying did. Andi winced.

The cops in the room said their farewells and 'call if you need us' to Cole and the cavalry outside started to recede, but the weight of the world settled itself on Andi's chest.

Ethan was in Cole's arms again. Emotions swirled in her head and heart. She ignored a shiver as a wave of guilt over Bella fought the rightness of her son and the man together.

"*Stop*, this is not your fault," Cole whispered, pulling her to his side with his free arm.

"I never said it was." Since when did he know her so well?

"It's written all over your face," he answered, a smile playing at his lips. He squeezed her against his side.

Cole held Andi and Ethan tight to him, dropping a kiss on her cheek. "We'll get her back. I promise." His tone held conviction.

She looked into his steel eyes and nodded, throat constricting, mouth dry, leaving unsaid, *Yes, but in what condition?*

When Ethan reached for her, she grabbed his small hand and clung to it.

Chapter Eighteen

Carlo tied the girl's hands behind her back in the dimness of the office at the rear of the warehouse. The same warehouse where he'd killed Gains and Reese. Blacked out windows offered no light, but he could manage with the lantern he'd got at Wal-Mart.

And if she didn't shut her goddamn mouth, he was going to gag the pretty little bitch. She whimpered when he yanked the ropes tighter.

"What do you want from me?" she demanded, her attractive mouth a hard line. Her dark eyes shot daggers at him.

Carlo smirked. "Your sweet ass."

He whipped her around and yanked her close, leaning down and pressing his lips to hers.

She yelped and tried to squirm away from him, but he jerked the rope and she froze, her breasts pushing into his chest. Small and firm, they needed a good squeeze.

"Don't touch me," she spat.

Chuckling, Carlo took a step back and pressed her into the chair, intentionally brushing her chest with both hands.

The girl gasped and bit her plump bottom lip. Her eyes were shiny as they caught the lantern light. He'd scared her. *Good.*

"Are you a virgin?"

She glared at him again. *Damn*, was the little bitch bipolar?

"Excuse me?" she asked.

Carlo looped ropes around her calves and ankles, securing her to the chair and flashing a smile as he straightened. He tugged his shirt in place and ran a hand through his dark

168

hair, propping his ass on the nearest desk top.

"Just a question." He shrugged.

Her eyes narrowed, but she said nothing.

With a growl, Carlo flew off the desk and gripped her face, digging his fingers into her jaw. She tried to shake him off by jerking back and forth, but he squeezed until tears welled again. He tilted her cheeks up, studying her.

Maybe he wouldn't care either way. He'd always liked the feisty ones. Sinking into her sweet body would be worth the loss of money if he'd be the one to pop her cherry. Her lips had hinted at her innocent flavour. Perhaps he should give it another go.

Carlo had time before Caselli's reinforcements were supposed to arrive.

"Have you ever had a real man? Blondie doesn't count."

Her eyes widened and she averted her gaze. A tremble racked her slender frame when he rubbed his thumb across her bottom lip. Tears cascaded silently down her cheeks, wetting his fingertips.

When he released her, she looked away, head hung low, dark hair curtaining her face. "How do you know about Matt?"

"So loverboy's name is Matt. Has *Matt* ever parted your thighs?"

She didn't look at him, but her face reddened and she shivered.

"Tell me the truth." Carlo tapped her shoulder. "Things will go easier for you."

"I'm a virgin." She met his gaze head on. "He *respects* me."

Carlo threw his head back and laughed. "Only because he's burying his cock in someone else's sweet pussy."

The girl gasped and he laughed harder. He caressed her cheek, but she yanked away from his hand.

"Oh, the things I could teach you if I had time."

"No." The whispered word was punctuated by the frantic shake of her head.

Grinning, Carlo cocked his head to the side. "You don't

get to pick, baby."

Her shoulders slumped and she bit her bottom lip. "Are you going to rape me? Is that what you want?"

"Unfortunately your virtue is safe from me...for now."

Breath exiting on a whoosh, she stared at him. "Then... why? What do you want?"

"What's your name, sweetness?" he asked, ignoring her question.

She glared. The spunk was back and his cock twitched. "Don't call me that," she snapped.

"I'll call you whatever I want." Carlo leant down, tapping her nose with his fingertip. He flashed a smile as he read the disgust in her eyes. "You're the one tied to a chair in this scenario, or did you forget?"

She set her jaw in a firm line. God, she was a hot little thing.

"Bella. My name is Bella."

Carlo grinned. "Figures. Fitting."

"Huh?"

"Do you know what your name means in Italian, sweetness?" He ran two fingers from her temple to her cheek.

Damn, he could barely keep his hands to himself. He needed to get laid.

Bella nodded, but Carlo spoke anyway. "Beautiful. It means beautiful, and that's just what you are."

"Don't touch me," she ordered, but her voice shook.

Carlo wiped her tears away with both hands, but Bella winced. "Aw, c'mon. I won't hurt you. Don't believe me?"

He continued his caresses down her neck, shoulder and arm as it curved around the back of the chair, but her tremors only increased.

He scowled. "Listen, *Bella*, relax, or I'll give you something to cry about."

Her dark eyes widened and Carlo leaned close, their noses almost touching. "Please don't hurt me," she whispered.

"Do what I tell you when the time comes, and you got

nothing to worry about."

"What do you mean?"

"You'll see." Carlo caressed her face. Her lip trembled, and he was torn between the hard-on his zipper was biting into and smacking some sense into her. But bruises damaged value, and this one was worth a shitload.

After bending over, he quickly undid the ropes containing her legs and feet, pulling her from the chair into his arms. She froze, uncertainty etched in her expression as he ran his hands over her long silky hair. "*Bella* Bella." Continuing to whisper to her in Italian did nothing to relax her in his hold, though her arms were still bound. But Carlo wasn't stupid enough to free them. The girl was still a firecracker.

He pulled her mouth up to his, claiming her forcibly. She fought him, wriggling, but he tightened his hold on her face, forcing her lips open and shoving his tongue inside. Damn, she was sweet, innocence palpable.

Could he keep her? Dangling her in front of Lucas would still get him to come after her. Bruno could still have the FBI agent, and Carlo could leave *with* the girl. If he could weasel enough money away from Caselli, it could work. Teeth sank into his tongue, the metallic taste of blood filling his mouth with the sharp agony. Carlo yanked his mouth away with a loud curse as her knee shot up. Hands on her upper arms, he tilted his hips just in time to save his boys, but her jab landed upper thigh, jarring his injured side as well as the bullet-ridden leg. Breathing was a struggle as pain radiated and he fought doubling over.

"Fuck. *Fuck*," he muttered through clenched teeth.

She slipped from his grip and spat. "Asshole."

As pain took over his form, he didn't have a retort ready as she darted from the office and into the darkened warehouse.

"Son of a bitch," he growled as he straightened, taking one deep breath, then another. Forcing himself to get it together, he reached for his gun.

Where the hell did she think she was going?

* * * *

"I don't need back-up, Liv. I have a whole PD. I was just letting you know what's going on," Cole said into his cell, pacing her living room.

Andi's eyes tracked him, her stomach in knots. Five hours and nothing, and now it was almost ten.

Maldonado had Bella. No telling what he was doing to her.

Don't think about it. Be a cop. Handle this.

Pete had taken Natalie next door, along with Ethan. Her friend had told her taking him would give her something to do. With the excitement, he'd been up way past his bedtime. Her partner had kept them both calm, but that was just Pete. Her little boy had even flashed a smile or two. He'd be fine—kids were resilient. Irony swirled around in her brain. How many times had she reassured parents with that phrase?

Chief Martin had SWAT on standby, so they would be ready at the drop of a hat as soon as Maldonado called—if he called. Despite Cole's assurance, Andi had doubts.

"I'll get him, Liv. You've just gotta trust me. I *know* Maldonado. He'll call. He won't be able to resist the lure. I'd bet money he promised me to Caselli. I know how his mind works."

Andi couldn't make out what his supervisor was saying, but she heard the even hum of her voice. Cole's shoulders slumped and she stared. What now?

"I don't need another agent butting around in my case." He paused. "Partner? Hell no, I don't need a partner. I don't *want* a partner. This case is mine."

She swallowed hard. It was a reminder of her place. She was his lover, but he was *stuck* working with her. Despite the progress they'd made, the fact that they worked well together, he would still rather be a solo act.

It shouldn't have been a shocker, but it smarted. She'd been working her ass off on this case. She wanted Maldonado as

172

bad as he did. Worse, now that the asshole had Bella.

"I don't have an hour and a half to wait for her." He shook his head, scowling. "Fine. But I'm telling you right now if I get a call, I'm acting. I'm not waiting around for *anyone*, even Agent Dawson." He paused again. "No, Liv."

Her answer was a hard, raised voice. Andi still couldn't make out the words, but the threat in her tone was clear.

"Then I guess you'll do what you need to do, and so will I. Goodbye, Olivia." Cole ended the call cursing under his breath.

She didn't bother asking if everything was all right. "Who's Agent Dawson?"

"She's a transfer to my office, out of the Dallas office, so she's still local here. Liv wants to send her over, because evidently, we'll be *working* together when I get back. My new partner." The scowl on his face matched his tone.

Her heart started to race. What if Cole ended up getting along with this woman like *they* got along? What if he took her as a lover? Was it routine for him when working with a female?

Andi jolted, sitting up straighter. What was she doing?

She needed to be focused on Bella, not...what...losing Cole? She was going to lose him when the case was over anyway.

It wasn't like they'd talked about their relationship. Was it even a relationship? They were just having sex. She winced. That made it...nothing. It was so far from *nothing*, Andi didn't have the right words. She'd spent the last week and a half in his arms and wouldn't have changed a thing about it.

Cole's jaw was tight and his fists clenched as he continued to pace in front of her fireplace, but he was still the most appealing man she'd ever seen. She wanted to comfort him, assure him it would somehow be okay. She had to believe that to get her through. But she needed him to believe it, too.

She wanted him. To be with him, near him. Always.

Oh, shit. I love him.

The realisation hit like a ton of bricks and she almost toppled off the couch.

His gaze found hers and he came towards her. "You okay?"

"Yeah, just worried about Bella."

"I know. I am too. But he won't kill her." He plopped down on the ottoman and grabbed her hand. "Listen…is she a virgin?"

She gasped. "I don't know. Why?"

Cole winced. "Virgins go for more. So, if she is, he probably won't rape her." He squeezed her hand.

"Oh, God," she whispered, crushing her eyes shut and taking a deep breath.

This was Bella they were talking about, not some unknown girl that Andi would have had empathy for as a police officer. This was her little sister in all but blood. A child she'd seen grow up from age seven.

"I know," Cole whispered. "We have to be realistic."

She met his gaze and nodded. "I know. I really do."

"We'll get her back."

"Matt's her first boyfriend. She told me the other day she thinks she loves him, but I don't know if they're having sex," Andi said. "And I don't know if Natalie would know. They have a pretty open relationship, but I'm not sure a seventeen-year-old girl would announce that kinda thing to her mom."

He nodded. "He'll call me."

As if on cue, his cell phone hopped down the coffee table as it vibrated. Caller ID flashed *Unknown Number*.

Pete appeared in the living room at the same time, standing over them.

Cole swished his thumb across the touch screen and activated the speaker. "Lucas," he barked.

The laughter that greeted them was maniacal. Andi's stomach twisted.

"Hello, Cole Lucas."

174

"Maldonado," Cole growled.

"Looks like you lost something. Want to come and get it?"

"Where are you?"

"Oh, don't worry, I think you know the place. Tell your *detective* girlfriend I said hello."

The line went dead, and the three of them exchanged a look.

"The warehouse," they all spoke at once.

Chapter Nineteen

Cole was *done* talking. They'd gone over the plan a hundred times. Get to the warehouse and take down the elusive bastard. Bella home safe and sound.

The SWAT team was ready to go and drooling, too. It wasn't often they got any real action in Antioch.

Andi was holding it together nicely, the consummate detective. Currently, she was arguing with Pete to go home as her partner strapped on his bulletproof vest, ignoring her. Chief Martin had already ordered him away, but had given up before continuing his part in the boring briefing. He'd left Pete in Andi's charge. But she wasn't getting anywhere either.

Not like Cole could blame the guy. Maldonado had put two holes in Pete. Like hell anyone would keep *him* from going after someone who'd shot him.

"Everybody got it?" Lieutenant Davis, the SWAT team leader, asked as he glanced around the briefing room at the PD.

Mass affirmatives were muttered and the lieutenant gave a curt nod. "Well, it's just after midnight. Let's get this done."

"Chief," a voice called from the doorway. A uniformed officer popped his head in, an odd look on his face. "There's an FBI agent here…"

Cole groaned.

"Show 'em in," Chief Martin barked from the head of the room.

A dark-haired woman stepped past him, hands on shapely hips. Silence descended and many of the officers straightened in their seats. There were quite a few throats cleared.

"Don't stop on my account, boys," she said, a smirk on her face. "I'm looking for Special Agent Lucas."

"Over here," Cole said, his tone dry as he waved his hand.

She made her way to him, and he scrambled to his feet to meet the thrust of her hand.

"Special Agent Selena Dawson. Call me Lee."

Lee made a show of looking him up and down, but he ignored it and gave her a firm shake. Eyes burned him, and he looked to his right. Andi was staring. He flashed a half-smile and motioned her over. "This is Detective Andi MacLaren. We've been working the case together."

The two women shook hands and Lee sized Andi up, too. Andi glared at her. What the hell? They both murmured 'nice to meet you's, then Cole introduced Pete, since he'd meandered over behind his partner.

"Let's go, people," Lieutenant Davis announced. The room started to clear out, guys and gear noisy as they shuffled.

"How we doing this?" Lee asked Cole. Her brown eyes were keen as he met her gaze. Not very tall, but she really was gorgeous, high cheekbones, naturally light brown skin, nice hour-glass shape. Probably Hispanic. But as his eyes swept over Andi standing next to her, his heart gave a thud. Lee wasn't even a temptation.

"How much do you know?" Cole asked.

"Agent Barnes briefed me. Maldonado took the girl as bait to reel you in. Trade the girl for you, a nice switcheroo to Caselli."

"That's my best guess. Only thing he was clear about was the place."

"SWAT's going in?"

"The lieutenant agreed just a few. The rest are back-up. I'm going in," Cole said.

"I am, too," Andi said.

Cole's instinct was to shout, *the hell you are*, but he kept his mouth shut. She was a cop. And this was Bella. Nothing would keep her out.

"I'm going in," Pete said, crossing his arms over his broad chest. No wince. That was good, at least. His mouth was set in a hard line. No one contradicted him, not even Andi.

"Count me in, then," Lee said, patting her sidearm and smiling.

Great, Liv was saddling him with some action-hungry freak. Just what he needed.

"Let's go get Bella," Cole said. "We have to get her now, or he'll move her. Back-up or not, the trading routes are vast. She'll disappear and we'll never see her again." His eyes swept over Andi, Pete and his would-be new partner. Pete nodded. Andi shifted on her feet, her wide sapphire eyes betraying her thoughts regarding his statement. Lee appeared indifferent but determined. She was new to all this, so he didn't take offence. The FBI agent was a fresh set of eyes. All he could hope was that she was good with her gun and a quick study.

He rode with a few members of the SWAT team in the APC, their brand new armoured personnel carrier. Andi, Pete and Lee did as well, which made it full to the brim. It was better not to risk holes in the Challenger anyway, right? God, he loved that car.

Andi sat beside him, stuck in her own head. He wanted to touch her, hell, even holding her hand would calm him—more for her benefit—of course, but keeping his hands to himself was better.

He'd done this a thousand times, it'd be easy.

They'd let two or three SWAT guys lead and clear the building. Then grab Bella, nab Maldonado and get the hell out. Take down any helpers Caselli might have sent.

Carlo wasn't stupid. He'd have his out all set up. There was no way Caselli's men would actually let him live after killing Gains and Reese, and Carlo would know that. No doubt he had a plan for it, too.

Cole shifted against the bulletproof vest Andi had insisted

he wear. Damn thing made him itch, even though it was the over-the-shirt variety.

Lee shot him a look, but he said nothing to his exotic new partner. He heard Pete's voice and looked in his direction. Seated next to Lee across from them, the guy had Andi's hand in his, their heads bent together as he spoke in low tones. Cole scowled. Her partner could take her hand, but he couldn't? *Bullshit.* He couldn't make out the words, but she kept nodding.

Rubbing his chest didn't make the vest's irritation stop, but he focused on the plan. They were close. Soon he would be slapping metal bracelets on Maldonado and putting the little bastard where he should have months ago.

There was a tiny, dark cell with his name on it.

The warehouse district was dead quiet, even after they were all set up. They posted across the street, the three guys from SWAT who were leading ready to go at Cole's order. The perimeter around the building was tight, too.

It was time.

The *shhht* sound of the radio caught his attention and he glanced at the cop next to him. "Go 'head," the guy said into his mouthpiece.

"A black Mercedes and silver Escalade are in the alley. No movement at the moment, but they're right outside the back door."

"Ten-four, stay on them."

"Ten-four."

"Bingo. Carlo's out," Cole said.

"Nice," Pete murmured, making a fist.

"Let's go get the bastard," Lee said, stepping up beside him, hand on her weapon.

Cole nodded. "Andi, you're with me."

Pete shot him a look and opened his mouth to argue, but she took a step towards him.

"Fine with me," Andi said.

Pete scowled and looked at Lee when the FBI agent tugged on his jacket.

"Guess that means you're all mine," she told him, looking him up and down.

Was his new partner a female version of him? Cole smirked.

"Ready?" the lead SWAT guy asked.

"Yup. Let's get it done," Cole said.

Their approach was silent, but the creak of the warehouse door could have woken the dead. It hadn't been like that the day Cole and Andi had checked the place out.

Nice touch, Carlo. "He'll be waiting for us," Cole told the SWAT officer in front of him.

The warehouse was dark and quiet with no one in sight, but he had his weapon ready. Andi was to his right in classic building clearance formation, her Sig up, her eyes sweeping the area. Pete, Lee and the other SWAT guys had spread out, all ready for anything.

Someone shouted 'gun' at the same time Cole heard the first shot. Who had fired first was a mystery, but soon he saw the bright flashes of three guns pointed their way and everyone was diving for cover behind pillars and stacks of pallets.

Cole's instinct was to grab Andi and get her down, but she dashed behind a dumpster and squatted low. He left the SWAT guy who was already returning fire and sank beside his woman. Hopefully Pete and Lee were holding their own.

"She's got to be in that container," Andi breathed, peeking around the edge of their reeking cover. How long had the place been closed down? The dumpster stank to high heaven. "The doors are ajar. I don't remember them both being open the day we came."

He gritted his teeth and met her eyes in the dimness. "I don't disagree, but we've got to get there."

"Cover me?"

"Andi, no. Wait until the guys burst in here. No doubt they will at any minute with the gunfire."

"I'm going to get Bella. You're going to get Maldonado. I

thought that's what we're here for," she barked.

"Dammit, Andi."

She leant forward and pressed her lips to his in a hard kiss. In the middle of a gunfight. "Let's go, Cole."

"I'm leading."

"Fine."

He inched around the dumpster, his gun high. Pete, Lee and the SWAT guys were returning fire from what Cole could tell, but there was a body on the ground near the container. It was too big to be Maldonado.

"Too bad we can't move the dumpster," she mused, fingers flexing on the grip of her weapon.

"It smells like shit."

She made an amused harrumph but said nothing. As soon as they were out in the open, another body hit the ground.

"Another one down," one of the cops shouted.

Gunfire stopped and everyone paused. The cops inched cautiously towards the container, and Cole kept Andi pinned behind him, but they moved together.

"I'm coming out! Don't shoot!"

Cole's head snapped around at the male voice.

A dark figure slid towards them, hands raised, no weapon in sight. His heart thundered, his stomach tight. It wasn't Maldonado. *Fuck.*

"Bruno *fucking* Gallo," Cole snarled. Caselli's right-hand man. He ignored the shock that washed over him at the high-positioned man. Caselli had sent the big guns. To ensure Cole's capture, no doubt. "Where's Maldonado?"

Lee rushed forward, Pete close behind her, his gun trained on Bruno Gallo as cover for the female FBI agent. She cuffed him and knocked him to his knees.

Cole smiled. He liked the badass after all.

"I'm not resisting, you bitch," Bruno spat.

"That's no way to talk to a lady." Pete holstered his gun and *accidently* knocked Bruno on the back of the head, then hauled him to his feet. The gangster muttered a string of curses, but Andi's partner grinned.

A door slammed. Cole's eyes narrowed to see the office door swing back and forth. The short hallway down from it led right out into the alley. Stupid to have missed that.

"The office," Andi barked.

"Shit. I'm going after Maldonado," Cole said at the same time someone from SWAT confirmed the container was empty except for a cheap lantern. No Bella. They didn't think she'd ever been inside it.

Andi ran towards the back door, and Cole had to sprint to catch up. He heard sirens before they hit the outside. Ambulance. So one or both of the guys that had gone down weren't dead.

Maldonado had managed to get out of the building with a teenage girl in the middle of a shootout. Slimy piece of shit. Cole's blood ran hot.

Damn, I need to put another hole in him for spite.

"Stop! Police!" Andi's voice was a hard order.

Carlo whirled around near the two vehicles in the alley. The coward froze before Andi as she trained her gun on him. Tears streamed down Bella's face as he pressed his gun to her temple. Human shield. *Son of a bitch.*

Cole scooted around the late model Mercedes. There was no way Carlo had seen him. Maybe they had a chance to take him from behind. If Cole could get there.

Andi's eyes darted to him and back to Bella. She'd caught on to his idea.

"Drop the gun, Maldonado, and let go of the girl," Andi ordered as Cole shimmied along the sedan.

"Pretend you didn't see me. We'll leave. She'll live. I promise," Carlo called back.

"I'll shoot your ass," Andi answered. "You don't have much time left to think about it."

Cole ducked down next to the black sedan, inching his way silently. He could see Bella's white sneakers and Carlo's black boots under the car. The light at the end of the alley wasn't the brightest, but he could still shoot the bastard in the foot.

Bella's sobs filled the silence. He took a breath and closed his eyes. No fucking this up. For the kid's sake, and for Andi's sake.

He moved on, hearing Carlo scoff at her every order. There was no way the coward was going to shoot Andi or Bella. He'd have done it by now. He was still convinced he would just get away. *Idiot.*

Okay, babe, get really talkative, please.

Cole slipped to the front of the Mercedes, gripping his Glock until his knuckles whitened. The Escalade was so close, the gap between vehicles about four feet. Could he dart forward without being seen?

"Maldonado, one last chance. Release the girl, drop the gun and I won't kill you," Andi said.

"Stop where you're at and I won't shoot you," Carlo said.

"You'd have to take your aim off the girl," she answered.

His lover's words were punctuated by a shot. Cole's heart dropped to his stomach. He straightened from his crouch so fast his head spun, just in time to see her dive for cover behind the black Mercedes. She didn't return fire. He couldn't either. *Bella.* "Hey, asshole. Let the girl go!"

Carlo swung around to meet Cole's shout, gun up. He fired and Cole ducked down behind the front quarter panel of the sleek sedan.

"Fucking *Lucas*," his old friend spat.

"Better watch those bullets, you'll damage your ride," Cole taunted, though his gut told him both cars were armoured, Caselli's standard procedure.

Andi sidled up to him and his eyes raked her face and body, his heart picking up speed. "I'm fine," she grunted.

Waving his gun around, Carlo sneered when Cole popped up for a position check. "Watch your head, Lucas. I'd hate to give you a hole in it."

"Would you now?" Cole asked. "I woulda thought you'd be fond of the idea."

Carlo snickered. "I'll leave you for G. Me and the girl... We're getting gone."

"The hell you are," Andi shouted, rushing to her feet.

Another bullet whizzed over their heads as Cole yanked her back down beside him.

"Don't be reckless," he growled.

She ignored him, throwing a glare.

"Federal Agent!" The shout accompanied the slamming of the back door of the warehouse.

Shit, Lee wouldn't know where they were.

Carlo shouted a curse and Bella darted away from him. If Cole had to guess, she'd stomped on his foot. *Good girl.*

A shot rang out and Carlo screamed, clutching his upper arm.

Pete, with a few SWAT team members in front of him as well as behind him poured into the alley with guns up. Lee took another shot at Carlo, one he returned.

Where the hell was Bella?

Standing, Cole aimed his Glock, feeling Andi do the same beside him. "Hold your fire!" he shouted. They needed to find Bella, fast.

Carlo was the only one who couldn't follow orders—he fired a few more times, slid to the driver's side of the Escalade and wrenched the door open. Gun aimed at Andi and Cole, he pulled the trigger of his Beretta two times point blank range.

Cole grabbed Andi and dived for the trunk of the Mercedes, covering her with his body.

The silver SUV roared to life and peeled out of the alley, crashing into the rear end of the cruiser posted there. SWAT fired, but the bullets just bounced off the armoured vehicle.

Meer moments and Maldonado would be gone.

Andi groaned beneath him and Cole hauled himself off her body. They made eye contact and she reached for him.

"Are you all right?" he demanded, eyes and hands raking her body as he put her on her feet. His gaze zoned in on the tear through the nylon of her navy police jacket, right biceps.

Holy shit, she was hit. The blood drained from his face.

She winced when he gripped her elbow and stripped the jacket from her without a word, but she didn't fight him. The red starburst on her white sleeve caused his stomach to plummet. "I'm fine, Cole. It's just a graze."

He ignored her and shouted for a medic. It took all he was made of not to grab her up, kiss her, hold her. He didn't give two shits that Carlo had got away. Again.

Sobbing took his attention and he glanced to the right. Bella was in Pete's arms—he was rubbing her back and whispering to her.

Relief washed over him—she wasn't hurt. So, even though he'd screwed up royally losing the slimy bastard again, Bella was safe. Score one for the good guys.

"Bella, I need to get to her," Andi said.

"No, you're getting that arm looked at."

Anger flashed across her blue gaze when their eyes met. "I'm fine. It's not even bleeding very much." Without giving him a chance to retort, she strode to her partner and the teen.

Lee met him halfway, but Cole threw a glare at her. "Shooting at Maldonado was reckless."

Squaring her shoulders, she glared right back. "I shot him, didn't I?"

Great, two pissed off female partners. Just what he needed. "The girl could have been hit."

"Not when I'm the one pulling the trigger." The smugness in her tone made Cole sigh.

He didn't want to fight.

"He still got away." Anger about that hovered, but he didn't have time to deal with it now. His gut told him he'd get Maldonado, it was just a matter of time. His mind was on Andi.

"PD is pursuing."

"Good."

Pete joined him and Lee, having relinquished Bella to Andi. Cole nodded. "She's hit. Did you tell her to get checked out?"

185

Andi's partner's eyes narrowed. "Of course. She won't do it for herself, but for Bella she will. EMTs are at the end of the alley. I'm giving them a moment before I drag her ass down there myself."

"Did he hurt Bella?" Cole asked, watching his woman with the girl. Despite the hole in her arm, she held Bella close. They both spoke, but he couldn't make out the words.

"Not physically," Pete said. "But they'll check her out. I've already called Nat to let her know we got her."

"What's the damage inside?" Cole asked.

"One dead, the other shot a few times, in critical on the way to the hospital. The dead one is a big son of a bitch," Lee said.

"I'll have a look to see if I recognise him," Cole said.

"None of our guys hurt," Pete said.

"Good," Lee and Cole said at the same time.

Lee eyed Cole up and down, her generous breasts heaving as she took a breath. "I'm gonna stick around. Hopefully Pete's boys will get that SUV. If not, we'll start the hunt tomorrow." She shot Pete a look. "Got a cot at the PD?"

"Yeah, a few in the locker room. But I have a couch."

"Nah, that's cool. Catch up with y'all in a few hours... later *this* morning." Her tone held irony, but she flashed a half-smile.

"I need to make a few calls," Cole said. Berto would be his first. Maldonado had big balls, but would he be that obvious? Berto's ranch wasn't all that far from Antioch—it was worth a shot.

"All right. Hope you both manage to get some sleep," Lee said, another smile curving her full lips.

"Catch up with you in the a.m.," Cole said, his mind twirling. There had to be money in Carlo's damn getaway ride. He would have never agreed to Caselli back-up without a sufficient cut. Too fucking bad he'd actually get the use of it.

Lee nodded then headed away, hips swaying. No way she'd have an issue hitting up a ride back to the station.

"She's somethin' else," Pete said with a whistle.

"She's not Andi," Cole answered without thought.

Pete's silence brought his gaze around.

What the hell did I just say?

"Glad to hear you say it," Pete said, a smile playing at his lips.

Oh, shit.

Chapter Twenty

"Cole, you've got to get some sleep," Andi said.

Her FBI agent ignored her and continued pacing in front of her fireplace, staring at his cell phone, willing it to ring.

"The guys lost him, it sucks, I agree, but if either of us is going to be any use by eight a.m., a few hours of shut-eye are in order. We'll find the bastard."

"Berto said he would make some calls," Cole barked.

"Like you gave him a choice." Andi tried not to let her tone sound dry. She swallowed back a huge yawn and glanced at the clock on her cable box. It was almost four in the morning. "He'll come through for us."

He ignored her, muttering something about crappy contacts and staring at the screen of his cell. He was probably thumbing through the address book on the device.

Cole wouldn't listen to reason and Andi was too tired to argue.

After returning Bella to Natalie and the tearful reunion that had followed, Andi had kissed Ethan as he slept in the toddler bed Natalie kept for him. She'd opted to leave her son at her friend's place. He was out like a light and Cole was too wired.

She intended to get into her own bed ASAP, but Cole was too busy beating the crap out of himself to want the same.

Her arm ached, though she'd been right about the minor wound. It hadn't even needed stitches. Her biceps was sore, exhaustion threatened to take her over, and her eyelids weighed about ten pounds apiece.

Andi's heart was heavy. They'd got Bella back, but Cole was so focused on Carlo Maldonado she couldn't get through to him.

He was back to being that guy she'd first met—obsessed with his case. Driven by the need to get his man, especially since the jerk had managed to get away. Again.

Where was she supposed to fit into that? Before her eyes, the man she'd got to know had receded. Her lover was once again unobtainable. She bit back a snort. She'd always known he would leave. Now he'd go even sooner.

As soon as he got the scent on Carlo's whereabouts.

"Andi, I don't want to sleep."

Her eyes locked with his, her whole body warming with the heat of that steel gaze. Crossing the room in two strides, Cole was on her before she could even unfold from her seat on the edge of the couch.

He parted her lips with his as the breath whooshed from her lungs and he crushed her against his chest, his kiss searing her. He shoved his tongue into hers and she pushed right back, taking over the duel.

Cole was in no mood for the slow, tender lovemaking that had become their routine, but that was fine with Andi. She needed rough, hot and fast to help process the night they'd had.

Shooting her arms around his neck, she held onto him as he slammed her against the wall of her living room, her legs wrapping around his waist of their own accord.

With fumbling fingers, he tried to open the top button of her shirt. He cursed into her mouth when it didn't cooperate. Gripping her shirt collar with both hands, he ripped downward. Buttons went flying, pinging off the wall and sailing to the carpet.

Andi moaned and kissed him harder, nipples peaking when Cole's touch teased through her cotton bra. She circled her hips against his, eliciting a groan as she rubbed the hardness in his jeans.

"I need inside you," he grunted, tugging at her belt. He spread kisses down her neck, sucking and nibbling her collarbone as his fingers worked her buckle, then tugged her zipper down.

Lifting her hips, she let him yank her khakis and panties off. She dropped her legs to the floor just long enough to stomp out of them and wrap herself around his body unencumbered.

Cole stepped forward, pressing her with his full weight, but she only wanted more. He sucked her nipples through her bra, making her cry out.

"Please... Cole..." she moaned.

He relieved her of her shirt and bra, and Andi was naked in his arms. It didn't matter that she was against the wall in her living room, or that he was still dressed. She was writhing and panting, and would die if he didn't come inside her.

Hands shaking, she reached for his belt and shoved his shirt out of her way just as Cole's hot mouth enclosed a taut nipple. Overwhelmed, she needed him so badly her blood was singing, her whole body quivering.

After forcing his zipper down, she freed his hard length, fisting him a few times. With another moan, his mouth found hers again and her name fell from his lips. He crushed his muscled chest into her breasts, flattening them against him.

With the heat coming off his body through the cotton of his grey T-shirt and the cool wall at her back, Andi was about to combust. She wiggled in his arms, kissing him harder.

Cole pushed his hand between them. He rubbed the blunt tip of his erection against her clit and she cried out against his mouth, the sound muffled as he deepened their kiss, his tongue shooting heat downward. Her sex throbbed.

Teasing, touching, but not entering, he brushed her slick folds until she was dripping and pulsing, undulating in his arms. Tilting his hips, he finally joined them in one quick jolt forward, filling her completely. Giving her no time to adjust to the sensation, he started to thrust, pleasure pouring over Andi in an intense wave that brought her close to the edge of release.

She bit her lip to keep from screaming and held onto him as he moved in and out of her, picking up speed with every plunge.

"Oh, God," he whispered into her neck. He kissed, licked and nibbled her heated skin, taking her mouth again.

Spearing her hands into his dark hair, she held him as close as she could. A whimper was all she could manage, though she agreed with his sentiment.

Cole sucked her bottom lip and thrust his tongue into her mouth in rhythm with his hips. It was too much for her. Andi shoved her pelvis against his as her body convulsed, and she screamed his name, every muscle tightening.

She threw her head back, panting as her orgasm roared over her. He grabbed her hips and propelled forward hard, burying his face in her neck and calling her name over and over. He stilled and stiffened, the warmth of his release filling her lower belly.

All Andi could to do was cling to him, otherwise she would slide down the wall and land in a puddle. Chest heaving against breasts, both struggling for breath, they said nothing. She held him close, love causing her heart to thunder in her chest.

God, she loved this man. And he was about to leave her. She didn't need to be a detective to know that.

"I'm sorry," Cole croaked.

Freezing in his arms, Andi took a deep breath. Had he read her mind? "What for?" she whispered.

He met her eyes, a smile playing at his kiss-swollen mouth. "That was rough. I didn't hurt you?"

She shook her head. "It wasn't rough, it was just what I needed." Her cheeks heated.

Chuckling, he pressed a quick kiss to her mouth. "Me too."

She unlocked her hold on his waist, her legs buckling as soon as her socked feet hit the carpet. He held her up, pulling her close and kissing her forehead. Her stomach quivered, chest ached. How could he be so tender?

"Should I say thank you?" Cole whispered.

She glared up at him, despite the tease in his tone. "If you want me to kick your ass."

He threw his head back and laughed.

Andi grinned. He'd finally lightened up.

They stared at each other for a moment. His gaze was intense, and she wanted to fall into him. Neither mentioned now they'd had sex twice with no protection. She ignored the voice that reminded her of possible consequences. Even well after Ethan's birth, she'd never got back on the pill.

"Let's go get a few hours," Cole said.

Before she could ask *of what*, he swung her up over his shoulder and smacked her bare bottom. Andi yelped, growling at his laugh even as he rubbed the smart away and carried her to the bedroom.

* * * *

He'd got fucking shot. Again. And his arm was bleeding like a stuck pig. Carlo gritted his teeth and glanced over his shoulder. The aluminium briefcase containing his fifty K was safe. That was all that mattered at the moment, though his blood boiled that he'd lost the girl. And Caselli was going to be *pissed* about Lucas. He'd send men after Carlo, despite G's *promise*.

Pulling the Escalade behind a gas station, he looked around. No one in sight, let alone a stupid cop. How long had he been driving? A glance at the clock told him it was five-oh-two a.m. So, about four hours. Just past the Arkansas border. Podunk, worse than the small Texas city of Antioch, from the looks of things.

He grabbed the new cell he'd picked up at a truck stop and cut it from the bubble pack with a cheap pocket knife. He'd wrapped his arm as tightly as he could, but it still stung like hell with the movement. He couldn't believe what he was about to do.

Activation and applying minutes took a second, then the phone was ringing.

"Hello," the gravelly voice greeted him. It was early up north, only an hour ahead of him, so he'd probably woken his old mentor, but desperation guided his actions now.

"Boss."

The pause was reminiscent of the conversation he'd had with Bruno.

"Carlo?" He heard age in the voice more than sleepiness.

"Yeah, it's me." Gulp. "I fucked up. I need help."

"Where are you?"

"Arkansas." Another silence made his stomach jump. "I have money." But would a bribe make a difference?

The cackle that greeted his ear sent a shiver down his spine. "I have money."

What the hell could he say to that? He didn't have the balls to demand that the man who'd taught Caselli the ropes help him. Since the falling out between the older generation and the younger, the two men, his old boss and his new, didn't speak.

He hoped.

Getting turned in to Caselli Junior would have the bite of betrayal if the man on the phone was the one to do it.

"Why are you so quiet, boy?"

"I'm here," Carlo croaked.

"Well, you need to be *here*."

Relief caused his breath to exit on a whoosh. How long had he been holding it? "When?"

"When you get here."

"Okay, I'll drive straight."

"Carlo—"

His name made his finger stop its hover over the red 'end' button. "Yeah?"

"This is the last time I clean up your mess with my son." The steel in the tone made Carlo's hand shake.

"Yes, sir."

He gulped as he tossed the phone to the passenger seat.

Upstate New York was going to be a hell of a drive, but he had little choice. He ignored the niggling reservations about what would greet him when he got there.

Chapter Twenty-One

Damn, Lee could argue. If Cole wasn't so irritated by the words coming out of her mouth, he might have had to grudgingly respect that she had the balls to argue with him, buck up to him. Even stick her finger in his face.

But it didn't matter. Berto's intel was correct—Cole's ass was going back to New York with or without her. *Without* was preferable. He didn't need a partner.

Rapping his knuckles on the table, his eyes darted to Andi sitting across from him in the briefing room. In silence, she assessed him like she hadn't in weeks. The bags under her eyes told him how exhausted she was, but there she sat, her head still in the game, pushing with Lee when he pushed back. Strategising, planning. His detective was a damn good cop.

His?

Cole swallowed back a sigh. Mixed emotions rushed him. The thought of leaving her, leaving Ethan...

It was going to kill him. But he had to go—he had a job to do, a case to work and a slimy bastard to apprehend.

Carlo had fled Texas—he had to follow. Was there was a reason for Cole to stay?

Chest aching, he took a deep breath and forced his gaze away from the woman who'd stolen his heart. How could he say goodbye?

"I trust Berto's info. I'm going to New York."

Lee rolled her eyes and crossed her arms. "Maybe you can talk some sense into his hard head," she muttered, throwing a glance at Andi. "I'm done." Shaking her head, his new partner headed out of the briefing room, cursing under her breath.

His eyes found hers. She bit her bottom lip and he reached for her hand. She didn't pull away as he entwined their fingers. Flashes of taking her against the wall, kissing her, and then holding her while she slept in his arms danced into his mind. The intensity of the feelings washing over him made Cole swallow hard.

Son of a bitch, he loved her.

"I have to go." Voice cracking, he ignored his sudden revelation.

"I know." A nod punctuated her affirmative.

He wanted to ask, *that's it?* But words wouldn't form. He didn't have the balls to ask her what she was thinking. "Tonight. I don't want to give Maldonado any more time to get lost."

"Okay." Andi's voice was low, but he couldn't read her expression when their eyes met.

She glanced away, her breasts heaving as if she'd taken a breath, but when she faced him again she wore a smile. "We've had quite a run."

Cole swallowed panic. She was shutting him out. "Yeah, you could say that," he managed, every word forced past the pain in his chest.

What the hell was happening to him?

"I've got a flight. I already let Agent Barnes know what's going on, since you have to be so damn stubborn." Lee's voice in the doorway made his breath exit on a whoosh.

He looked Lee's way, not missing her keen dark gaze honing in on his and Andi's joined hands. When Andi yanked away, Cole let her go, his chest tightening all over again.

"I'm driving," he said.

One of his new partner's eyebrows shot up.

Cole shrugged. "I bought my rental. Gotta get it home, is all."

"I don't know why you're so sure you can trust this guy, Lucas," Lee said, taking a seat across from him, next to

Andi.

"I was under for fourteen months, that's how. I trust his intel. The guys he contacted were all mine. Caselli's father always had a big mouth, but it's never without a purpose. My guess? He's double crossing Maldonado and trying to get back into Junior's good graces. The money tree is yielding more for the son than it ever did for the father."

Lee nodded, but her expression fairly bled scepticism. "I'll meet you at the office then."

"Sounds good to me."

"I'm out, gonna head to DFW Airport." Standing, Lee thrust her hand out to Andi. "Nice working with you, MacLaren. Tell that partner of yours I hope to see him again. And don't worry, I'll take good care of your boy, here."

Andi muttered pleasantries and shook his new partner's hand, but her jaw was tight as Lee winked.

Was she jealous? It wasn't the first time he'd thought so when it came to Lee. His lover didn't relax until Lee was gone, but Cole tamped down the hope that popped up. Just because Andi might be jealous, it didn't mean she cared about him. Did it?

"We should go," Andi said, clearing her throat. "I want to get home to Ethan and make sure Bella's doing all right."

"Yeah." *I need to get on the road,* he left unsaid. Maybe he could ignore facing it for a little while longer.

The ride home was silent. Words wouldn't form, so Cole didn't push her to talk. What the hell could he say, anyway?

He'd been stabbed in the leg when he was seventeen, shot twice as an adult. Even had appendicitis. Nothing compared. He'd never been in so much pain in his life. Every breath stuck him like a dagger, his chest was torn open and his stomach felt like it was riddled with ulcers.

When Ethan flew into his arms after greeting his mother in the living room, Cole almost lost it. He buried his face against Ethan, breathing in detergent, soap and clean little boy. Cheek to the kid's chest, Cole needed a moment to gather himself.

Natalie was there. Her voice, along with Bella's and Andi's, sounded far away. He heard the door shut. Jerk that he was, he hadn't even said goodbye to mother and daughter.

Cole barely processed Andi explaining things to her son.

"You hafta go?" The little boy's voice trembled, but he didn't cry.

He was proud of him for that. "I do." His voice cracked.

Ethan met his gaze and nodded seriously. Cole was able to smile genuinely—the kid was a mini adult sometimes.

Andi cleared her throat and their eyes met. God, she was beautiful. He wanted to kiss her, but not touching her was a plan he needed to stick to.

Coward.

He didn't have the balls to tell her he loved her.

"Do you have everything?" she asked.

"Yeah." He glanced at his black duffle. As with his hotel, he'd never unpacked. He'd always kept his life grab and go.

"Don't want you to go." Ethan's voice was small.

"I have to, buddy."

"When you comin' back?"

"I'm not sure." He hated lying. But he couldn't look Andi's son in the face and tell him he might never see him again.

Damn, how could a three-year-old look so solemn? It was killing him. Cole kept his eyes glued to the little boy. He couldn't look at Andi. God, his gut ached.

If he looked into her blue eyes and saw hurt—even sensed it—the composure he was fighting for so hard would dissolve.

Was she dying inside like him? She'd never professed love, either. He had no idea what she felt for him.

He wanted to yank her into his arms and kiss her to find out. Was it worth the risk?

Yes, a voice whispered. He ignored it and tightened his hold on Andi's son.

198

"I'll see you when I can," Cole whispered.

Ethan flashed a brilliant grin. "I love you, Cole." He squeezed his arms around Cole's neck, almost too tight.

His heart dropped to his stomach. Sucking in a breath, he buried his face against the little boy to hide his reaction. Caressing Ethan's copper curls, he was still unable to meet Andi's eyes. "I love you, too," he croaked.

Closing his eyes, Cole set Andi's son to his feet. The little boy slid his hand into one of his.

Her gaze found his and he swallowed hard against the lump in his throat. It was time to go. Before he did something stupid or weak.

"Good luck. No doubt in my mind you'll get him." She swallowed, making Cole want to kiss her throat. "Then you'll have a tough road getting back to normal after being under so long."

You and Ethan are my new normal.

He didn't give a shit about getting settled back in at work. Cole could only nod. Digging deep, he forced words out of his mouth. "It'll be good to get back." *Liar.* "I'm sure I'll be fine." *Double liar.*

"I figured you would be," Andi said, grabbing Ethan's free hand.

The little guy looked up at his mother then at him, contentment in his expression. Cole's heart flipped.

His eyes swept over their joined hands. *Rightness* settled over him.

This was *it.*

Ethan and Andi were supposed to be *his.*

Releasing Andi's son, he took a step back, loss hitting him in waves. Every breath was tight, painful. "Well, I need to hit the road. Take it easy. Say goodbye to Pete for me." His words were rushed.

Just go. You need to leave. Now.

"I will."

Reduced to small talk? They were lovers. *Had been lovers.* Pain threatened to cave his chest. Cole bit back a cringe and

199

planted his hands at his sides.

Get. It. The. Fuck. Together.

He shot a look at the door and shifted on his feet.

"Drive safe, okay?"

Mouth dry, he nodded. No way he could talk.

Squeezing his eyes shut when he heard Ethan shout one last goodbye, he closed the door to her house.

Fucking coward. What the hell is wrong with you?

Tossing his duffle in the back seat, he slammed the car door shut and pounded the steering wheel as soon as his ass hit the bucket seat.

Was leaving a mistake? Couldn't Lee get Carlo? He'd briefed her on his whole case history. She was more than capable. Why didn't he have the balls to let it go?

He was losing them. The only woman he'd ever loved and the kid he couldn't bear not seeing every day. Was he walking away from his...future?

Andi had stood there wishing him luck with a smile on her face.

Did she feel anything for him at all? Was he arrogant to think so, to wish so?

She didn't cry or ask if he'd come back. Tell him she cared about him...even loved him? Why had they never talked about it?

Because, asshole, you wanted it that way.

Why would she have risked herself with him when he'd never offered her the same consideration? He'd never told her a damn thing, other than confessing to *needing* her. That was a drop in the bucket compared to how he felt now.

So, the joke was on him.

He was the one who'd fallen in love.

Cole should have kissed her goodbye. But if he'd touched her it would have been over. He'd have told her he loved her. He may have even *begged* her to let him come back when Maldonado was behind bars.

With one last glance at the door, he started the Challenger. He still loved the car, and now it was truly his. But Andi and Ethan were not.

"Fuck," Cole muttered, shaking his head.

He shoved the car in reverse and gunned it to the street. Long drive meant he'd better get the hell on his way.

* * * *

Andi had struggled for control the whole time he'd stood talking to her. Like *normal*. Like everything was okay. Like he wasn't ripping her heart into pieces with every word.

When the door shut, she fell apart. Knees buckled, her ass hit the couch hard. Damn good thing she'd been standing so close.

Tears cascaded. How could this be happening? The man she loved…leaving her. Again. A voice whispered he hadn't wanted to leave, that he'd had to go. He said nothing about coming back.

He'd told Ethan he loved him. What about her? Why didn't Cole love her?

"Mama, Mama." Ethan's panicked tone made her force one breath, then two.

What the hell was she doing?

Get it together, Andi. Now.

His blue eyes as wide as saucers, Andi forced a smile and ruffled his hair. She swiped at her face with her free hand, but the tears wouldn't quit.

"Mama. Crying? Mama, don't cry!" Ethan grabbed her hand and squeezed.

She gathered her little boy onto her lap, burying her face against him as his small arms shot around her neck. Cole's clean masculine scent clinging to his T-shirt tickled her nose. Her eyes slipped closed.

Oh, God.

How was she supposed to get past this?

Ethan patted her back and hugged her tight. "Mama," he whispered.

Forcing a breath, she pulled back as her son nestled closer

on her lap. "I'm okay, buddy."

His gaze was confused and she bit her lip. She needed to get it together. *Fast.* If not for herself, for Ethan. It wasn't fair for him to see her like this.

"I'm okay," Andi repeated, sniffling. "I'll be okay."

He nodded and patted her cheek. She smiled and grabbed his little hand, pressing a noisy kiss into his palm that made him giggle.

"I miss Cole, Mama."

She blew out another breath, her heart stuttering. "I do, too." And it was true, God, it was true. Gone only ten minutes and her heart...her *life* would never be the same.

Andi ran her hand against Ethan's soft curls, fighting another sob.

Letting Cole go because it was what he needed was the right thing to do.

Right?

Case aside, his life was sixteen hundred miles away. Not in a small Texas city. Not even for Andi and Ethan. After he caught Maldonado, he could get back to the matter at hand—getting Caselli. Despite his undercover work, the surface was barely scratched. He *needed* to be in New York. That should have comforted her.

Being his lover was always going to be a temporary thing. Andi had gone to bed with him—had him in *her* bed—with both eyes open. Cole had never promised her a damn thing. So why the devastation?

Because you love him, stupid.

And it wasn't Cole's fault she'd fallen for him. *Fool.*

He'd always seemed to sense what she needed. After their interlude in the living room, he'd held her until she'd fallen asleep. Tender touches, soft kisses leading the way. No pressure to do anything but be together.

Why hadn't she told him then? His eyes had been deep pools of molten steel, tender heat that had affected her as much as his hands on her body. Feeling that had made her burn for more.

Andi should have told him she loved him.

Today he'd stood across the room, away from her, Ethan the only one in his arms. How could someone so close be so far away? Untouchable.

Now he was gone, without so much as a kiss goodbye.

He was *gone*. He'd *left*. No word about a return.

Pain threatened to double her over and she clung to Ethan. The metallic tang of her own blood hit her tongue. She'd bitten into her lip to stave off more tears. Unsuccessfully. "Oh, God."

"Mama?"

Shit, she'd spoken aloud. "It's okay, Ethan." Her voice shook.

He looked even more confused. Andi caressed his cheek and his eyes welled with tears.

No, please. Don't let him cry.

"I want Cole." His bottom lip trembled.

She held him closer. The little boy sniffled loudly, a tear sliding down his cheek.

"Don't cry, baby."

I can't take it if he makes you cry, too.

She tried to swallow back her own sob and lost the battle. Her vision blurred, her chest heaving.

"I want Cole." Ethan's stubborn demand was punctuated with him crossing his arms over his small chest.

"I do too, buddy, I do too."

"Why'd he go?"

Andi crushed her eyes and bit the inside of her cheek. "He had to."

Ethan's eyes were misty and earnest when she met his gaze. "I want him home."

Home. How did she tell him Cole had *gone* home? His home wasn't truly *their* home.

Wiping his tears, she rocked him in her arms.

Neither of them would ever be the same again. The only question was who would cry more?

Chapter Twenty-Two

She had to sprint away mid-sentence. Andi made it to the ladies' room just in time to throw up. Pete would likely come after her. His concern would even be genuine, but what the hell was she supposed to say to him? *None of your business* never worked with her partner.

The menacing tiny blue plus sign popped into her mind, as fresh as it had been four weeks ago when she'd taken the test because Mother Nature had been two weeks tardy to her monthly party. Now she had a nine month suspension notice — well, more like seven and a half.

Tears streaming hot, sobs had racked her body, as she'd stood at her dresser in her bedroom after taking the test, staring at the wedding ring she'd taken off only about a year before — at Pete's urging. Iain's ring. What had she been crying about? Andi still wasn't sure exactly. Loss. Love. Life?

Cole was gone, too. They'd both left her with a child.

Heart pounding, Andi stood and reached to flush the toilet, then brushed off her khakis. Wobbly legs took her to the sink. She rinsed her mouth out, splashed cold water on her face and prayed for control.

Pete wasn't stupid. He'd been there when she was pregnant with Ethan. She'd been sick as a dog the first four months.

If her partner hadn't followed her to the bathroom — she was lucky he hadn't burst inside — the third degree would descend before her ass hit her seat.

He'd been gone almost two months. Andi's gut clenched, but it wasn't nausea. Pain threatened to double her over.

She rested her hands on her knees and panted.

No calls. No texts. No emails. Hell, not even snail mail. It was as if she'd never existed to him.

He made you no promises, a voice reminded. She crushed her eyes shut and took a deep breath, then another.

Cole could pretend all he wanted that they had never been, but proof grew safely inside her. Andi rested her hand low on her belly and tried to calm her heart and her thoughts.

What had she expected—that he would get back to New York and they'd talk every day? Skype? Carry on a long-distance relationship? They'd barely had a *relationship* at all. He hadn't even called to let her know he'd got there all right.

The rational side of her brain reared its ugly head. He was working his case. He was...busy. Right?

Andi had been trolling the news—TV and websites—hell, even watchdog websites. Nothing. No human trafficking king pin apprehended, not even a low man on the totem pole like Maldonado.

Pete's brother Nate was the assistant district attorney assigned to the Gains and Reese murders, and knew nothing new either. Texas still waited for its turn with Maldonado.

Wouldn't Cole or Lee let them know they'd got him? Were their ties *that* severed? Andi worried her bottom lip, teeth sinking in with a sting she ignored.

As soon as she'd made it back to her desk, Pete's gaze was appraising. She glanced around the room. Damn good thing everyone was out. He would be blunt, and it would be now, at work or not.

"Sorry. I think I'm coming down with something." Her breath released on a sigh as soon as her butt hit the chair.

Pete leaned on the edge of her desk, crossing his arms over his chest. She disregarded the memories of Cole in that same spot, same posture. Hell, even with the same look on his face.

"I'll say," he said, his green gaze sharp.

Well, it was worth a shot. Andi tried for a quick subject change. "Want me to get you some coffee? Mine's cold." Grabbing her cup and peering inside, she swirled around the brown contents.

Her partner threw his palm up. "Uh-uh."

"No coffee? Well, I'm gonna get some." She shot to her feet.

"I think not. Park it. My bullshit meter is screaming. You and I both know what's *ailing* you, Andi MacLaren."

"We do?" she croaked.

Pete gave her a long look. "What did Cole say?"

"About?"

"Andi." Pete glared.

She sighed.

"What'd your man say?" he prompted.

"He's not my man," Andi said, frowning. She bit her lip when tears threatened and swallowed against the lump in her throat. She would *not* cry at work.

"The man has a right to know he's going to be a father."

She closed her eyes, but tears leaked then poured.

He tried to pull her into his arms, but she pushed him away. It wasn't her partner's comfort she wanted.

"He left. I know he had to go, but…" Her voice broke on a sob, and she allowed Pete to wrap her into an embrace.

"I think he loves you," Pete whispered against her hair. "And sure as shit you love him."

She would have denied it, but he'd see right through her anyway. Her partner always did. "I do. I love him." Pain hit square in the chest and Andi closed her eyes against Pete's shoulder, inhaling his woodsy cologne. It was a pleasant scent, but it wasn't Cole's.

"Look, I'll be here for you no matter what, you know that. But you need to tell Cole Lucas what he's left behind."

"I can't. He's needed in New York. He…has his case. It's what he cares about most."

Pete scowled, but wiped her tears away with gentle hands when she pulled out of his arms. "Don't think for the man."

"He made no promises. Cole's not coming back." She sank into her chair, gut twisting. Besides, Andi didn't want him if he was obligated to come back for her...them. Cole had to want her like she wanted him.

"You never gave him a reason to stay, Andi."

Anger flared and she glared at him. "Should I have had to? If *you're* so sure he loves me, why the hell didn't *he* say that?" She sniffled, but took the tissue he yanked from the box on her desk when he offered it to her.

Sighing, Pete shook his head.

Andi was dying inside without Cole. How would she ever get over him? So far, the time apart from him had only served to make her miserable. He haunted her thoughts, dreams and days. But she wasn't sorry she was having his child. Andi would have a piece of him to hold in her arms.

"Are you surprised?" she asked, studying Pete's disapproving expression.

"That you love Cole, no. That you got knocked up, hell yeah. There are tons of contraceptives available these days, partner." One corner of his mouth shot up.

Heat rushed her cheeks. "Yeah, well..."

Pete snorted and she looked away. "Are you happy?" he whispered when her eyes welled with tears again.

She snatched another tissue. "About the baby?"

"That too, but I meant in general. Are. You. Happy?" He dragged out the words and she nodded, wiping her eyes. He tweaked her nose. "Liar," he said softly.

"I'll live."

"I know. You're a survivor. You'll have this baby and raise him or her with Ethan. I'm not worried about that. What's bugging me is that you'll be unhappy about it for the rest of your life. Cole Lucas changed you for the better. You changed him, too. I saw it with my own eyes. And I don't think he'd be all that upset about the baby. Even if he would—I'll kick his ass, worry not—he has a right to know."

What could she say to that? She agreed, but hated he was

right. Guilt slowly rose from the pit of her stomach. She couldn't hide behind the *he's busy with his case* thing forever. He might not love her, but Cole was a good guy. He might offer to come back.

Andi couldn't do that to him. A ready-made family was a trap for a guy like him. He'd said on day one he didn't do small towns.

Was she afraid Cole would reject her, Ethan and their child? Or was she trying to punish him for leaving? Ignoring her. Getting back to his case—his life—with a new *female* partner and no contact. Was he *busy* with Lee? Was that the *real* reason he hadn't called?

Her chest tightened, and it hurt to breathe. She couldn't speak.

"Heartache sucks ass, I know," Pete said. "But *regret* is even worse. You'll regret it for the rest of your life if you don't tell Cole about his kid. And what you'll regret even more than that is not telling him you love him. I know you too well, partner."

"I just can't, Pete," Andi whispered.

"It's not worth the risk, then?" His eyes bored into her. His logic burned.

"What do you mean?"

"You're miserable now. He's there, you're here. Fifteen plus hundred miles away. He has no idea how you feel, or that he's left something so important behind—and I don't just mean the baby. What's a phone call going to hurt?"

"I couldn't tell him over the phone, anyway," Andi protested.

"Obviously you're not willing to see if you're the only one hurting. Don't you want to know how he feels about you?"

"I just *can't*. Not right now anyway. Drop it, okay? We have work to do. I don't want to talk about it."

"Coward," Pete muttered.

Bingo. Andi scowled. She didn't need to hear it from him.

Her partner glared right back. "It doesn't matter if I drop it now or later. It doesn't change the fact that Cole has the right to know about his kid, bottom line. I've never had a problem telling you how I really feel and I'm not gonna start now. I'll continue to bring it up until you change your mind."

"Dammit, Pete," she said, crossing her arms. "He told Ethan he loved him." It was supposed to be a retort, but it had come out choked, pained.

Pete closed his eyes for a moment, his expression sympathetic. "Wow, sounds like a real asshole to me."

She forced a breath. No more tears at work. "I didn't say that. We didn't get along at first, but…that changed. We… worked well together."

"*Working well together* must have extended outside of work, or you wouldn't have fallen in love with him."

"Will you stop saying that?"

"Why? It's true. Only, I wasn't the one who needed to hear it."

"I just want to work, Pete. We have a case."

"The case can wait. Our meeting with the new CI isn't until one anyway. This issue isn't going to go away."

"I don't have an issue."

"God, you're so fricking stubborn." Pete dragged his hand down his handsome face. "If you want to be miserable for the rest of your life, so be it."

Andi sighed. The last thing she needed was a pissed off partner. "Just let it go for now. Please."

"Fine," Pete said.

"I know you don't like it, but it's my life," Andi whispered.

"Damn right I don't like it. If it was my kid, I'd want to know."

Glaring, she leant forward. "So much for dropping it."

"I will. For *now*. But your belly in a few months won't. There're gonna be questions around here. You prepared to answer them?" Fair brow raised, her partner studied her.

She groaned and closed her eyes. Maybe no answer at all would shut him the hell up.

The phone rang. They both jumped and Andi grabbed it.

Thank God it was regarding the burglary case they'd just picked up.

Chapter Twenty-Three

Even if they caught Maldonado tomorrow, this case was going to kill Cole. The slimy bastard had been just out of reach several times. Two attempted raids. No juice. Lost a few more contacts. An arrest by accident that hadn't appeased him in the least.

Cole had always loved his job. But right now, he'd gladly change careers. Bag boy at the grocery store might work.

Stupid fucker Maldonado. He'd blame it all on the weasel.

Who was he kidding? He was stuck. He loathed his new *normal*.

He couldn't get back into his routine and couldn't blame it on the investigation, let alone being under. The transition had never bothered him before. Granted, he'd never been undercover for as long as he'd spent with Caselli's organisation, but working wasn't what was killing him. It was the two sets of big blue eyes haunting him.

Cole hadn't been able to sleep worth a shit in the three months he'd been home. The bags under his eyes were a new constant, as well as odd looks from people who'd known him for years—Olivia included. She'd even pulled him into her office to see if something was wrong. Well yes, but hell no, he didn't need a shrink.

Dex had looked at him like he'd grown a second head when he'd declined going to the strip club they'd always frequented. It'd only taken his buddy two seconds to figure out what was up with Cole. He'd walked away shaking his head, muttering something about a new best friend.

Working with Lee was all right. She was passionate, hard-working and cared about the case. But her hair was too dark, she was too short and her eyes weren't blue.

"Fuck," Cole muttered, shoving his hand through his hair. He needed to get it cut, but he didn't give a shit about much.

He watched the FBI logo flip around the screen of his computer.

When he couldn't take it anymore, he moved the mouse and his desktop appeared. What had he been doing, anyway?

The red flashing light on his phone caught his eye, indicating that he had a voicemail message on his direct line. Cole hit the speaker button.

"Enter your password, followed by pound," the female voice said.

He sighed as he did so, and pressed one for new messages when she specified.

"Cole..." Her voice caused his heart to go into overdrive. He swallowed hard. "Listen, we need to talk. Uh...call me." *Click*. Dial tone.

It took all he was made of to not replay it...a hundred times.

Andi...her sweet, even tone rang in his ears, in his heart.

Was something wrong? No clues in her voice, despite her pause after his name. God, he missed her.

"To save message, press two. To delete, press three," the voice prompted. Forcing his finger down on the number three was accompanied by a deep breath and closed eyes.

He'd call her later. Maybe.

"Gonna call her?" Lee's voice made him jump.

"Jesus," Cole cursed. He swivelled his chair around. She had two Starbucks cups in a drink crate, one corner of her full mouth raised.

"Woulda never pegged you for the jumpy type."

"Only when my partner is eavesdropping," he muttered.

She laughed, handing him one of the cups. He thanked her and hung up the phone. "Done checking up on me?" Cole glared as she slipped into the chair between their two

212

desks.

Lee shrugged. "I'm just observant. And you like your speakerphone." Unapologetic, she studied him. He wanted to squirm. "I know it's none of my business and all, but—"

"You're right. None of your business. End of."

She sighed, but her dark gaze was keen, reminding him of Pete. "You know Texas wants to sink their claws into Maldonado. You'll end up back there for the trial *when* we get him," Lee said, sipping from her cup.

He wanted to snap at her that it didn't matter. But it *did*. Cole said nothing. Even though he'd have to go back to Texas to testify, it was too late for him and Andi. He ignored the voice that asked *was it really?*

"I talked to the ADA that'll be handling the case. Nice guy. Nate Crane." She grinned. "I think you know his brother."

"Ah, yeah." Pete's brother was an assistant district attorney? News to him. But he'd heard of the guy only one time, when he'd been eavesdropping on a phone call himself. Shaking his head, his stomach tightened.

When was he going to stop thinking about her? *Never*, a voice whispered.

"Bruno Gallo's safely in protective custody, by the way." Lee's voice grounded him. "They got him in his own cell. The warden is investigating because it took too long for the guards to break it up. Someone was probably paid off."

Cole banished his thoughts about what could never be and focused on the case that was far from over. "After the attack the other day, I'm actually glad to hear it. Did you get the full medical report? He's okay?"

"He was beaten pretty bad, but he'll be fine. Still agreeing to testify against Caselli." Her slight Texas accent headed his thoughts back in the wrong direction.

He cleared his throat. "Glad to hear it."

"Lucas, Dawson. We got a tip. We need to move. Now."

Heart racing for a different reason now, Cole's eyes locked onto Special Agent Clint Downs' hazel ones. "Maldonado?"

"Yup. We got intel he's brokering a deal at a snazzy five

213

star downtown. We heard he's even got the girls with him. Let's go."

Lee was already on her feet and tossing her coffee cup in the trash can. "About damn time."

"I'm getting the bastard this time," Cole growled.

His gorgeous partner flashed a feral smile. "Hell yeah we are."

Downs nodded and turned on his heel. "Whole team is ready to go."

Cole followed his team as they rushed downstairs and into the parking garage to two black vans. During the whole ride across hectic New York City, he couldn't sit still. Probably should have driven to keep himself busy. Lee kept shooting him looks he ignored. He adjusted his vest and tried not to think about the last time he was on his way to a raid.

"You good?" Lee asked.

Nodding, he looked out of the window. The nondescript, dark van was supposed to help them blend in, but Cole was more in sore-thumb territory in his head.

"We're doing this." His partner's confident tone made him nod again.

Cole didn't want to talk—he didn't want her to worry about him—so he kept his mouth shut, watching their surroundings as they moved through the heart of the city.

His original hunch that Caselli's father, Antonio Caselli Senior, former head of the vast crime organisation, had indeed backstabbed Maldonado. From what they'd learnt, Carlo had been fixed up by the old man's personal physician and had got out of Dodge before the son's men had come for him. But the move hadn't patched things up between Tony and Antonio. There'd been a shootout at Senior's vast mansion.

How Carlo had remained in the state and on the run was a mystery, but now he had both Casellis and the FBI on his ass. It was a race against the bad guys.

Dead wouldn't look bad on Carlo, but Cole would prefer

a small dark room. Besides, after all the asshole had put him through, death was too easy for Maldonado. And he'd shot his woman. Minor wound or not, he had to pay for that.

Wincing as Andi danced into his mind, he shook his head. He didn't need the distraction. Again.

"Let's go," Lee urged him from the van.

His team—him, Lee and nine other agents that made up their human trafficking unit—fanned out, following their plan. Full cooperation from the place helped, and soon they were ready to apprehend Carlo and his buyer.

The fancy suite was visible through the previously placed cameras. The agents had been able to learn the layout of the room, and could see the people inside from their own room across the hall. Carlo had three girls with him, all young, barely dressed and shivering.

"He a mark?" Cole asked the agent manning the cameras, pointing to a skeeze in a cheap suit with slicked back, blonde hair.

The man shook his head. "Nope. Not one of ours. You don't know him?"

"Not from my time under."

"Maybe he's new to the life?" Lee asked. She stood next to him, staring at the screen. "Damn, those girls aren't even fourteen."

"Carlo likes them young." Cole sympathised with his partner's shock. Human trafficking hadn't been her speciality in Dallas. "How'd you get the cameras in?" He made eye contact with the other agent.

"Dex did it last week. It was for a sting that's now been postponed. We happened upon Maldonado by accident."

"We're ready," Downs said, hovering in the doorway.

"Money changed hands," the agent at the cameras confirmed.

Good, now they got to arrest the skeeze, too.

"Let's go," Lee said.

Cole took some satisfaction from the look on Carlo's face

when they burst through the door of his suite. The girls screamed and two semi-automatic handguns hit the carpet at the first shout of, "Federal Agents!"

"Fucking Lucas," Carlo spat, not fazed in the least that Cole's Glock was trained on him. "Thought you were in Texas?"

"Aww, Carlo, you know I couldn't help but follow you. You and I go way back."

Maldonado scowled, but his shoulders slumped.

After chasing Maldonado for months, and all the close calls, Cole couldn't believe it was going to be this easy.

Was it really going to be this easy?

Carlo's buyer cussed Clint Downs to hell and back as he cuffed him. The Russian accent caught Cole's attention, but he didn't tear his eyes from his nemesis. Smart of him to deal with someone new, though. Had Caselli broken into the Russian market too or was Carlo slyer than he looked?

"C'mon, Carlo, don't tell me you're not gonna fight me," Cole said as he approached slowly, kicking the Beretta farther out of Maldonado's range.

"Fuck you, Lucas."

"No thanks." He flashed a grin at the dark look Carlo shot him.

"Cuff him, partner, I got your back," Lee said from behind him.

Carlo growled, but didn't fight him as he reholstered and slipped behind the bastard. A wave of satisfaction washed over him as he wrenched the guy's injured arm down and back to cuff him. Other than the curse he muttered, Maldonado said nothing, so Cole held back the jibe he had ready, and restrained the urge to knock him on his ass.

The click and snap was the best sound he'd heard since he'd left Texas. Lucky and easy had an odd taste on his tongue. But they'd got him.

"Better you than Caselli—either variety," Carlo whispered. "What do you want to know, Lucas?" he asked a moment later, his voice steadier and louder.

"Hmmm, general population not looking so good, Maldonado?" Lee asked, winking at Cole. Being in a regular pod—even Federal prison—could get Carlo killed, given his affinity for sex with young girls. The bastard would want to aim for protective custody, even if he had to beg for it. Surprisingly, even convicts didn't like paedophiles.

Chuckling at his partner, he addressed the slippery asshole he'd chased too long. "Maybe we can talk."

"Maybe?" Carlo barked, dark eyes wide. "Anything you want to know, I promise."

"A promise from you doesn't mean shit."

Maldonado shook from head to foot, his Adam's apple bobbing up and down.

Members of their team hovered. Cole said nothing, exchanging a look with his partner. He took a breath and crossed his arms. "Get him out of my sight."

Agent Downs stepped forward, grabbing Carlo's upper arm. "I'll take him out the back way. Roberts, Morris, you're with me. Two thugs known to be associated with Caselli the younger were spotted in the lobby."

"Wow, Maldonado, you're popular indeed," Lee said, one corner of her full mouth lifted.

Carlo went white, trembling in Clint Downs' grip, his step sluggish as the other two agents stepped forward. Cole swallowed a curse. They'd been closer to losing him than they'd thought.

"Lucas, I want to talk. I want to talk, man," Carlo shouted as he was led away.

The three teens sobbed, arms around each other as one of Cole's fellow female agents moved them against the far wall and tried to urge them into the plush chairs in the room. As soon as they calmed, their interviews would begin. Hopefully their families could be located—there would be no telling if they were Americans or illegals until they'd talked to them.

"You're gonna listen to what he has to say, right?" Lee asked, taking his attention from the true victims of this whole thing.

"Oh yeah. But I have to let him stew for a while." Cole flashed a smile.

* * * *

The rest of the day was a whirlwind of interviews and evidence. Carlo's Beretta was shipped off to the lab, no doubt the murder weapon Texas would need to prove he'd killed Gains and Reese, though the coward had already confessed on paper to Cole. Andi and Pete would be pleased.

Two of the girls were sisters and their family was located in Montana, where they'd run away from six months before. The third girl was apparently an orphan, and had been taken into custody by Child Services. Hopefully they'd find her a decent foster family.

Saving three girls was a drop in the bucket, but it did renew his faith in his job. A bit. He still wanted Caselli. But Andi and Ethan kept dancing in and out of his thoughts.

He stared at Lee as they debriefed with fresh coffee in their shared office. His partner was more than capable to lead the team with Agent Clint Downs at her side. Could he give up control? Was his place in New York or Texas?

"Great job today, Lee," Cole whispered.

Dark eyes widening, she studied him. "Thanks. You too."

"Carlo's intel will actually further the investigation." And secure his ass a place in protective custody. Cole had relented on the bluff even before Maldonado had opened his slimy mouth.

"Caselli's thugs were gone before Downs and the men hit the lobby with Carlo. Bet he was relieved," Lee said, sighing.

"Not like we could have brought them in. It's not illegal to hang out in public, anyway."

"If we could only get back in," Lee mused, turning her cup and looking at the label that said her name.

"I know it, but I am pretty sure Maldonado screwed that

up. Or I did, anyway."

"Nah, you did what you had to do."

Cole nodded. "Thanks."

Silence descended and once again he wanted to squirm under that dark, appraising gaze. "You know, for what it's worth, I think you should go back to Texas," she said.

Blinking, he wanted to assert a quick denial. Snap that it wasn't any of her business. But his tongue was glued to the roof of his mouth.

"I thought it would be more exciting, working with the great Cole Lucas" — Lee flashed a grin — "but your head's not in the game."

What the hell could he say? He'd known her three months, and she'd pegged him one hundred per cent. "It's not affecting my job," he managed.

"Today proves that, and besides, I didn't say it was. But you're not yourself." She shook her head when Cole scowled. "Don't give me that *you don't know me* crap. You're a lot like me. And I know that look. You *are* off your game. You're functioning, not living. You should do something about it." Her tone took on a sadness that made his stomach flip. "Before it's too late." The whisper was an afterthought, and her throat bobbed as she swallowed hard, pain flashing across her dark eyes.

So, she'd been through some shit too. He sympathised, but what could he say?

"I don't want to talk about this," Cole muttered.

One corner of her mouth lifted and the constant amusement he was used to was back. "Who does? Ever?"

A string of curses fell from his mouth and she laughed.

"Yeah, cover it up. Typical guy."

He shrugged and Lee shook her head.

"How's your adjustment been, anyway?" he asked. It was the first time he'd bothered to check on her. And this morning's nosiness aside, he *was* interested in her answer. "New York growing on ya?"

She cocked her head to the side, long hair shifting with

the movement. "My place is too small, too expensive, and I will always be a Texas gal, but everyone here has been great."

"Except your shit of a partner." He shook his head. "Sorry about that. You're right, about everything you said."

Lee laughed. "Nah, even my shit of a partner has been all right."

Cole smiled and she grinned.

"The question is, Lucas, what are you going to do now?"

Chapter Twenty-Four

When Cole got back into Antioch, the first place he went was the toy store. Ethan's fourth birthday was in about a week. He got the kid something nice, and would sweep him up into his arms and pull Andi tight to him. He'd never let either of them go.

He'd never laid his heart open to a woman, and if Andi rejected him, he'd have to deal with it. His fate was sealed. He was out of the FBI—he wouldn't go back even if Olivia would have him.

Olivia had called Chief Martin for him with a glowing recommendation, as well as giving him a letter to deliver. He had a job, if he wanted it. And Cole did. Small town detective was going to be a change for sure, but one that could only be for the better. He belonged in Texas...for the rest of his life.

If things didn't go as planned, he'd have to get over her, move on somehow. Deal with seeing her every day at work. He'd love her for the rest of his life, and he could only pray that she'd forgive his pigheadedness for not realising it. For leaving like a total asshole. Under the guise of work, when there were others who could take up the cause.

Cass had been overjoyed that he was giving up the FBI, but even more that her baby bro had *finally* found *the one*.

If she would take him back, anyway. His sister had told him to follow his heart when he'd told her about Andi and Ethan.

Cole smiled. She'd threatened to be on the next plane to Texas. He'd had to bribe her to keep her away. It wasn't that he didn't want them to meet...but he had to explain everything to Andi and hope she'd have his sorry ass. Almost four months. Too damn long.

Chief Martin had been pretty open with his start date, so he'd called and left a message for his new boss. The city would have him show up at HR to fill out paperwork sometime in the coming week. He'd even asked dispatch which detective was on call. It wasn't Andi or Pete. Good, it meant she was probably at home, spending Saturday afternoon with Ethan. After a two-day drive, and only stopping about six hours to catch a nap, all he wanted to do was collapse, but he had to see Andi and Ethan.

He ached every time he looked at the wallpaper on his cell phone. Ethan's grin warmed his heart and Andi's smile flipped his stomach. He'd snapped the picture not long before he'd left. Cole had never intended on taking the photo, let alone using it on his phone, but now it was a lifeline, pure hope of a future.

His heart thudded as he made the turn off the main thoroughfare into her subdivision. It sped into overdrive when he hit her street and Cole actually gulped as he pulled into her driveway. He forced a deep breath and had to prise a white knuckled hand off the steering wheel to put the car in park. After swiping his thumb across his cell, he kissed the picture of Andi and Ethan as it popped up.

Pete's grey pickup was parked next to Andi's silver SUV. *Don't lose your nerve now, coward.*

Her partner was a big part of her personal life. He might as well accept that right now. He wasn't jealous...exactly. He just wanted his face in one piece, an unbroken nose and no bruises.

Cole grabbed the huge teddy bear from the back seat and slipped it under his arm, ignoring his roiling stomach. He jogged up the three steps and stared at her front door, stepping onto the welcome mat. Bile rose and he swallowed against the lump in his throat.

This is it. Please, God, let her love me back.

Cole made a fist, hesitating for only a moment before

knocking hard. His knuckles smarted, but he clung to the sting.

Minutes were more like hours and he shifted on his feet. Finally the door opened.

She gasped, then their eyes locked. They stood frozen and staring.

"Cole…" His name was a whisper that fell from her lips and snapped him out of his stupor.

Eyes trailing her body, he froze again, glued to Andi's stomach. It was…distended…round. Her light blue tee did nothing to hide it, especially tucked into her cuffed denim capris.

No. Shit.

Pregnant.

Pregnant?

Blood drained from his head, but his heart thundered in his ears. He swayed on his feet.

A baby. *His baby.*

He should be scared shitless…but he wasn't. But what *was* he feeling?

Ethan's oversized bear slipped from his grasp and hit the porch.

"Why didn't you tell me?" The words tumbled out. Not the demand he'd planned, but a cracked whisper. Cole cleared his throat.

He wanted to shout, but wanted to hold her, kiss her and wipe the shocked look from her face, too. His hands remained at his sides — he couldn't reach for her. Was he afraid?

"Andi, who was at the door?"

He heard Pete's voice before the man appeared around the corner, Ethan on his heels.

"Cole!" The little boy bounded towards him, and Cole squatted down just in time to catch the kid as he jumped into his arms.

Ethan kissed his cheek with a loud smack and Cole hugged Andi's son tight.

223

God, he smelt good, just like Cole remembered. Sunshine, detergent and all little boy. He closed his eyes and buried his face in Ethan's soft red curls, taking a deep breath. This kid was his son. It didn't matter that they shared no blood.

"Well, it's about damn time," Pete muttered.

Andi's partner threw his hand out for a shake. Cole propped Ethan on a hip and gripped Pete's hand, letting his comment slide. If he'd known Andi was carrying his child he would have been by her side. Hell, for all he knew, Pete could think he'd known about the pregnancy and didn't give a damn.

"Hey, man," Cole said. He almost sighed at the appraising look Andi's partner gave him. Pete hadn't changed in the time he'd been gone.

"Good to see ya," Pete said, returning his shake. "Too bad it wasn't sooner." He shot a look at Andi.

Pete knew she hadn't told him about the baby. *Interesting*.

One glance at Andi and his heart stuttered. Her eyes shone with unshed tears. Cole made himself look at Pete and be polite. "I'm here now."

"Glad to hear it," Pete said.

Ethan noticed the stuffed bear and leant down in Cole's arms. "Mine?" he asked.

Cole set Andi's son to his feet. The little boy grabbed the bear's arm and righted it, his big blue eyes wide.

"Yes, sir," Cole said, squatting in front of him. "I know your birthday isn't until next week, but Teddy said he couldn't wait to meet you."

Ethan grinned and wrapped his little arms around the stuffed animal. Pete chuckled and Cole couldn't hold back his grin. The bear was almost as tall as the kid.

Andi was much too quiet, but Cole straightened when she sniffled. He'd made her cry. *Great* – add one more point on the asshole list.

God, he needed to touch her. He smiled but her expression became even more fragile.

"Thank you," Ethan said politely, hopping up and down.

224

Cole ruffled his hair. "You're welcome, buddy. Anytime."

The little boy beamed up at him, still latched onto his new toy.

"Well, squirt, I think it'll just be me and you for lunch," Pete said, taking the bear from Ethan and tucking it under his arm.

She said nothing, but Andi's chest heaved as if she'd taken a breath. Cole watched her rounded tummy, his heart flipping. There was a piece of him — them — growing there. He was going to be a father. She was still gorgeous, even puffy-eyed and pregnant.

"Gonna stand on the doorstep all day?" Pete asked, one corner of his mouth lifting.

Pete led the way into the house. Cole rested his hand at the small of Andi's back like he'd done dozens of times. She jolted, but didn't pull away as they headed into the living room, Ethan tugging his bear from Pete's arms.

Plopping onto the couch with the giant stuffed animal beside him, Ethan beamed, unaware of the growing tension in the room.

"We were actually going to head out for lunch, but I'll take Ethan. You two need to talk," Pete said, giving Andi a pointed look before his intense gaze landed on Cole.

He managed a nod to Andi's partner. He agreed completely.

She paled, her blue eyes wide. Was she afraid of him? Cole's gut ached. Obviously she was planning on having his baby, but what if she didn't want him? What if she didn't love him?

Andi swiped at her cheeks and took an audible breath.

"C'mon, squirt," Pete said, holding out his hand.

Ethan slipped off the couch, his eyes wide. "I want to stay with Cole." He looked up at Pete, then back at him, shifting on his little feet.

"C'mere, buddy," Cole said, sitting on the edge of the couch and gathering Andi's son to him. "You go have lunch with your Uncle Pete, okay? When you get back, I promise

I'll be here. I'm not going anywhere." He kissed Ethan's forehead and looked at Andi, making sure she'd heard his vow, too.

She worried her bottom lip with her teeth, her hands clasped tightly in front of her. God, he wanted to hold her. Comfort her. Make her worry free. Always.

"Promise?" the solemn question quavered and he met Ethan's innocent gaze.

"Promise," Cole said.

Pete flashed a smile that broadcasted approval. "Ready?"

"Okay," Ethan said, scrambling off his lap.

"Work it out, Andi," Pete said, his low tone carrying.

Heart dropping to his stomach, Cole forced a breath. Pete was on his side, after all.

The door closed.

He crossed the room in two strides and wrapped his arms around her. She tugged against his hold, hesitating for a moment, but then she came to him, her arms shooting around his waist and squeezing him almost too tight. Sobs were muffled by his shirt as she buried her face against his chest.

Andi's heart pounded against his, and he rubbed her back, letting her cry. It was killing him, but she needed to get it out so they could talk. *Really talk.*

He rested his cheek against her soft hair. It was loose and fell past her shoulders in soft waves he needed to touch. The strawberry scent tickled his nose. She smelt the same, felt the same in his arms, except for the firm roundness of her stomach pressing into him.

Cole closed his eyes and inhaled. How had he lived without her every day?

He loved her so much. The three words should have been out of his mouth first thing, but were clogged in his throat. "Andi…" When she lifted her head, he cupped her face and thumbed her tears away. "No more tears," he whispered.

She closed her eyes and he couldn't resist. He lowered his head and covered her mouth with his. He moaned as

226

she opened for him and their tongues mingled. She tasted as sweet as she always had. Deepening the kiss, he pulled her closer.

Chapter Twenty-Five

Andi didn't resist him. How could she? She slipped her arms around his neck, burying her fingertips in his thick dark hair. It was longer than she'd ever seen it, but she liked it. He was still gorgeous, and being in his arms was even better than before.

She needed this, needed him. She loved him more than words.

Moving closer, her firm round tummy pushed against his hard abs. She wanted him to feel their baby. *Their child.*

He'd never returned her call, but could she have told him over the phone? Guilt rose up, but she ignored it, kissing him harder. Cole groaned. His erection pressed into her and her heart tripped over itself. His body wanted her, but did he? His body alone wasn't going to be enough this time. She needed his heart.

She should've told him about the baby. Andi wouldn't blame him if he was angry—he had a right to be. But his reaction on the porch had been shock.

Andi would have to answer for not trying overly hard to contact him. She would be devastated if Cole didn't want them—her…the baby…Ethan.

Springing a child on a man was a bad idea no matter what. A guy like Cole? It was amazing he hadn't run screaming on the doorstep after dropping that ridiculously large bear.

And now he was kissing her. Should she question it?

His hands shot down her back and around her bottom. He squeezed and rocked against her.

Andi's stomach flipped. Confusion, hurt and desire warred as her tears slipped down her cheeks. She tasted saltiness as it mixed into their kiss.

Cole was unrelenting, devouring her mouth hungrily until his moving lips swallowed her moan and her legs wobbled with need and love for him.

She still wanted him. She always would.

"Andi." Her name was a half-moan as he yanked away and cupped her face. Confusion clouded his steel gaze and he wiped away her tears. "I want you, but we need to talk."

He wanted her, but he always had. She saw more in his eyes, but could she believe it? She swallowed back another rush of tears.

"I'm sorry," Andi blurted, clinging to him. Burying her face in his neck, she was ashamed to meet his eyes. There was nothing she could say, no excuse that was adequate enough for not telling him about his baby. No magic justification. Pete had been right.

He said nothing as he held her. He rubbed her back. It was so good to be in his arms again.

But the silence was killing her.

"Let's sit," he whispered.

Andi bit back a gulp and nodded, slipping out of his arms. As she was about to turn away, Cole grabbed her wrist. She jumped as he laid his palm on her stomach. Her vision blurred as the baby moved and his eyes widened. He stood frozen, but his Adam's apple bobbed as he swallowed. His expression was tender.

"It's moving?" His tone held wonder. He followed the baby's movement with his fingers, his eyes misty. *Misty.*

She nodded, unable to speak.

Was he...happy? Wasn't that too much to hope for?

"I'm so sorry, Cole. I should have told you... I..." Her voice broke on a sob. She didn't bother accusing him of not calling her back. She should have tried harder.

He guided her to the couch and pulled her back to him as soon as they were seated. "Shhh, don't cry. It kills me." He kissed her cheeks and forehead before pressing a quick kiss to her lips.

There was no way Andi could hold it together with him looking at her that way, with tenderness and…love? "You didn't even call. It hurt so badly…" Words tumbled with no thought.

"I'm a shit," Cole said, his voice thick.

What should she make of that? She closed her eyes. Nothing but truth and hurt would pour out, but she needed him to hear it.

"You left. I know you needed to go, but you never—"

"I should have stayed."

"Pete said I didn't give you a reason." She met his eyes, her breath cut off as she saw his open gaze.

"I had reason enough. I was just too pig-headed to believe it. I'm sorry." His expression was pained, and more honest than she'd ever seen.

Andi's heart stuttered. "You had a reason?" Her voice cracked, and more tears coursed down her cheeks.

Cole cupped her face and wiped them away with the pads of his thumbs. "Two, actually. Looks like I have three, now." His gaze dropped to her swollen tummy, a tender smile on his lips.

"You're not angry with me? I don't blame you if you are."

"I'm not angry. I was surprised. Not telling me was no less than I deserved. I understand why you didn't say anything. My case aside, I left you… Never called… I'm…an asshole. I hurt you. I hurt myself, too. But I'm done with all that."

"What are you saying?" She stared into his grey eyes.

Cole grabbed her hands and squeezed. "I love you, Andi. I love you, I love Ethan, and…" He threw his head back and laughed before meeting her gaze again. "I love this baby beyond words."

She bit her bottom lip, but it couldn't stop the sob. Cole loved her. He loved *them*. "You… You want…us?" Andi sniffled.

Nodding, he pulled her back into his arms, resting a hand on her tummy and his cheek against her forehead.

"The question is do you want *me*?" he whispered against

her hair.

"I love you, too." Pulling away from his chest, she met his gaze.

The tears in his eyes startled her. She leaned up to brush her mouth against his, but Cole slid his hand to the back of her neck and yanked her to him, crushing her lips under his. She clung to him, kissing him back with all her might.

She tugged at his tight black T-shirt, needing bare skin. "Let's go to bed," Andi pleaded, fisting the material with both hands.

Cole nodded, his fingers brushing her breasts through her blue tee. Her nipples peaked even though the touch had been fleeting. Continuing downward, he followed the curve of her stomach with his hand. He froze and pulled back, meeting her eyes. "Wait. Can we...is it safe to...?"

"Yes," she breathed, kissing him again.

When they parted, she hurried to her feet, tugging on his hands.

"Are you sure? I mean, the baby—"

"Cole, if you don't take me to bed this instant, I'm—" Andi's statement was cut off by his mouth on hers again as he also gained his feet. She moaned. Her legs were water. Damn good thing he had her pinned to his chest.

He chuckled as their kiss ended. "Okay, babe. You've convinced me."

She flashed a smile and led him to her bedroom, a tangle of fumbling touches and stumbling kisses.

Cole kicked the door shut and ripped his shirt off. Her breath caught as his muscles rippled. He was just as beautiful as she remembered. His hands froze on his zipper and their gazes locked.

"You have clothes to lose," he growled.

She blushed to her toes. He'd seen her nude before, yes, but not when she was almost five months pregnant and awkward. Her stomach was no longer flat, her breasts were already huge. She was so...ungainly. Nerves fluttered and she stilled at the end of the bed.

Cole stepped out of his jeans and shoved down his boxer briefs, his erection jutting free. How could he even want her?

"Andi?" he whispered. "What's wrong, babe?" He pressed a kiss to her lips as soon as he stood before her.

Her voice was gone, so she just shrugged.

Staring for a moment, he tugged on her shirt until she lifted her arms and he helped her slip out of it. The rest of her clothes followed slowly, as if he was unwrapping a present.

Andi averted her eyes when she finally stood naked before him, her cheeks burning. She made a grab for the sheet, but he stopped her, gripping her wrist gently.

"Oh. My. God. You're so beautiful," Cole breathed.

She shivered as he caressed her cheeks, both sides of her neck, her shoulders, and reverently followed the curve of her belly, dropping a kiss over the place where their child grew.

Cole laid her down, worshipping her body with his hands and mouth. He started a trail of warm, wet kisses down her neck and nibbled her earlobe. She moaned and arched into him as he cupped her breasts and lowered his head to kiss each one.

Andi panted his name as he added his tongue to the kisses. He was setting her on fire, just as he had all the other times they'd made love, but this was different. He'd finally said the words she'd longed to hear and it meant so much more now.

He was in no hurry as he continued nibbling and kissing downward, until he nudged her thighs apart with hot palms and settled his shoulders between her parted legs. The first touch of his tongue against her aching sex made her cry out, and she held him in place with her fingers buried in his hair.

Humming against her most sensitive spot, Cole pulled her into his mouth and slipped a finger, then two, inside her. Andi screamed, lifting into him. It wasn't enough.

Friction, pressure, she needed more.

"Cole," she moaned. She wanted him inside her.

He ignored her and laved her clit, moving his tongue in circles until her hips undulated. She was so close. Cole gave her no mercy, sucking her into his mouth as he moved his fingers in rhythm.

"God, you taste good," he said, the vibration of his words making her clench her thighs. He licked her again, then nipped.

The little nick of his tooth sent her spiralling. She threw her head back and called his name, hips bucking. Her arm flailed, but he grabbed her hand, entwining their fingers and stroking her inner thigh with sure touches, helping her ride out the orgasm.

She shivered, her chest heaving. "Cole…"

He settled his body over hers, holding his full weight back with his elbows, then sucked on her bottom lip. Andi trembled, tasting herself on his lips, and wrapped her arms around him, keeping him close.

"That was for you," he whispered before dipping down for a deeper kiss.

The heat of his erection burned her hip and she throbbed. Climax had been intense, but she was far from done. She wiggled. "I want you," she whispered against his mouth.

"Good, I can't wait any longer."

Andi lifted, rubbing against him. Cole groaned.

"Don't wait," she said.

He left her body cold as he pulled back, but he guided his erection to her, teasing her inner thighs with his tip, and pushing against her, but not entering. After caressing her breasts and her stomach tenderly, he slid a hand between her legs, parting the dark curls at her centre.

Andi whimpered as he moved his hands over her. "I thought you couldn't wait," she panted.

He grinned and pressed his swollen head into her engorged clit. They both moaned.

"Cole… Please…" She writhed against him.

Finally, he gave her what they both wanted and slowly pushed inside.

Both cried out. She gripped his biceps as he started to move and he leant down to kiss her again, his tongue mimicking his thrusts.

They made love slowly, tenderly, until it wasn't enough. She needed more. Cole gave her what she wanted, panting heavily over her as she parried his every plunge, resting her hands on his rear end, squeezing, kneading, encouraging.

Andi cried his name, throwing her head back. Release hit her just as hard as before, her whole body tightening. He was right with her, grunting her name as he stiffened, burying his face against her neck. The warm rush of his release made her shiver along with the jerk of his penis inside her.

As soon as he lifted his head, she pressed her lips to his in a frantic kiss he didn't hesitate to deepen. He slipped from her body and rolled onto his back, pulling her tight against his chest.

"I love you so much," Cole whispered.

Cuddling closer, Andi panted. She rested her hand on his hard pec and looked into his eyes. "I love you too." She cursed her tears.

He cupped her cheek, his gaze concerned. "Did I hurt you? Why are you crying?"

"No, no. I'm happy." Shrugging, she tried to smile, but it was wobbly.

"Okay..."

"It's a girl thing."

"As long as I didn't hurt you." Cole wiped her tears, his expression worried.

She shook her head. "You didn't. Promise."

He flashed a smile then brushed a kiss against her mouth. Andi's heart flipped and she nestled closer, resting her head against him. She closed her eyes and listened to his heartbeat.

"How's that Jared Manning guy to work with?" Cole

asked, breaking what had become a companionable silence.

"Why?" She lifted up, looking at his handsome face.

"Chief Martin gave me a job. Manning's going to be my partner, since my wife already has one."

She blinked.

Her heart pounded and she stared. "Wife? Job?" she croaked.

Cole chuckled and cupped her face in his hands. "I want it all. I want you to marry me. I want to be Ethan's father."

Andi licked her lips then opened her mouth to speak. Nothing came out.

"That was my speech before I knew about *our* baby, of course," he said, his brow furrowed. "So, I guess I need to add something. I love you. I want to raise Ethan and our child together. I can't see the three of you all the time and have it any other way. I'm pretty rough around the edges without you."

Her vision blurred with more tears and she absently swiped at them.

"No more tears, babe," Cole whispered. He caressed her cheek.

"I'm happy, like I told you," she insisted. Never in a million years did she think he'd want to marry her.

He grinned, flashing dimples. "Is that a yes?"

"Can you be happy here? I mean... I don't..."

"Andi, you're killing me. Can I have an answer?"

"Did you ask me a question?" she teased, regaining her composure with a breath. Joy washed over her and a giggle bubbled up.

He glared and she gave into the laugh. So, he wasn't going to take her bait.

Cole kissed her hard. Just when she was getting lost in it, he pulled away. Colour spread across his cheekbones — was he blushing?

"Yes, Agent Lucas, I'll marry you."

"That's Detective Lucas." He cocked a half-smile.

"I know," Andi said, grinning. "I just wanted to hear you

say it. Are you sure about this?"

"I've never been so sure about anything in my life."

"I love you," she whispered.

"Thank God," Cole said, squeezing her in his arms.

"I'm really sorry I didn't tell you about the baby," she whispered, looking away.

He rested a hand on her naked stomach, and she met his eyes. "It doesn't matter."

The baby moved and his hand followed, making soothing circles that shot a shiver down her spine. Andi cuddled closer. "You're not scared? It's a big thing to spring on a person."

"I came here today to ask you to marry me. That decision was made before I even left my place. The baby shocked the hell out of me, yeah, but it changes nothing."

She bit her lip to stave off tears. God, she hated the pregnancy hormones. She rested her hand next to his on her tummy. "Want to see the first ultrasound?"

"I don't want to miss another moment," Cole breathed. He swallowed hard against the lump in his throat, but it didn't dissipate.

She slipped from the bed and he watched her naked body. God, she was stunning. Never had he thought he would *ever* be sexually attracted to a pregnant woman, but as Andi leaned slightly to dig in a bag on her dresser to get the DVD and her breasts swayed, his cock stirred. He wanted to run his hands all over her again. Taste her skin. Lavish attention on the place where *his* child grew. She and the baby were his. Ethan was his, too.

His family. His heart thumped.

Smiling at him over her shoulder, he had to restrain himself from grabbing her.

"Can you hand me that remote?"

"Sure." He tossed it to her from her nightstand and scooted to the end of the bed, wrapping an arm around her when she sat beside him.

Andi kissed his cheek then leaned into him. She turned the TV on and an image popped up on the screen.

Cole froze.

Sure, he'd seen those little printouts of a little white blob with a black background and a ruler on the side. Cass had sent him both Kelsey's and Lacey's, but this was different.

Movement on the screen ensnared him. His vision blurred as he fell in love all over again. When was the last time he'd cried? It didn't matter.

Andi squeezed his hand. Cole couldn't speak as love and wonder settled over him like never before in his thirty-three years.

A tear made its way down his cheek and she wiped it away. "I'm sorry it was my fault you missed this," she whispered, looking down.

When he guided her face back up, her eyes were misty and his heart clenched. "I didn't miss it. I'm seeing it now and that's all that matters. And I'll be by your side next time. I love you." He kissed away her tears. A slight smile curved her lips and Cole tugged her into his arms.

"I told Dr Hayes I don't want to know the sex. I want to be surprised, is that okay?" Andi said, tucking her face against his neck. Her warm breath tickled him and a shiver slid down his spine.

"That's the best kind of surprise. I just hope he has your eyes."

She lifted her face. Her lopsided grin made him smile. "Or she."

Cole acted like he had to think about it, cocking his head to the side, and Andi poked him. "Okay, okay. Or she." He chuckled and rubbed his pec. "That hurt, ya know."

Her grin widened and he laughed as she kissed the spot with a loud smack.

"I still hope *she* has your eyes. And freckles, she has to have freckles," he said, caressing her cheek.

She laughed. "What if he or she has your eyes and no freckles?"

"Then we'll get it right next time." Cole kissed her nose.

"Next time?"

"No more kids?" he asked.

Andi shrugged. "I hadn't thought about it. I didn't know you'd come back for me." Her eyes flashed with pain and he kissed her hard.

She was it for him. A real family, a wife, two kids…maybe more. Forever. "You're not a single mother anymore."

"I'm glad." Her smile was watery and his stomach somersaulted.

"Tell you what," Cole said, winking. "No matter how many kids we have, let's never stop doing what it takes to make them."

She laughed and shook her head, but he pulled her onto his lap and fused their mouths. Andi straddled him, his hard cock pleasantly trapped between them as their bodies touched in all the right places.

"Again?" she breathed against his mouth, wrapping her arms around his neck and rocking in his lap.

Cole moaned. "Yes."

"I love you, Cole Lucas," Andi whispered as she lowered herself onto him.

"Colliding with you in that hallway was the best thing that ever happened to me."

She kissed him in answer. Forever was getting a damn good start.

Epilogue

Andi pulled into the driveway with a sigh. She eased her cumbersome body out of the car, smiling when the baby moved. She only had six weeks to go, and she couldn't wait until the pregnancy was over. Being pregnant in a Texas summer sucked.

She glanced to the right, spotting Bella and her boyfriend on the porch swing next door. "Bella, where's Ethan?" she called.

"Cole insisted he had things under control, so I left about two," Bella said, coming to the porch steps.

The teen was doing well, all things considered, after the ordeal with Carlo Maldonado. She'd agreed to testify against him without protest, and was seeing a counsellor. In the long run, she'd be fine and Andi was more than relieved, she was proud of her.

Bella and Natalie were excited about the new baby. In just a few days they were hosting a baby shower. She'd told them not to make a big deal about it, but of course, she'd been disregarded. There'd be tons of people there.

She waved to Matt. He called a hello, and she flashed a smile. He was a good kid. He'd rushed to Bella's house the night she'd been taken by Carlo, just as frantic as Nat about her.

Matt had definitely scored cool points when Bella had told Andi about the virgin conversation she'd had with Carlo. The boy respected her — hopefully he'd keep that up.

She waved goodbye to the young couple and headed up her steps, biting back a yawn. Andi was still working, but on light duty, not leaving the station much. Her shifts

239

were mostly normal business hours and she was out of the on-call rotation until after the baby was born, so that was a relief. But the guys at work were killing her with their overprotection, her husband and partner, of course, leading the charge. She couldn't even get up to pee without interrogation and some male freaking out.

Cole and Jared Manning were getting along now that their mutual posturing and 'guy stuff' — according to Cole — had passed. He'd been over to their house a few times for dinner, and Andi was getting to know him better, too.

They were too much alike, so she had to bite her tongue when her husband complained about him, but so far, so good. They'd be great friends...eventually. The few cases they'd worked had gone well, so at least they could be professional.

Their current case had finally broken the night before, but Cole and Jared had literally been up all night. He'd just pulled in the driveway when Andi had been on her way out that morning. He'd have the chance to get some much needed sleep, since Bella had Ethan all day in the summer, as he and Jared had been working overnight for a few weeks, and both had been sleep deprived.

Over the past two and a half months, Cole had been settling in well, both with her and Ethan, and at work. Chief Martin was already bragging about him, and she'd heard him say Antioch wasn't so bad after all.

Andi grinned. She loved him so much, and couldn't imagine her life without him. When she thought about Iain, she could finally smile. The sadness and grief had faded. She missed him from time to time — she always would — but her first husband would have wanted her — them — to be happy. It wasn't something she'd convinced herself of to feel better, it was just who Iain had been as a person.

He would have wanted Ethan to grow up with a man to guide him. Cole was proving to be one hell of a dad to her son. She had no qualms that he would be just as fantastic with his own child, and any others that they might have.

The baby moved and Andi rubbed the spot, smiling. Cole wouldn't treat Ethan differently from his own blood, and it only made her love him more.

Closing the door, she listened hard. Silence descended as she put her gun away and headed into the living room. The scene before her made her heart stutter.

Ethan was asleep in Cole's arms on the couch, nestled against his chest. Both husband and son were snoring softly. She couldn't help the smile that curved her lips.

Her son's favourite book was upside down on the floor, as if it had fallen there. She laughed. Ethan never made it through the whole story when they read at night. Looked like Cole couldn't last this afternoon, either.

Andi brushed Ethan's curls out of his face—too long again—and kissed the top of his head. She caressed Cole's stubbled cheek and leant down as best she could to kiss his forehead. Both her boys were perfect.

Cole's eyes fluttered. "Hey." His tone was heavy with sleep.

"Hey."

Her husband shifted on the couch, sitting up and making room for her to sit with them as he cuddled Ethan closer. He threw his free arm around her then pressed a kiss to her lips.

She leaned into him, giving a contented sigh.

"What time is it?" Cole asked.

"Almost four. I left early."

"Everything okay?" His steel eyes widened, more alert.

"Absolutely. Just wanted to get home to you guys." Andi patted his cheek. "You should have let Bella keep him and gotten more sleep."

Cole shook his head. "I wanted to hang with him. I feel like I haven't seen you guys in forever. Besides, she's leaving for camp tomorrow, she'll be gone for the rest of the summer, remember? That counsellor gig. I told her to go pack."

Ethan roused, yawning as he rubbed his eye with a small

241

fist. "Mama," he said when he noticed her, flashing a sleepy smile. He threw himself at her and Andi caught him up, hugging him tight and laughing.

"Ethan, careful," Cole admonished.

The little boy leaned against her and she ruffled his hair. "He's fine. But thanks. I'm more worried you didn't get enough sleep."

"I got enough, babe," he told her, caressing her cheek. "Besides, me and Ethan had guy stuff to do."

"Yeah!" The four-year-old agreed.

He put his hand up and Ethan slapped him with a loud high-five. Andi laughed.

"But we missed you."

"Yeah, Mama." Ethan pushed up to his knees and kissed her cheek.

"I missed you guys, too."

Cole flashed his dimples. He still made her heart race, and that would never change.

Her son splayed his small hands against her stomach and looked down. "Hello, little brother," he announced.

"Was this one of the guy things you had to do?" Andi asked, quirking an eyebrow.

Cole grinned. "I'll never tell."

She rolled her eyes and cupped her son's face, meeting his big blue eyes. "Ethan, you might have a little sister instead, is that okay?"

"Like my Bells?"

"Yes, a girl, like Bella. You'd have to protect her. You're her big brother."

"Boys are better," Ethan said, nodding seriously.

When Cole laughed, Andi glared at him.

"I didn't tell him that, I swear." He put his palms up in surrender and shook his head, fighting another grin.

"Daddy," Ethan said, scrambling off the couch. "I wanna play blocks."

Andi's heart skipped a beat, as it always did when her son said that word.

"Go for it, buddy," Cole said, his lips curving in a tender smile.

They'd left the choice up to Ethan as to what he would call Cole. He'd asked if Cole was going to be his dad the very day he'd come back into town. She'd cried, of course. Pete had beamed, and Cole's eyes had been a bit misty.

Ethan had called him Daddy from the moment he'd got a yes to his question.

"I guess I'll have to address that later with him," she grumbled, and her husband chuckled, earning another glare.

Cole yanked her closer and kissed her. "I love you."

She smiled. "I love you, too."

"You know I wouldn't mind having a daughter, anyway."

"I know," she said, putting her hand next to his on her tummy when he followed the movement of their very active baby.

"I wish you'd call it quits already. Pete and I agree."

"Cole," Andi warned. "I worked up until the week before Ethan was born." Did they really have to go over this again? "Dr Hayes says we're both healthy, and there's no problem with me working. I'm stuck at a desk, for God's sake. That's bad enough."

He didn't say anything, but he glowered.

"I don't want to argue with you," she whispered.

Cole's expression softened. "I know, babe. I'm not trying to argue. Just expressing my opinion."

"For the thousandth time," she muttered. "Besides, with the whole detective squad on your side, what do you have to worry about? I can't even get my own damn decaf. I get escorted to the bathroom. They practically have the paramedics on standby. You'd think this was my first baby."

"I wouldn't complain about being waited on hand and foot, if I were you. And this is my first baby. So I'm bound to be a little neurotic."

"That's one word I'd have never described you with." She

bit back a laugh.

"Hmmm... Well, some things can change a man," Cole said, gazing into her eyes.

"For the better?" she asked, her heart flipping.

"For the better." His lips hovered over hers, his warm breath tickling before his soft kiss. "I wasn't alive until I met you and Ethan," he whispered.

"I was only half alive, I think. Until you came along and showed me it wasn't wrong to love again."

Cole held her close, like he would for the rest of his life, and Andi snuggled into him. Ethan called them to look at what he'd built. Andi and Cole exchanged a smile as they watched their son play.

Chance Collision

Excerpt

Chapter One

The paper aeroplane sailed down the long hallway, heading towards Chief's office. Pete cringed as the click of high heels registered at the same time as the feminine yelp.

Ethan dashed around the corner, and Pete hurried to follow.

"Hey, squirt, slow down," Pete called, but his partner's son was already out of sight.

Nikki, his boss's administrative assistant, bent down towards the little boy. Ethan's copper curls were several shades lighter than the young woman's, but Nikki's hair was as natural as the kid's. Usually neatly coiffed at the back of her neck, today her locks were loose and flowing. *Appealing.*

"What do you have there?" she was asking Ethan when he reached them.

"I'm sorry," Pete said. As she straightened, Nikki had a smile on her face. *Thank God.* "Didn't realise I'd get that kinda air."

Ethan retrieved the paper creation and slid a small hand into one of Pete's, looking up at both of them.

"It's no problem, just startled me. Not like a paper plane collision can do much damage." She smiled at the little boy, then met Pete's eyes.

"Yeah, except for maybe a paper cut?" Pete shrugged.

Nikki's smile slid into a grin and he got swept into the deep pools of her big brown eyes. She shoved her hair over a shoulder and Pete swallowed hard. The soft, wavy sea of red begged for a touch. A light floral scent tickled his nose with her pleasant perfume. It made her more intriguing.

Gorgeous. How had he never noticed before?

"Somehow I think I'll live." She laughed. The sound was sweet and he found himself grinning back. Like a besotted idiot.

"Unca' Pete. Did you see? It went faaaaaaar," Ethan piped up, tugging on his hand and jumping up and down. He veered the plane back and forth with his free hand.

"I did, squirt."

Ethan grinned, his blue eyes wide and bright. "What's your name?" the four-year-old asked Nikki.

Her white billowy skirt moved as she bent down and offered her hand. The fabric stopped at her knees. Damn, she had killer legs.

Pete averted his gaze from her asset-hugging lilac top and the cleavage peeking out as she moved to the child's level.

"I'm Nikki. Ethan, you're getting big! I know your mommy. Andi's my friend."

"And my daddy is Cole!" Ethan tugged his hand out of Pete's and shook Nikki's outstretched one.

A smile played at Pete's lips as he watched them.

"I know him, too. We all work together."

Ethan eyed her up and down. "Where's your gun?"

"Oh. I work for Chief Martin. I don't have a gun. I'm not

246

a detective like your parents and Detective Crane," Nikki explained.

"C'mere, squirt," Pete said, hauling his partner's son onto a hip. "Hungry?" His shoulder didn't even twitch. *Good.* Never could tell when his year-old bullet wound would bother him. How much of *that* was in his head?

"Yeah," Ethan said, nodding.

"How'd you get little guy duty?" Nikki asked, brown eyes dancing. As she squared her shoulders, her lilac top hugged her breasts more.

Pete's stomach fluttered. He must be hungrier than he thought. He was too old for her, even if he didn't consider her off limits. Unlike his partner, he didn't date — or marry — at work. "Andi went into labour this morning."

"Ah, I hadn't heard."

Shifting his feet, he met her gaze. "Yeah, and Cole's with her, of course. Bella, his normal babysitter, is a camp counsellor for the rest of this summer down south in Livingston, and Andi's mom is on her way. She moved to Ohio a few years ago when she remarried. Cole's sister's even coming in from Seattle later today. But for now, I'm it. I don't mind, really. Me and Ethan are cool."

Nikki's eyes widened as she took in all the info he'd thrown at her.

Babbling? Really?

Come to think of it, that soliloquy was probably the most he'd ever said to her. He cleared his throat.

"My cousins are coming," Ethan announced.

"That's nice," Nikki said, an easy smile back in place.

Pete had never noticed the dimple in her chin before. He tried not to stare.

"My mama's having a baby," his partner's son continued.

Nikki ruffled Ethan's hair. "You're gonna be a big brother?"

Pete chuckled as the little boy nodded. He looked at Nikki's slender hands. She'd been close enough to touch his face. What would that feel like? Her skin against his —

247

Jesus, what is wrong with you? Lusting after a kid. What was she, twenty-five?

"I'm gonna be the bestest big broder ever!"

Her laugh jolted him. It was as tempting as she was.

"I bet you are," Nikki told Ethan, holding out her hand. The little boy slapped a loud high-five.

The buzz of Pete's phone offered him the excuse he needed to tear his attention away from the Chief's lovely administrative assistant. He offered a wave and turned away. He admonished Ethan to hush while he brought the phone to his ear.

"Crane," he said.

"How's Ethan?" Cole asked.

"Howdy to you, too, bud," Pete answered, hiking the little boy up higher on his hip. Kid was getting heavy.

Cole's sigh was all the answer he got.

"Everything okay?" he asked his partner's husband.

"Yeah, I guess."

"Isn't your wife, I don't know, having a baby or something?"

"Not yet. I just wanted to call and check in," Cole said.

Pete's bullshit meter lit up like a Christmas tree. He set Ethan down on his desk in the Criminal Investigations Division room—where all the detectives officed—as they reached it, handing his partner's son the foam apple he kept around to squeeze when he was stressed.

Ethan made motor sounds as he steered the paper aeroplane around, then rammed the apple into it, making explosion noises.

More books from
C.A. Szarek

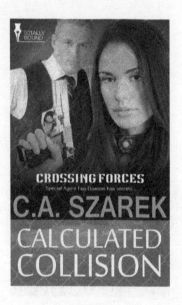

Book three in the Crossing Forces series

Special Agent Lee Dawson has secrets. Secrets that forced her from Dallas to New York City in disgrace two years ago.

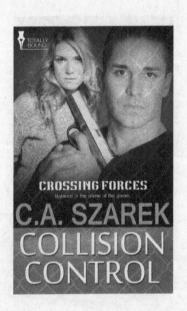

Book four in the Crossing Forces series

A one-night stand can't possibly mean forever…

About the Author

C.A. Szarek

Bestselling, award winning author of romantic suspense and epic fantasy romance, C.A. loves to dabble in different genres. If it's a good story, she'll write it, no matter where it seems to fit!

She's a hopeless romantic and always will be. Risking it all for Happily Ever After is what she lives by!

C.A. is originally from Ohio, but got to Texas as soon as she could. She's happily married and has a bachelor's degree in Criminal Justice.

She works with kids when she's not writing.

C.A. Szarek loves to hear from readers. You can find contact information, website details and an author profile page at https://www.totallybound.com/